BRIDE
AND
GROOM

BOOKS BY RONA HALSALL

BRIDE
AND
GROOM

RONA HALSALL

bookouture

Published by Bookouture in 2024

An imprint of Storyfire Ltd.
Carmelite House
50 Victoria Embankment
London EC4Y 0DZ

www.bookouture.com

ISBN: 978-1-80314-166-4
eBook ISBN: 978-1-80314-165-7

This one is for Gillian Mitchell, a lovely, kind-hearted friend and an enthusiastic beta reader, who sadly passed away earlier this year. Rest in peace, Gill xxx

PROLOGUE

I will never forget the sound of the body as it bounced off the bonnet of the car. The sickening thump, the floppiness of the limbs as they cartwheeled out of sight. My foot stamping on the brake too late to stop it from happening. My heart jumping out of my chest with the shock of it. The sheer horror of what had happened tearing at my brain, shredding my thoughts into a million scattered pieces.

Then the silence, pressing on my head.

Both of us gaping at each other as time stood still for a moment. Just long enough for reality to make itself known. The weight of dread landing in the pit of my stomach, a buzzing starting up in my ears, the thumping of my heart throbbing at my temples.

It was pitch-black and raining, the headlights reflecting off the puddles, raindrops splattering against the windscreen before the wipers cleared them away. We were travelling home after a night out, our last dinner invitation before our wedding in three days' time. An evening meal at Stacey's house, the queen bee of our social group who loved an excuse to invite people round to her home and show us her latest renovations. It had been a chance to make sure the final details were planned for our big day, to be clear about what was happening and when, who was picking up what from where.

It had been a fun evening, the champagne making everyone giddy and I didn't think about how much I was drinking because we planned to get a cab home. Stacey was going to drive our car back the following day, but there were no cabs available, so we'd decided to drive. It was fifteen minutes at the most back to our house, and we could cut down a back lane. It was the only solution, other than sleeping on Stacey's sofa.

A safe option, we'd told ourselves as we fastened our seat belts. It was late and who would be out in this weather anyway?

All of that flashed through my head as I sat and stared, waiting for the person to stand up and dust themselves down. Wanting to believe that something horrendous hadn't happened.

A voice spoke into the silence.

'Oh shit. I think... Did we hit somebody?'

Hearing Ethan saying it out loud made it more real. My chest felt tight, my breath catching in my throat. Suddenly my lungs wouldn't work; I couldn't get the air to go in or out. My mouth opened, gasping like a fish out of water, but my body had stopped doing what it was supposed to do. A hand grabbed my arm, shaking me.

'Oh God, what's happening?'

My hands slapped at my chest, desperately trying to shock my muscles into action. I'm going to die, I thought, as dots filled my vision. Right here, right now, I'm going to die.

I passed out then, coming round later in our cottage, a two-bed rental in Cononley, a village not far from Skipton, North Yorkshire. My memories were muddled, as blurry as the view through the rain-spattered windscreen, refusing to come into focus.

I might not be able to remember exactly what had happened, how things had come to pass. But I knew with a dreadful certainty what I'd done.

CHAPTER ONE

Nicci looked up as Ethan brought her a glass of water, crouching beside her and stroking her hair from her forehead. She took a sip, then another, thankful for the cool of the liquid as it ran down her throat. She knew she'd had a panic attack, something she'd been prone to since her mum had become ill, all those years ago, when she'd been in her last year at school. They always left her feeling dazed and exhausted, sticky with sweat.

Thankfully, Ethan had witnessed her going through these before and knew what to do. He'd driven her home, carried her inside and laid her down on the sofa, covering her with a blanket. Seconds later, her Jack Russell terrier, Mack, had burrowed inside the blanket, giving her worried licks, sensing something was wrong.

The cottage was in the middle of a long, stone-built terrace, the old weavers' cottages that used to house workers from the disused mill at the bottom of the village. Ethan said it was too small, but she enjoyed living there, with the views of the hills at the front and fields at the back. It was a simple layout, easy to keep clean and tidy. There was a living room at the front of the cottage, the kitchen at the back and the stairs running up the wall between the two. Upstairs there was a double bedroom at the back, a smaller bedroom at the front with a narrow bathroom next to it. The décor was tired and dated, the furniture well worn, the bathroom suite avocado, but it was homely.

The front room was small enough to be termed cosy by the letting agent, only big enough for the sofa and a chair, positioned in front of the fireplace, a dining table pushed against the far wall. Ethan must have put another log on the stove because she could see orange flames licking the glass.

'You okay, love?'

His voice snapped her out of her daze and she murmured a 'Thank you' as she handed the glass back to him. Her body felt limp and weak, a headache banging at her temples. She leant back against the cushions, closing her eyes, wondering if her mind was playing tricks on her, making her imagine things. It had happened to her before, panicking about events that might happen but didn't, coming round from an episode thinking the worst. She knew she'd had a panic attack but were the images in her mind real?

Ethan put the glass on the coffee table and stood, pulling a hand through his dark, wavy hair. He looked rumpled, his blue eyes wild, a shadow of stubble on his normally clean-shaven chin. 'I think I should go back and check,' he said, eyes darting towards the door. 'Make sure they're okay.'

His words brought a replay of the accident into her mind, a slow-motion reel that made her heart start racing again. *Oh God, I knocked someone over.*

A tear escaped and rolled down her cheek. A lovely evening flipped into her worst nightmare in a matter of seconds. It didn't seem possible.

She watched him go, feeling anxious and helpless, praying

that the person they'd hit was okay. Her body was shaking, a chill seeping into her bones as her mind conjured up the worst scenario. Her teeth were chattering and she pulled the blanket tighter, hoping to wake up from this nightmare.

Only ten minutes later, he was back, locking and bolting the door behind him before perching next to her on the sofa. He blew out a long breath, like he was trying to calm himself down and she waited for him to tell her what was going on. Her hands found each other under the blanket and she pulled them to her chest, needing to cling on to something, wanting to know, but not wanting to hear what he might say.

'An ambulance was there. And the police.'

Nicci felt her muscles relax a little, her chest not quite so tight, her breathing a little easier. That's what she'd needed to know. The person they'd hit was getting medical attention.

'Were they... okay?' she whispered, hardly daring to ask.

He grimaced. 'I didn't hang around because I thought that would look suspicious and the police had blocked the road. But...' His lips pressed together, like he didn't want to tell her any more. He sighed. 'Two paramedics were bent over them...' His forehead creased, uncertainty making his voice waver. 'I think they were okay.' He nodded to himself. 'They were definitely alive. I'm certain of that.' His eyes met hers. 'We didn't kill anyone.'

She swallowed, her voice robotic, unable to connect with her words. 'That's good, then.'

Her mind was not in the room, travelling back to the scene of the accident, trying to remember exactly what had happened. But it seemed the harder she tried to bring things into focus, the more blurred her recall became. How had she not seen them? It wasn't as though she'd been speeding. In fact, the opposite had been true. Or was that what she wanted to think? Was her mind making things up, rewriting history to make her feel better?

She was too hot all of a sudden, sweat gathering under her arms, making her clothes stick to her back. She threw off the blanket, Mack grumbling about being moved as she sat up, wiped her face with her hands.

'I suppose...' She grimaced, her mind only now starting to think about the consequences. 'We ought to tell the police?' It came out as a question and his eyes widened. He looked scared. Exactly how she felt. This was going to ruin everything, touch their lives in so many ways. Guilt clutched at her neck, squeezing her throat.

'The police will know we've been drinking,' he said, his voice low and urgent. 'We'll be arrested.' He reached for her hand, held it tight and she wondered if this was as much for his own comfort as hers. 'If we go to the police, we'll have to cancel the wedding.' He paused to compose himself, his voice thick with emotion. 'I love you so much, Nicci. I want you to be my wife. More than anything in the world, I want us to be married.'

She bit her lip, panic rising again. Cancelling the wedding was not an option, because it wasn't just about her and Ethan, it was also about her father. And the business, their financial future. Imagine what would happen if word got out they'd run someone over while over the limit.

She squeezed his hand. 'The weather was awful,' she murmured, trying to mitigate their situation. 'It was dark, visibility was rubbish.' She caught his eye. 'Would they think it was anything other than an accident?'

He stood, started pacing the floor, a hand tugging at his hair as he worked it through in his mind. 'I suppose it depends on what the person we hit tells them, doesn't it?' Then he shook his head. 'No, we can't, Nicci. We can't. They'll do a breath test. It's standard procedure.' He leant against the mantelpiece, his head bowed. 'There's no getting away from the fact we should not have been in that car driving home. They'll charge us with drink driving.'

A thought surfaced, making her groan with dismay. 'You're supposed to report it if you hit someone, aren't you? Like, straight away. Otherwise, you can be charged with leaving the scene of an accident.' Her voice was getting weaker, all the strength draining from her body. 'That's what we did, Ethan. We didn't just hit them, we *left* them. A hit-and-run.' She spoke the last words carefully, trying them out.

The awfulness of their situation was starting to penetrate her foggy brain. The feeling she was drowning swept over her, making her gulp in big breaths, choking as her emotions clogged her airways. She clutched at her throat, feeling dizzy as she struggled to breathe.

'Hey, calm down,' Ethan said, dashing to her side, his eyes full of concern as he sat and pulled her to him, shushing her and rubbing her back. Slowly, the panic started to subside and he kissed the top of her head as she leant on his shoulder, exhausted. 'Come on, love, you need to try and keep it together. Getting yourself all worked up isn't going to help. Let's think about this rationally.'

She closed her eyes and nodded, her heart still racing. At least she didn't have to do this alone, she thought, grateful for his support. It made her appreciate the value of their partnership from a new angle, this knowledge that he was there for her whatever life threw at them. She was the guilty one, she'd been driving, but here he was, determined to protect her. They sat in silence, his arm tight around her body as her breathing began to slow.

'Nobody will know what happened,' he said, carefully. 'If I remember rightly, that person had their back to us. I don't think they would have seen the number plate, or clocked the make of the car. So... I think we're okay.'

She sat with that idea for a moment, the suggestion they

should not own up to what she'd done, and it felt dark and heavy. Not something she'd want to carry round with her for the rest of her life.

'That person was wearing dark clothes on an unlit road,' he continued. 'If we hadn't been talking about the wedding, instead of...' He faltered, left the end of the sentence hanging.

Nicci's guilt twisted in her gut. If only she'd waited until they'd got home to have her say none of this would have happened. It was her fault. She pressed her lips together, tears stinging her eyes.

'Let's agree to keep this to ourselves. Not tell anyone,' Ethan murmured and she pulled away from him, her eyes searching his face. He was deadly serious. This was his suggestion, the way they were going to deal with this terrible situation. Her heart clenched. Could it be that easy? Just pretend it hadn't happened?

'But what about the car? There must be damage.'

He gave a derisive snort. 'It's an ancient Land Rover Defender that's spent half its life up on the moors pulling other four-by-four's out of peat bogs. It's already battered.' She realised this was true. Ethan's hobby was off-roading and most weekends he'd be out in the wilderness somewhere. One more dent wouldn't be noticed.

'I don't know.' Her fingers massaged her temples. 'It doesn't feel right.'

'The thing is... what good will it do anyone if we go to the police?' He paused a moment before carrying on, sounding like he was trying to convince himself as much as her. 'It'll just mean we can't get married, we'll break your dad's heart, ruin the business and lose all our friends.' His hand dropped from her waist and he slumped back against the cushions. She could feel the despair leeching out of him. *I've done this*, she thought. *I've ruined our lives.*

'Let's face it,' he continued. 'The consequences, not only for us, but for those around us, would be pretty catastrophic.' He blew out his cheeks. 'Whoever we hit got medical help pretty quickly, so ask yourself this... who rang for help? There was nobody else around, was there? Which means they must have been okay enough to ring themselves.' She hadn't thought about that, but his logic made sense. He nodded. 'They'll be okay.' She noticed a determined set to his jaw. 'I promise you, love. We weren't going fast. They'll be fine.'

Hearing him lay it all out sent a wave of doubt surging through her body. Although she could accept some of his arguments as valid, it felt so wrong.

'We've broken the law. Doesn't that bother you? That we might get found out?' They stared at each other, the silence thick with things unsaid. 'If this catches up with us somehow, the punishment will be twice as harsh. We need to go and own up now.'

Still, he said nothing, but she could tell by the way his mouth was working from side to side that his conscience was tussling with the moral dilemma.

'The truth is, there's no easy way to deal with this,' he said eventually. 'But this is what I think we should do. Let's slip something into the marriage vows, something only we know about. Promise each other we won't tell a soul, then we can both be comfortable going forward.' He slid off the sofa and knelt in front of her, took her hands in his. 'I know that's going to be hard, but it's the only way we get to keep living our lives.' His eyes were pleading with her, his reasoning persuasive. 'The minute we tell someone, that's it. We're criminals. The business goes to the wall. We have no income. No future. We'll probably go to prison.'

She whimpered as his words hit home. He was right. There was no palatable option, that was the truth of it. Keeping it secret was the easiest solution, the path that led to the least damage, both to themselves and those around them. She nodded. 'Okay,' she whispered, hating herself more in that moment than she'd ever hated anyone in her life. 'That's what we'll do then.'

Questions filled her mind. What if somebody had seen them, and they'd rung for an ambulance? Or the person they hit remembered the car and the two people in it? Could they possibly escape unscathed?

CHAPTER TWO

Nicci was awake when the sun rose on her wedding day. It was 5.16 a.m. and it looked like it was going to be glorious, judging by the golden glow that seeped through the crack in the curtains. Surely the fact the sun was shining was a good omen. But the worries that had been chewing at her brain, waking her up every night since the accident refused to go away.

Did anyone see us? Is it too late to tell the police?

She sighed and climbed out of bed, feeling sluggish and dopey. Another sigh. The day would feel so much better if her mum could be here to share it with her, and almost two years since she'd died, she still forgot sometimes that she was gone.

Her eyes settled on her wedding dress. Ivory silk with hundreds of crystals sown into the fitted bodice. It was sleek and elegant and made her feel like a princess. She gave a sad smile, sure her mum would have approved.

But would she have approved of Ethan?

Unfortunately, she'd never had the chance to meet him as he came into Nicci's life shortly after her mum's death. At a point in time when she was shocked and vulnerable and quite lost. As she was happy to tell anyone who'd listen, Ethan had glued her back together. Not just Nicci, but her father too. He'd been a tonic for both of them and her dad had often said that hiring Ethan was one of the best decisions he'd ever made.

She opened the curtains and gazed out into the garden, her elbows leaning on the windowsill. She'd stayed in the family home for her wedding night, her dad insisting it would be bad luck if she spent the night with Ethan in their cottage. Silly superstition, but she was happy to see him so cheerful and had gone along with it. In a way, it had been good to have some time on her own, a bit of space to think.

She could see the little summer house at the far end of the garden, nestled in a corner, the first garden building her parents had built together. Her dad a joiner, her mother an interior designer, they'd made a brilliant team. They'd had so many compliments about it, people asking if they could make one for them, they decided to set up a business and the rest, as her dad would say, was history.

Now the company employed eleven people, including herself, Ethan and her father. Lockdown had been a blessing from a business point of view and they'd shifted their focus away from summer houses and more towards home offices. When the cost-of-living crisis hit and house prices increased, they'd developed larger living and bedroom spaces for grown-up children who couldn't afford to move away from home. They'd also started to develop 'Elder Spaces' for people who needed to keep a close eye on parents, but wanted them to retain an element of independence. All Ethan's ideas. He was full of plans and enthusiasm and was so charming to potential clients they rarely said no.

Yes, business was booming, their future assured for the time being and she should count herself lucky. Still the air of gloom hung over her. It wasn't just the aftermath of the accident that was weighing heavy on her mind, though, there were other troubles vying for attention.

She could see her reflection in the glass, a ghost version of herself, her shoulder-length chestnut hair tousled from sleep, her fringe standing on end, wide-set brown eyes looking anxious. This was supposed to be the happiest day of her life, marrying a man who adored her. And they got to live and work together. Lots of people dreamed of this exact scenario.

Except Nicci didn't want to be an accountant, which was her current role in the business. Payroll and invoicing and chasing money and ordering goods and keeping the books and... Oh God, it was tedious and not the job she'd wanted for herself at all.

It had been her mum's role, and over the years, she'd taught Nicci how the systems worked. When Nicci was at school, she'd helped out in return for a weekly allowance. Later, when her mum was ill, she'd postponed her teacher training course at university, and taken over the admin and finance role. It wasn't going to be forever, her mum kept telling her, constantly thanking her for putting her plans on hold to stay at home. After her mum died, though, she'd stayed because her dad was struggling. He said he didn't trust anyone else to look after the money and he'd begged her. 'It won't be forever,' he promised, echoing her mother. 'Just until I can find someone else.'

That was two years ago. Now, at thirty-one, she was resigned to the fact she wouldn't be going anywhere anytime soon. *You can train as a teacher later*, she promised herself. Anyway, it was probably better to do it when she was a bit older, with more life experience.

One day she would follow her dream, and marrying Ethan was the first step in the right direction. By marrying him, she was securing the future of the business. He would be part of the family, his place in the firm beyond question. Really, he'd already earned that right with his hard work and innovative thinking.

Ethan was a plumber by trade, but had soon moved into

sales. They'd met when he was a sales rep for the company they bought kitchen and bathroom fittings from. Even then, he'd been full of ideas, happy to spend time looking at different options. It had been a bit of a surprise to everyone when Nicci's dad, Pete, offered him a job.

The three of them had been talking through a problem in the office, when Ethan came up with an answer and Pete slapped him on the back. 'That's genius! Come and work for me, lad, you're exactly what we need.' When Ethan didn't respond straight away, he added, 'I'll pay you more than you're earning now.'

Nicci gasped and shot a wary glance at her father. Could they afford another salary? She did the books and knew the answer to that was no.

Ethan laughed. 'You're having me on, Pete.'

But her dad shook his head, looked deadly serious.

'It's a genuine job offer. We need someone to help. I can't do it on my own and I struggle with sales now Jean has gone. I'd much rather be supervising the building side of things.'

A big grin spread over Ethan's face and Nicci realised she was grinning too. Her dad was right. Ethan had always been pleasant to work with, nothing too much trouble and she could see that his customer service ethos was exactly what they needed to boost sales.

Ethan looked from Nicci to her dad and then nodded. 'Alright,' he said, shaking both their hands. 'I'd like that.'

Was she attracted to him at that point? Perhaps. Because who wouldn't want to run their hands through that dark, wavy hair? Who wouldn't enjoy looking at that chiselled face? Those blue eyes, with a bit of a twinkle in them when he was teasing her. A deep voice and a booming laugh. If she was being honest with herself, she'd enjoyed sharing a coffee with him whenever he came into the office. Looked forward to it, in fact.

Having him around would be fun, she told herself, and she

knew it would brighten her days, making the job a lot less boring. That afternoon, she hummed as she did the invoicing and when she answered the phone, she sounded cheerful for the first time in ages.

Three months after Ethan had started working with them, he asked her out on a date. There was no doubting the attraction at that point, but she'd been unsure about mixing business with pleasure. She'd put him off a couple of times until her dad overheard their conversation, heard her refuse him and took her to one side, insisting she give him a chance.

'You could do a lot worse than Ethan,' he'd said. 'I like the guy. I like him a lot.' So she'd humoured her father and realised she liked Ethan a lot too.

Almost eighteen months later, when Ethan had asked her to marry him, her dad had practically exploded with joy.

Yes, Ethan was the answer to a lot of problems, she told herself now, as she straightened up and stretched. Being his wife would make life easier in so many ways and after the accident, he'd been one hundred per cent supportive, totally committed to their future. But there were new complications to deal with. The first of which was this guilty secret they shared, a secret they'd vowed to keep.

The second complication was something that made her seriously question if marrying Ethan was the right thing to do...

CHAPTER THREE

She went downstairs and made herself a coffee. The house was silent, her father not yet awake. Sitting in the conservatory at the back of the house, she watched the sun rising higher, lighting up the gritstone bluffs that sat on the edges of the rolling hills. But instead of thinking about her wedding, her thoughts took her back, as they always did in quiet moments, to the night of the accident, making her relive it again and again.

She could hear the slosh of the tyres going through puddles, the murmur of her and Ethan's conversation, as though she was sitting in the back seat as an observer, rather than a participant in the horror that was about to unfold. The flip-flop of the wipers on the windscreen. Ethan shouting at her to watch out. Then that thump. A blur of flailing limbs. Her own terrified scream.

She shuddered and shook the thoughts from her mind, pulling the throw from the back of the chair, and wrapping it round her shoulders. Had they done the right thing? A pointless question because it was too late to go back now. *What's done is done.*

She'd gone through everything a thousand times in her

mind and she knew Ethan's analysis of their situation was right. Their lives would be over if they confessed and the thought of prison terrified her because she'd have no idea how to look after herself in a place like that. But the effect it would have on her dad had been the real deciding factor. He'd struggled so much since her mum's death and the stress had seriously impacted his health. He had a heart condition now and he suffered from high blood pressure. The trauma of finding out what she'd done, and the impact on the business could kill him.

The thought of the consequences made her tense, emotion swelling in her chest, tears pricking at her eyes.

Remember the vows. Nobody is ever going to know.

She grabbed onto that thought and held it close, shutting her emotions down. Not only were they going to promise to be there for each other for the rest of their lives, they would promise to keep their secret safe too.

She finished her coffee and went back upstairs, lifting her handbag onto the bed. She pulled out the folded piece of paper with her wedding vows written on it and read it through. It had taken a while to get the wording right, something they were both happy with, but they'd finally agreed on a version:

I vow that I will protect our truth until my dying day. As we go forward, we do so together, as a partnership, bonded by our love and trust in one another to do what is right for us as a couple. I promise to always put us and our well-being at the centre of my world. You are the one, my only one. Always and forever. Until death us do part.

Could she say that in church without breaking down, knowing what it really meant? That they were vowing to hide their criminal activity for the rest of their lives, or at least until one of them died?

She picked up her phone and checked the news site for an

update on the accident, but there was nothing. The day after, there'd been a short report about a hit-and-run victim, a male, early thirties, as yet unidentified. They said he was critical but stable in hospital. The police had been appealing for witnesses, but as there'd been no further reports since, she had to assume nobody had come forward. At least she hoped that was the case, because if there had been a witness then... well, it didn't bear thinking about.

A knock on the door made her jump. 'You up yet, love?' her dad shouted. 'Can I get you a coffee?' She pinned a smile on her face and opened the door a crack.

'A coffee would be lovely. I'm going to get a shower, then I'll come down, okay?'

'I'll get breakfast on, shall I? What do you want? A fry up or...'

Her stomach growled, but the thought of food made her feel nauseous, the nerves having kicked in now. This was it: she was getting married. The enormity of what she was about to do made her feel a bit light-headed, conflicting emotions building inside her like a hurricane.

'Toast will be fine,' she said, keen to close the door and sit down before she keeled over.

'Right you are,' her dad said with a grin. 'Your mum would be so proud. So very proud.' He leant forward and pecked her on the cheek. 'I'll see you downstairs.'

She shut the door and leant against it, her legs like jelly, as she blinked back tears. She didn't think her mum would be proud at all. Not if she knew the truth.

Five hours later, the limo pulled up outside the Holy Trinity Church in Skipton, a beautiful medieval building nestled at the top of the high street. It had always been Nicci's dream to get married here, right from when she was a little girl. She was often in the town centre on a Saturday, shopping with her mum, and they'd always stopped to watch if there was a wedding going on. She'd been bewitched by the dresses, the happiness shining from the bride and groom's faces. Now, she hesitated for a moment in the back of the car, and took a few deep breaths. Her father, sitting beside her, reached for her hand.

'Are you okay, love? I've got to say you've been looking a bit... I don't know... worried. Anxious. A bit absent.' He squeezed her hand. 'You should be feeling happy on your wedding day.'

She mustered a smile. 'I'm just nervous, Dad. You know what I'm like with crowds of people.'

'There's nothing to worry about.' He patted her hand. 'You're going to be fine. And the man you're marrying, well I couldn't have chosen better myself.' Nicci looked at her fingers, at the pearly pink nails that matched her flowers and the bows at the end of every pew in the church.

'You look absolutely stunning.' There were tears in his eyes. 'Your mum...' His voice cracked. 'She would have loved to see you in that dress.'

His words brought a fresh surge of emotions and she dabbed at her cheeks, trying to keep her make-up intact. If only her mum had been here, perhaps she wouldn't be in the mess she was in now. She'd always been so close to her mum and knew she could have shared her feelings with her, explained her uncertainties, the dilemma she'd found herself in. Instead, she'd had to rely on her best friend, Stacey, to be her sounding board and she had very definite views.

'The problem with you, Nicci, is you're too *nice*,' she'd said a couple of weeks ago when they were sitting at her kitchen table, finalising the items to go into gift bags for the four brides-maids. The way she said it made it clear it was a criticism rather than a compliment.

'What?' she'd said, feeling stung by her remark. 'How can

you be *too* nice. I'm working with the "be kind" ethos.' She studied the shopping cart in the online jewellery shop and clicked the buy now button before closing her laptop. She gave a satisfied smile. 'I like it.'

Stacey tutted. 'I don't mean that.'

'What do you mean, then?' Nicci had been having issues with Stacey all morning. She was in one of her restless, critical moods and she wondered if her relationship with her husband, Greg, was as harmonious as she liked to make out.

'Well, I know you want to thank your bridesmaids with a lovely gift bag. But I also know your credit card is maxed out. Because you told me the other day. So, what do you do? Instead of settling for something that would be perfectly acceptable and within budget, you get a new credit card so you can get the bridesmaids the more expensive gifts.'

Nicci pulled a face. 'I know. But I don't want to disappoint you all. It's important to me that I get you gifts that are memorable, that you'll all love.'

'It should be about doing what's right for you. And taking on more debt can't be a good idea, can it? You're people pleasing again.'

'Oh, Stacey. Don't be such a killjoy,' she laughed. 'When did you get so... grown up?'

Her friend looked at her then, an appalled expression on her face before she burst out laughing. 'I wish you'd listen to me, though. You do it with Ethan as well. And your dad. In fact, you do it with everyone.' She leant towards Nicci and pulled her into a hug. 'I want you to promise me that at some point you will stop and think and do whatever it is that *you* want, not everyone else. I mean, you've given up the career you wanted for your dad. That'll come back to bite you on the bum at some point.' She gave her a pointed look. 'You'll be consumed by seething resentment.'

Stacey had trained as an actress and she put such feeling

into the last two words, accompanied by matching facial expressions, that Nicci burst out laughing again. But Stacey was undeterred, wagging a finger at her. 'You can't keep yourself suppressed forever, you know. That sort of behaviour makes people ill.'

Nicci held up a hand, still giggling at the theatrics. 'I know, I know. Okay, I appreciate the concern, but I do things out of love and it makes me happy to see other people happy.'

'I think you're deliberately misunderstanding my point here.' Stacey gave a frustrated huff, hoisted her bag on her shoulder and stood up. 'I better get off. Meals to cook, husband to please.' She'd given Nicci a wink as she walked away and she knew Stacey was making another dig at her. Yes, she did do all the cooking, but... She sat for quite a while, thinking about her friend's words, wondering if she was right. But she enjoyed making people happy and there was nothing wrong in that, was there?

Now Stacey's words loomed large in her mind. There was no doubt that going through with the wedding was as much about pleasing others as it was about pleasing herself. Life was full of compromises, though, nothing was perfect and Ethan would be a wonderful husband. He would.

But, in all honesty, could she vow to keep this terrible secret? Was that a sensible basis for a happy marriage?

CHAPTER FOUR

She took a deep breath. There was no alternative. Not now. This was the only way forward.

Ethan's lovely, she told herself. *He loves me. And I love him.* And that was all that mattered. She'd make it work.

The driver came around and opened the door for her. 'Let's rock and roll,' Nicci said, pinning a broad smile to her face as she stepped out of the car. Her father held out his arm and the look of pride in his eyes made her heart swell. Wasn't it worth her compromises for that alone? The pleasure this was giving her dad was invaluable.

It doesn't have to be forever, she told herself, a recurring mantra in her life. Words that had kept her going for over a decade and would continue to serve her well now. Her bridesmaids rushed to greet her, cooing their approval, Stacey fussing with her veil, while the others organised the train of her dress.

As she walked into the church, waiting for her cue to go down the aisle, she scanned the pews for the rest of their friends, ticking people off the guest list like a school register. She noticed that Louise and Joel were missing, but she was seven months pregnant, so maybe she'd felt this was too much.

Dom was missing too. He was a fairly recent addition to their group, but had become an integral part of their lives.

He was someone she'd kept bumping into at the sandwich van on the industrial estate. She'd overheard him talking on the phone in Spanish one day and had struck up a conversation, as she was learning the language. That sparked a friendship and when she introduced him to Ethan, they realised they knew each other from school. He'd moved over from Spain when he was ten and the two of them had moved through the education system together, although not in the same friendship group. She remembered now that he'd mentioned the possibility of having to go back to Spain to deal with family matters, so it looked like he wouldn't be joining them. Everyone else who'd been invited was there, though. Many more on her side than on Ethan's.

Nicci had a big family; both her parents had three siblings, who all had children. Ethan, on the other hand, had no family present at all. He was estranged from his parents and had been since he was in his late teens. A falling out over his career choice, apparently. They'd wanted him to study medicine. He'd wanted to learn a trade. His father had bullied him relentlessly, trying to make him change his mind, but he'd held firm and suffered nothing but abuse because of it. They felt he'd let them down and had never forgiven him. She didn't think he'd forgiven them either and knew his ambition and his work ethic were all to do with proving his father wrong. His side of the church was filled with friends from the off-roading club and schoolfriends he still played five-a-side football with one evening a week. Plenty of people loved him, despite what his family might think.

As the music started, everyone stood up, their guests turning to greet her with encouraging smiles. Already there were tears. And Ethan standing at the front, his best man Steve giving her the thumbs up.

Ethan turned and beamed at her, love glowing in his eyes.

She readied herself as she walked towards him. Her dad kissed her on the cheek as they reached her groom, then stepped aside as she carefully lifted her veil. Ethan's hands felt sweaty as they clasped hers and she fixed a smile to her face, hoping she'd get through this. That she'd be able to speak her vows, be able to keep smiling, despite the turmoil in her heart.

She glanced down the aisle towards the wooden doors where she'd entered, felt too hot, claustrophobic and the impulse to run was almost overwhelming. But then she saw all the expectant faces and knew it was too late to back out now.

It's nerves. Just nerves, she told herself, thinking if she got any hotter, she was likely to faint.

Ethan held her hands a little tighter, as though he'd felt her waver. The vicar started to speak and she was frozen in place now, unable to move even if she'd wanted to.

Her heart was racing and when the vicar asked if anyone knew of a reason why she and Ethan couldn't marry, she opened her mouth to speak. *We're criminals*, she wanted to shout. Being in this holy place, about to making binding vows, she felt unbearably guilty and desperately wanted to confess. But no words came out. She caught Ethan's shocked expression and manufactured a sneeze, flashing him a smile. He smiled back, his hands tightening their grasp.

They sung the hymns that she and Ethan had chosen so carefully, said the prayers and then they came to the vows. Her voice kept cracking and she had to stop a couple of times to catch her breath, push the emotions back down. *This is the right thing to do*, she told herself as she caught a glimpse of her dad, dabbing at his eyes with his handkerchief. She looked at Ethan, standing tall and proud, giving her a smile of encouragement and she forced herself on, stumbling over the final couple of sentences, but she made it.

He looked relieved when she finished and by contrast, when it was his turn, his voice was loud and crisp and certain.

He was totally committed, that much was clear and she hoped her performance didn't give the impression that she was struggling with the sentiment of the words.

With the service finally over, Ethan bent for a kiss, the pressure of his lips on hers making her sink into his embrace, to cheers and coos of delight from their family and friends. *This is my life now*, she thought. It was better to accept that nothing could be changed than worry about the past and what might have been. *Onwards*, as her mother would have said. *Tomorrow is another day.* A new day in a new life, as Mrs Nicola Watts, where their secret would be safe.

Once they'd taken the photos outside the church, they drove the short distance to the country house hotel on the edge of town for the reception. It was a stone-built manor house, set in lovely gardens, with a large conservatory extension which served as a function room. She tried her best to enter into the spirit of things, but in quiet moments, she was struggling. All those years ago when she'd dreamed of this, she never imagined that her wedding day would be a trial to get through rather than a happy celebration to enjoy.

She kept replaying the accident in her mind. All through the reception, she found herself locked in her thoughts, watching a dark and rainy night, hearing the slosh of the tyres driving through puddles, feeling the slam of car brakes. Several times people had been speaking to her and she hadn't realised until they physically touched her, asking if she was okay. She would flash them a smile and tell them she was fine, just a bit overwhelmed by the excitement of the day. But she'd seen Stacey watching, concern in her eyes.

When Nicci headed off to the ladies' toilets for a bit of alone time, Stacey followed her in. 'What's up?' she asked, once the door was closed and she'd made sure there was nobody else in any of the cubicles. 'You're so pale. And you keep drifting off.

It's like you're not here half the time.' She rubbed her shoulder. 'Aren't you feeling well?'

'I'm fine,' Nicci said, trying to smile, but it quickly slid off her face as she fought back tears. In the presence of kindness, it was impossible to keep her emotions at bay.

'Hey,' Stacey said, wrapping her in a hug. 'It's okay. I suppose it's all a bit difficult with your mum not being here.'

Nicci nodded, glad to have been given an excuse, because not even her best friend could know the real reason for her tears.

Stacey rubbed her back, and pulled a handful of tissues from the box on the counter by the sinks. 'Come on, let's get you cleaned up,' she said, dabbing at Nicci's face, trying to save her make-up.

A few minutes later, she stood back and declared, 'That looks better.' Nicci wasn't so sure, her face still blotchy after the crying, and smudges of mascara had somehow found their way onto her dress.

She sighed. 'I'm sorry, I'm being an idiot. I'm not sure what's going on with me at the moment.'

Stacey's eyes widened, her voice reduced to a whisper. 'You're not pregnant, are you?'

Nicci shook her head. 'No, definitely not pregnant. Tired, I think. I didn't sleep well last night and I was awake at the crack of dawn.' She glanced at herself in the mirror again. 'I'm a mess, aren't I?'

'You are not,' Stacey said, emphatically. 'You are nothing like a mess, you look fabulous. Ethan thinks you're gorgeous. I mean, the way he looks at you...' She gave a dreamy sigh. 'I wish my husband looked at me like that. And those vows you both wrote.' She rolled her eyes up to the ceiling. 'Oh my God, I just welled up. You should have warned me about those.' She stood next to Nicci at the mirror, put an arm round her shoulder and gave her a reassuring hug. 'It was so special and you two are going to be great together.'

Nicci laughed. 'Well, you've changed your tune. Are you the same person who warned me off him? The same person who ends up arguing with him every time we meet up?'

Stacey grinned. 'You know it doesn't mean anything. We're just different personalities, aren't we? And anyway, I'm not the one married to him. You two never seem to argue. Not like me and Greg.'

Nicci thought about that and knew it to be true. They didn't argue. That didn't mean she always agreed with Ethan but she'd been brought up not to sweat over the small stuff and let things go, because they didn't really matter. Having been through the trauma of her mum's illness and death, she'd learnt that lesson years ago.

Now, though, she'd let a big thing go. The hit-and-run. And that did matter. She gave an involuntary shudder and Stacey frowned. 'Are you a bit cold? These old stone buildings look lovely and everything, but it is a bit chilly in here.'

Nicci rubbed at her arms, 'I'm okay. It's warmer out there, though. Come on, let's go.'

While they walked back to the party, arms linked, Nicci gave herself a pep talk. It was time to start enjoying her big day. The whole thing was costing a fortune and she wanted her dad to know she appreciated the effort he'd gone to in order to make the day so special for her. Even if she was conflicted inside, on the outside, she was determined to show that she was happy to be married to Ethan, happy that her family and friends had come to celebrate with them. And it wasn't fair on Ethan, because he deserved for her to be mentally present and enjoying their day together.

After another glass of champagne and something to eat, she

started to feel better and surrounded by so much laughter and banter between friends and family she began to brighten up and join in.

Ethan took her in his arms for their first dance, his body tight against hers as they moved around the floor to the slow number. She allowed herself to think that the worst was over, the past was done with and she could enjoy their life together. Who wouldn't be happy with a man like her new husband?

As she looked into his eyes, she could tell how much he adored her. What they'd done wasn't his fault, and his idea for the vows was his way of protecting them both, showing her that although she was driving, and clearly at fault, he was backing her all the way. Sharing the responsibility. And she loved him for that, knew he would always be on her side, no matter what happened.

As the evening wore on, Ethan went to talk to his friends and she had time to chat to her bridesmaids, who were huddled together at the end of the top table, whispering to each other.

'I have a little something for each of you, to say thank you for being here to celebrate this day with me.' She gave them each their gift bag, handing a different bag to Stacey. 'Thanks for being my rock. Honestly, I couldn't have got through the day without you.'

Stacey welled up when she saw the extra gifts that Nicci had bought her, something special to let her know she was her best friend and her maid of honour. It was odd that someone as confident as Stacey would need constant ego boosts, but Nicci knew that the real Stacey was different to the public persona. She'd come through some tough times in her life in the care system and, as an adopted child who hadn't been taken in by a family until she was twelve, if anyone deserved to feel special, it was her.

Not long after that, when everyone was dancing, and she was sitting back watching, she caught a movement out of the corner of her eye. Ethan and Stacey. They were going outside, his hand on her back while she smiled up at him.

Now that's odd, she thought to herself. Because the two of them wouldn't naturally seek each other out. Stacey was Nicci's friend and Ethan tolerated her when he had to. He hadn't come straight out and said he didn't like her, but that was the impression he'd always given her. So... what was going on?

CHAPTER FIVE

The next morning, Ethan lay in bed beside his sleeping wife, a wonderful glow of well-being filling his heart. They were staying at the hotel where they'd had the reception and the honeymoon suite was suitably grand, fitted out in red and gold. It had plush carpets, a big bay window and a king-sized four-poster bed, with red velvet drapes. It also had a huge double-ended bath, which he was hoping they might try out later. It must have cost Nicci's dad a fortune, but he'd insisted on paying for everything. Nothing was too good for his only daughter. And now Ethan, by marriage, was his only son. Honestly, life didn't get much better than this.

He snuggled in to his pillow, thinking this might be the comfiest bed he'd ever slept in. Who would have thought, in three short years, he would have gone from sofa surfing, living from hand-to-mouth, to this? When he'd left home at sixteen, he'd struggled to manage his money and got himself into all sorts of bother with loan sharks. It had taken him years to pay off his debts. Thankfully, that was all in the past and he'd learnt a valuable lesson. He didn't even have a credit card these days, determined never to get himself into that situation again.

The wedding had been fun in the end, once Nicci had controlled her nerves and they'd got through the service. For one terrifying moment, he'd thought she was going to do a runner. He could see it in her eyes, feel the tension in her body, but then she'd settled down, thank goodness.

What would he have done if she'd run away?

It didn't bear thinking about, their plans in tatters before they'd had a chance to get started. But anyway, that didn't happen, and now they'd made their vows, he trusted Nicci to keep her side of the bargain. She was solid like that and he had every confidence that her word was her bond. Like father like daughter. That's what you got with the Bale family. Trustworthy with a capital T.

It was one of the qualities he most admired in his father-in-law. None of this double talk, saying one thing and thinking or doing another. He'd had enough of that with his dad. Status was all his parents worried about. What mattered most to his dad was how he'd look to the rest of his family and his pseudo-friends at the golf club. He was so competitive in all aspects of his life and proud of the way he'd managed to work his way up through the ranks in the council, by fair means and foul, until he finally became leader. It was all about impressing people and Ethan hated that about him. A master manipulator, knowing who to suck up to in order to get his promotions, knowing how to connive to knock his competition down. There was something in him that was downright nasty and when he reached the top of the organisation, he became insufferable. He thought he knew best about everything, constantly belittling Ethan and undermining his confidence.

'You'll never come to anything, you stupid little shit.' That's what he'd said to Ethan when he told him he was leaving school after his exams to take up a plumbing apprenticeship. What father says that to their son? Those words had left an indelible mark on Ethan's psyche and he could remember the rest of the conversation as clear as if they were having it right now.

'University is a mug's game,' Ethan had responded. 'I know I've got the grades to do well in science and stay on for another couple of years, but I don't want to. I'm ready to work. I don't want to spend years building up a huge student loan and all that stress of being a doctor. It's not for me.' He'd picked up his rucksack, packed with his clothes and not much else. 'I'm leaving.' His best friend's mum had said he could stay for a few weeks while he got himself sorted out. She knew what the score was, had seen a video he'd recorded of his dad having a go at him and had been shocked by the cruelty of his words.

'You are clueless,' his dad had shouted, his spittle spraying Ethan's skin. 'You mark my words, you'll be crawling back home, begging for help.' He jabbed his finger inches away from Ethan's face. 'But if you walk out, I don't want you coming back. You understand me?'

Ethan pushed past him and out of the door, slamming it behind him. He didn't blame his mum for not standing up for him, he knew she was bullied just as much as he was. She couldn't help him. Nobody could. It was a matter of helping himself.

However hard leaving home had been, it was better than suffering his dad's constant jibes, being made to feel he wasn't good enough because he didn't want to follow the career path his dad had chosen for him. He knew what he wanted to do, knew what his goals were, and he'd decided he would find his own way to achieve them.

His greatest ambition in life was to be way more successful than his dad, then the stupid man would have to eat his words. It would hurt him and that's what he desperately wanted. Because his father's actions had caused Ethan untold distress and hardship over the years, leaving mental scars he knew would never heal. He hated him with a passion that felt hard to control sometimes, but instead of letting it eat him up, he used that anger to fire his ambition, make himself work harder. One day, his father would have to admit that Ethan had been right and he'd been wrong. That his shocking behaviour towards his son had been undeserved. That Ethan had won.

Thinking back, he was so grateful to Pete for his job offer. It had marked a turning point in his fortunes. Mind you, he'd worked his socks off proving he would be a valuable employee, bending over backwards to help them. He'd spotted an opportunity early on, when he'd first started supplying the business and could see the potential, things they didn't seem to recognise themselves. For some reason it had taken over his brain, all these ideas he didn't know what to do with, new products they could develop, new markets they could exploit. Something clicked in his head and he knew this was what he wanted to do.

There was no way he'd be able to raise the funding to start his own business and anyway, he didn't have all the skills. But he did have an instinct for sales. It probably came from his grandfather who'd been a market trader, selling hardware and household items. That's how Ethan had learnt how to sell, it was part of his DNA. Even if his father liked to gloss over that part of his family history.

Pete soon realised how useful he could be, liked his ideas and the way he worked with them. But Ethan knew he had the wits to make the business truly thrive. He wanted to be part of it, one of the team, driving things forward.

Now he was not just part of the business, but part of the family too. Not something he'd anticipated happening at the start, but it couldn't have worked out better. His future was secure and that was a wonderful place to be after his rocky start to adult life.

Nicci stirred and he rolled over, stroked her arms with his fingertips until her eyes opened and she gazed at him for a long moment, no words. Sometimes he felt they didn't need to speak to know what each other was thinking. Sometimes he hadn't a clue what was going on in her head. Today was one of those days.

'Good morning, Mrs Watts,' he murmured, his fingers moving to caress her cheek. Her eyes closed and she took a deep, contented breath. He took that as a sign, and let his hands roam over her body. 'I believe we have unfinished business to attend to,' he whispered, as he took her in his arms.

Much later, they actually got out of bed.

They had decided to postpone their honeymoon because business was hectic in the summer months and they couldn't leave Pete to manage on his own. They were going on a winter cruise in December instead, when business tended to go quiet, so today was their only day off. Ethan was determined to wring every last drop of pleasure out of it.

He went for a shower, whistling as he washed his hair, until he heard Nicci shout to him from the other room. She sounded frantic and he didn't think twice about dashing into the bedroom, even though he was dripping all over the floor.

'What is it?' he asked, puzzled, because everything was how he'd left it a few minutes ago. She was propped up in bed, the remains of breakfast on a tray on her lap.

She pointed at the TV on the wall, turned up the sound so loud it made him wince. He caught a reporter saying:

'The victim of the hit-and-run is still in hospital. His condition is improving and doctors are hoping to bring him out of his induced coma. They are still no closer to identifying the man, but hope he will be able to give them more details once he is conscious. However, due to the nature of his head injuries, doctors have warned there are no guarantees that his memory will be intact or if he'll be able to speak. That's why officers are appealing once again for information. If anyone was in the area at the time of the accident, or think they might know the

identity of the victim, then please get in touch using the number on the screen.'

The report finished, switching back to the main newsreader. Nicci turned off the TV, her face ashen.

'Oh God,' she said, her voice fluttering with panic. 'What if someone comes forward? What if the man knows something that will identify our car? What if—'

'Hey, hey, come on, love. Let's not get worked up about things that might not happen.' He sat on the edge of the bed, put an arm round her shoulders and drew her to him, kissing the top of her head as she leant against his shoulder. 'Nobody saw us. Don't you think the police would have been round by now if they had? No, we're okay.' He kissed her again. 'But we won't stay okay if you're going to panic every time a news report comes on, or someone starts talking about it.'

He could feel his heart racing, could feel Nicci shaking in his arms. It was hard to sound calm when he was as jumpy about the accident as she was, but one of them had to stay strong and he knew the role was his.

'You can't know that,' she insisted, her voice shrill. 'Somebody called an ambulance. What if they were just behind us? What if they saw? Or somebody could have been walking their dog and seen it happen. Or cutting through to the new houses, coming back from the pub. People walk past that corner all the time, don't they?'

Ethan took a deep breath, trying to keep his voice even and patient, while his brain was scampering round inspecting all the possibilities. His one priority was to keep Nicci calm and rational. She'd given him a scare in the church and she was starting to scare him again now.

'It's going to get easier. I promise it will.' He leant to kiss her on the lips, soft and gentle, but she didn't respond in the way she usually did. Instead, she shrugged him off, wriggling from his embrace. The breakfast tray went flying, tipping coffee dregs all over the pristine white bedcovers, croissant crumbs sprinkled like confetti.

'Oh hell,' she said, reaching to put everything back on the tray, trying to gather the crumbs, mopping at the coffee stain with a serviette. 'Look what I've done now.'

He watched her for a moment before speaking again. 'Once the person is a bit better and can tell them who they are, all this will die down. Let's be clear, it was an accident.'

'Or they might remember what happened and they will be able to track it back to us.'

Nicci was losing it. He'd thought she was stronger than this, but he accepted it was a big thing to deal with. He was able to keep his emotions in check better than she could, it was a man thing, but that didn't mean he wasn't feeling it. He knew how hard it was, but what if she couldn't keep it in? What if she blurted their secret out to someone? Like her dad. Or Stacey...

CHAPTER SIX

Nicci was on edge all morning, restless and unable to settle to anything now she'd seen the news. She didn't want to go out, didn't want to stay in. Didn't want Ethan touching her. In the end he'd taken himself out for some fresh air. His frustration was clear and she knew he was trying to help, make things better, but his presence was doing the opposite, amplifying her fears.

She was glad to be alone, which is not how it was supposed to be the day after your wedding. The aftermath of the accident was consuming her, rolling through her mind, squashing any other thoughts until it was all she could think about. An obstacle she couldn't find a way past.

Her phone rang, startling her from her thoughts and she saw it was her dad.

'Hiya!' she said, forcing a cheerfulness into her voice.

'Hello, love. I'm so sorry to bother you.' He sounded a bit emotional, his voice thick, like he was on the verge of tears. She snapped to attention, immediately on red alert.

Since her mum had died, her dad had struggled with bouts of depression. He'd been upbeat yesterday, but it sounded like his mood had crashed now the excitement was over and he was on his own. She'd been worried this might happen, another reason for not having the honeymoon straightaway.

'Dad, don't be silly. You're never a bother.'

'I don't know how I forgot this, but today would have been thirty-four years since my first date with your mum. After the wedding yesterday and then you not being here on a Sunday... I mean, you're always here for Sunday lunch, aren't you? Well, I —' His voice cracked and she heard him sniffing, unable to finish what he was saying.

'Hey, Dad, are you okay?' Her heart fluttered, her mind already working out how she would get herself to his house to check. He was an impulsive man and she didn't want him doing anything untoward. It had been enough of a shock the last time, finding him unconscious, seeing the empty packets of painkillers, rushing him to hospital, the stomach pump, the nervous waiting. Thankfully she'd found him soon enough and there was no lasting damage, but a repeat attempt at ending his life was unbearable to contemplate.

'I don't know that I am.' She heard him gulp and it was a moment before he could find his voice. 'I'm feeling so low and I know it's daft. It's not like you've gone anywhere. Not really. I've got myself in a right state about being without your mum. Even though she's been gone for a couple of years now.' He sniffed, blew his nose. 'She was my soulmate and seeing you with Ethan in the church brought it all back, you know? You look so like her, I kept thinking it was Jean I was seeing. But then I kept having to tell myself she's gone.'

Nicci's heart went out to him. Her dad was a romantic, someone in love with the idea of being in love. He'd always bought her mum flowers and little presents. Every week they were married there would be a gift on a Friday. A thank you for being his wife. Once Jean had died, he'd showered his love on Nicci, keeping up the weekly tradition. Now she was married, she supposed he felt that his place had been taken. He was on the sidelines. On his own.

'That's understandable. It was an emotional day for both of us, wasn't it? But nothing's changed just because I've got married. I'm still here for you.' She checked the time, making up her mind. 'Tell you what, shall I come over?' Ethan had made arrangements for them this afternoon, but she'd have to tell him to cancel. Her dad's welfare was more important.

'No, no, don't do that!' He sounded horrified at the idea. 'You've only got today until you're back at work and I'm sure you're exhausted after the wedding. All that planning and the socialising.'

She looked at the empty bedroom and thought she'd rather be with her dad than sat here on her own. 'Honestly, it's no bother. I'd like to come and see you. Ethan's gone out for a bit of fresh air so—'

She heard a gasp. 'You've not been arguing, have you? What man goes out for fresh air on his bloody honeymoon?'

'No, not arguing.' Nicci was quick to refute the suggestion, but although they hadn't been shouting at each other, there had been a smouldering tension in the air. 'He's the sort of person who needs his own space now and again. I mean... getting married is a big thing and he needed a breather. But he should be back soon.'

'Don't you worry about me. I'm being silly. I don't want to drag you away from him.'

Nicci's mind was made up now and she realised there was a compromise solution. 'Look, we'll both come. In fact, why don't we take you out for Sunday lunch? Ethan booked us a table at The Angel. I'm sure they'll be able to fit you in too.'

'I haven't been out for Sunday lunch for years.' Her dad sounded brighter and she could tell he liked the idea. 'We usually cook it together, don't we?'

'We do and won't it be lovely not to have to bother?' She

heard the door open and Ethan came back inside. 'In fact, he's here now. Get yourself ready. We won't be long.'

She ended the call and Ethan looked at her. 'We won't be long for what?'

'Dad's having a wobble. I always get a bit worried when he's like this, you know... since that trouble after Mum died. I don't want him to be on his own.'

Ethan's brow creased with concern. 'I suppose it's to be expected. He was looking a bit tearful yesterday at times.' He came and gave her a hug, which was exactly what she needed and she could tell his earlier frustration had gone. He bent to give her a kiss. 'Shall we pick him up on our way over to lunch? I'm sure they'll be able to fit one more in.'

And that was what she loved about Ethan. Nothing phased him. He didn't mind if plans were disrupted. Flexibility was his middle name. She looked up at him, pulled an apologetic face. 'I hope you don't mind, but I already invited him.'

Ethan grinned. 'No worries, love. You know I enjoy Pete's company. He's always been a father figure to me. In fact...' His grin broadened. 'I can call him Dad, now, right? I might start practising.' He hesitated. 'Do you think he'd mind?'

Nicci's heart melted. This was another of the things she loved about Ethan. He saw himself as part of her family. Perhaps it was because Ethan wasn't close to his own parents, but it was a wonderful thing.

'Mind?' She laughed. 'God, no. He'd love it. In fact, I think that's exactly what he needs. I think he's feeling a bit left out.'

He kissed her again and it was a few minutes before they came up for air.

'Anyway, Mrs Watts, it's time we were heading off if we're going to pick your dad up on the way.'

She smiled at the sound of her married name and slipped on her shoes, grabbing her bag and a jacket as she followed Ethan out of the door. She was thankful that the tension had dissipated, Ethan's mood now buoyant, and she looked forward to giving her dad a treat after the money he'd lavished on their wedding.

It was a delicious meal and as they were finishing, Pete turned to Ethan. 'I don't suppose we could head up to the cemetery on the way back, could we? I'd love to say hello to Jean.'

'No problem at all... Dad,' Ethan replied.

Nicci watched her father's eyes widen, a happy smile spreading across his face. He gave Ethan a soft punch on the shoulder. 'Thanks... Son.'

They both laughed and Nicci was touched by this show of affection between the two men in her life, confirming she had made the right decision. Ethan would be a wonderful husband, and a fantastic support for her dad. She had to push this silly idea that there was a problem, a compromise, out of her mind. Everything had worked out exactly as it was supposed to and she was lucky to be married to this gorgeous man.

Ethan glanced over at her. 'Nicci was saying how hard it's been not having her mum at the wedding.' He leant over and rubbed Pete's shoulder. 'We can go and tell her all about it, can't we?'

Tears stung Nicci's eyes. Ethan was so intuitive with her dad, it made her heart fill with love. And he was right, it would ease her own heartache to go and see her mum's grave, have a chat with her. He even stopped at the petrol station on the way and picked up a bunch of flowers. That was Ethan all over. Thoughtful and kind. The perfect husband in so many ways.

What had she been thinking yesterday when she'd nearly run out of the church? It was going to be fine. Absolutely fine.

They pulled into the car park at the cemetery and her dad hesitated before getting out of the car. 'I was going to drive up here myself, you know, but I'd got so upset I had a nip of whisky and I didn't think I'd be safe driving.' He frowned, his face colouring. 'I'd never forgive myself if I hit somebody.' He gave an angry shake of the head, his voice hardening. 'People who've been drink driving, or know they're not fit to be behind the wheel, should be locked up for life. That's what I think. There's no excuse in my mind.'

Nicci's eyes met Ethan's and she swallowed, her reply stuck in her throat. In her mind, she could see her and Ethan at Stacey's, the champagne flowing. How many glasses had she drunk? She couldn't remember, but nobody would be able to prove anything now. Not all these days later. She checked that thought, wondering if she was right.

Already she was remembering the feeling of horror when she heard the body hit the car, the deafening silence afterwards, her hands clawing at her throat as she tried to breathe.

She imagined what her dad's reaction would be, the hate in his eyes as he realised his daughter was not the person he thought she was. His devastation as customers shunned his business. His despair when he faced financial ruin.

Whatever happens, Dad must never find out.

'You okay, love? You're looking a bit pale?' Her dad was frowning at her and she realised she'd stopped walking. He came back and hooked her arm through his. 'I know this is tough, but we can do it together.'

She could never knowingly cause this man harm, but words from her childhood came flooding back, spoken in her mum's voice. 'The truth will always come out.' She could see herself standing in the kitchen, an empty chocolate wrapper scrunched in her hands, hidden behind her back. 'I know there was a chocolate bar on the worktop and it's not there now, so where do you think it might have gone, hmm?'

On that occasion the truth had come out because she had chocolate all round her mouth. There was evidence. Her mother was just giving her the chance to confess and redeem herself, but she chose to lie and get caught out. The punishment was no sweets for a month, which felt severe at the age of five, especially after her mum told her if she'd owned up straight away, she would have had a telling off and that would have been the end of it.

Is there evidence now? she wondered, thinking they should at least give the car a thorough clean. And what would the punishment be if they were caught?

Her legs felt weak and she leant on her dad. She was stuck in an impossible dilemma. The urge to confess was getting stronger as the pressure of keeping the secret grew. *The truth will come out.* Was it better to lie and chance being caught out, or confess in the knowledge that the punishment for her and Ethan would likely be less, but the impact on her dad would be severe?

He was innocent, just as the accident victim was innocent. Doing what was morally right in confessing, could be morally wrong if she was certain it would harm her dad. Was that how it worked? Her head ached; her thoughts tied in a knot. This secret was making her feel like she was going mad.

CHAPTER SEVEN

The weather had been a bit mixed, but now the sun was breaking through the clouds, shafts of light illuminating the higgledy-piggledy gravestones at the top of the cemetery. They were ancient, some hundreds of years old. Her mum's ashes were buried lower down, reunited with her own parents. Ethan strolled around the graveyard while she and Pete had some quiet time with her mum, taking turns so they each had a few moments on their own to share what they needed to say.

'You've got yourself a good 'un there, love,' her dad said, as they watched Ethan, looking relaxed as he sat on a bench at the top of the cemetery.

'I know,' she said, giving him a wave to tell him they were finished. He waved back and strode towards them.

'I've got something I want to say to you both,' Pete said when Ethan arrived at the graveside. 'And I think this is exactly the right place and the right time.'

Nicci looked at Ethan and her dad, not sure what he'd got in mind.

Her dad rocked back on his heels, his hands jingling the small change in his pockets, his eyes on his wife's grave, lost in thought for a moment. Then he smiled, a big beaming grin, that lit up his face. 'I had a word with Jean, and I know you're going to think I'm a bit mad, but I sense your mum believes this would be the right thing to do as well.'

He took Nicci's hand, then Ethan's, looking from one to the other and back again. 'I want to make you both directors of the company.'

Ethan's eyes lit up.

Nicci's heart sank.

This was the last thing she wanted. She'd hoped she could slide herself out of the business, by hiring someone to gradually take her place so she could finally get to university. She didn't want more responsibility in the family firm, but how was she going to tell her dad that when he thought he was giving her a gift?

She said nothing while Ethan gasped his thanks. 'Wow, Pete... Dad. I wasn't expecting that. Not at all. Christ... I'm so grateful.' He grabbed Pete's hand with both of his and pumped his arm in an enthusiastic handshake.

Pete laughed, his face lit up with delight as he finally let go of their hands. He held up a finger. 'There's one more thing. Ethan, I'd like you to be managing director. I want to step back a bit. I'm starting to feel my age. I can't do the hours I used to and I'd much rather be looking after production than dealing with the office side of things. Nicci here does a brilliant job, so I think it would be right for her to be finance director.'

Ethan was lost for words, his mouth hanging open. 'What? Are you sure that's what you want?'

'Yes, Son.' Pete clapped him on the back. 'It's exactly what I want. I think the business will be in good hands for years to come with you two running it. Hopefully it'll always give you a decent living well after I'm gone.'

Nicci felt her world falling apart beneath her. The life she'd planned torn away from her grasp and she couldn't think of a way to prevent it from happening. Not without throwing her dad's gift back in his face and giving Ethan the impression she wasn't going to be there to support him.

Her mind took her back to their wedding vows. They hadn't just been about keeping their secret safe. They'd been about keeping their marriage safe too. But now she felt like she'd locked herself in a box and thrown away the key. How was she going to get herself out of this without alienating the two most important people in her life?

Her body swayed, the ground coming up to meet her as she felt herself falling. Ethan grabbed her arm to keep her steady.

'Whoa, careful, love.'

Her dad frowned, concerned. 'What's up, Nicci? Do you think you're sickening for something?'

She closed her eyes, clinging on to Ethan as she waited for the world to stop spinning. 'I'm fine, Dad. It's just... a bit of a shock.'

'A nice shock, I hope,' he said, tentatively.

'Wonderful,' Ethan said, quickly, as if he was worried her dad might change his mind. 'The best shock we've ever had.'

She forced herself to open her eyes, smiled and nodded, not able to say what she really thought. Not now. Stacey's words floated into her mind. *People pleaser.* She was doing it again, but had no idea how to stop. She was complicit in a crime she couldn't admit to and tied into running a family business that she'd never wanted to be a part of.

If she was going to be true to her wedding vows, there was nothing she could change. She was trapped.

If she was going to be true to herself though... What would happen, she wondered, if those wedding vows were broken?

CHAPTER EIGHT

Ethan couldn't sleep. It was now half past two in the morning and he was enjoying the buzz of contentment, a cocktail of happy hormones keeping him awake. Honestly, he'd never been so excited in his life. *Managing director.* Didn't that have a wonderful ring to it? He was going to be the managing director of a successful business. He couldn't wait until he told his dad. Imagine the look on his face. The utter disbelief that the son he wrote off fifteen years ago had made good. That would show him. But this was just the start. *Slow and steady wins the race.* That's the rule he lived by and look how it was paying off now, everything suddenly slotting into place.

He'd get business cards sorted straight away. That would be his first job in the morning. And get Nicci some with finance director on them. A proper power couple. He chuckled to himself as he lay in bed, his hands underneath his head, looking at the drapes on the four-poster bed. It was their last night of luxury in the hotel and then back to their poky little home.

He thought about the cottage. The musty smell of damp in the kitchen. The neighbour on one side who played dance music all night at the weekend. And on the other side there was a dog that howled like a wolf when its owners went out. Thank goodness they were only renting – the knowledge that he wouldn't have to live there permanently was the only thing that made it bearable. Maybe now they could think about a mortgage, getting a place of their own. They'd talked about it often enough but it had always seemed like a faraway dream.

Then his mind took him to the four-bedroom house that Pete was living in on his own, feeling lonely and left out. He was a constant worry because his mood was prone to take sudden dips, and after he'd tried to take his own life, the fear that he'd do it again was always at the back of their minds.

Pete was a great boss, and hadn't he loved being called Dad? Ethan noticed he'd called him Son a few times as well. He'd have to admit it did give him a glow. What a pity you couldn't choose your parents. This man wanted him to be his son, not like his own family. He evicted them from his mind before they could intrude on his happiness. No way was he sharing any of this with that bunch of losers. Not yet. Knowing his dad, he'd find a way to make a negative out of a positive, a way to make him feel bad about things he wanted to celebrate. One day he'd tell his dad what a success he'd become, but now was not the time. Because there was more he could achieve, he was certain of it.

The evening before, when they'd dropped Pete off, they'd stayed at his house for a celebratory drink and a bit of wedding cake. Shook hands again on Pete's offer, and when they'd left, he'd seen the glisten of tears in his eyes.

It was no secret the guy was emotionally unstable, which was a bit of a problem. He wasn't safe to be on his own. How many times had they dashed over to check on him when Nicci had one of her 'feelings' that things weren't right? Too many to count and she'd usually been right.

In fact, she'd been so anxious about leaving her dad on his own it had almost made her back out of their marriage. She'd definitely had a wobble at the altar and as far as he knew, that was the most likely cause. But then...

Ethan turned and looked at his sleeping wife, her back towards him. Was he imagining it, or was there something else troubling her?

CHAPTER NINE

On Wednesday, Nicci was meeting Stacey for lunch and she was glad to get out of the office. It had been a weird sort of morning already, one of those days when everything that can go wrong, does go wrong, and she could feel her temper rising. She needed a change of scenery, and a laugh with her friend, to put it all in perspective. The perfect distraction to stop her from snapping at people.

Relieved to get out of the office, she made her way to the coffee shop where they often met for lunch. It was just off the market square, down a little side street and only had a few tables inside, most of their business being takeaways. The coffee was the best in town, though, and they always had an interesting selection of sandwiches and cakes. If the weather was fine, they would get their coffees and lunch to go and find a quiet spot outside, but today the rain was pelting down, so they were sitting in.

'How's married life treating you?' Stacey said as she pulled out the chair beside Nicci and flopped down, her bag on her lap. She looked tired and fed up, a little bedraggled, her make-up smudged under her eyes.

Nicci grimaced, unsure how close to the truth she wanted to sail. Stacey was like a terrier when she got a sniff of a problem, worrying away at it, asking endless questions until she got to the truth. If Nicci was a people pleaser, then Stacey could be described as a problem solver. She always had the best intentions at heart but was prone to interfere in the name of helping, always thought she knew what was best for everyone, and the results were not always positive.

Nicci wasn't in the mood for an interrogation, hoping she could have a vent about a few issues and leave the marital stuff alone.

'Um... Let me say it's not been quite what I expected,' she said, carefully.

'Oh no. I hope everything's okay? What's happened?'

Of course, Nicci couldn't tell her everything that was bothering her, but there was one thing she did want to discuss. Her dad's behaviour. Ever since the wedding, he'd been a bit odd, all maudlin and melancholy, and she wanted a second opinion.

'Well, first off, Dad has made me and Ethan company directors.'

Stacey gasped, her effusive congratulations coming a few seconds too slow to be genuine. Nicci knew she'd be jealous, because she was always going on about how lucky Nicci was to be working in the family firm, with a secure job, whereas Stacey had been made redundant three times in the last four years. Her acting career hadn't taken off in the way she'd hoped, and she'd come home from London to a series of temporary admin jobs.

'Ethan is going to be managing director and Dad wants me to be finance director.' She pulled a face. 'I hate to sound ungrateful but you know this isn't the career I want and I don't know how to get out of it without offending Dad and Ethan. They're both so passionate about the business but...' She sighed. 'It bores me to tears. You know this, don't you? Honestly, every morning I go in that office I could weep. I only stepped in to help when Mum was ill, but I've been stuck there for years now. And if I'm finance director, I feel like I'll be there forever.'

'Oh my God!' Stacey's mouth gaped open, speechless for a few seconds. 'A director. You're getting all the lucky breaks. I wish Pete was my dad, that's all I can say.'

'But I can't accept it, can I? Not when I don't intend to stay.'

Stacey frowned. 'What does Ethan think?'

Nicci sighed, looked at the table. 'He's ecstatic about becoming managing director. That's his dream come true right there. I haven't spoken to him about my role yet because I know he'll be upset that I don't want to do it. He sees us as this dream team. But I've had a horrible morning chasing up overdue invoices and sorting out deliveries of materials that haven't arrived and doing the payroll. And I just thought... this is destroying me. I can't do it.'

She pressed her lips together, knowing she'd tried her hardest to shed a positive light on her situation and failed. Whatever she told herself, whatever spin she put on things, she knew she'd waited years to be able to follow the career she wanted and now the door had closed on her dreams. 'I feel like I've been given a prison sentence and the walls are closing in.'

Stacey looked dumbfounded and fished her purse out of her bag before standing. 'You need a strong coffee and a talking to, my friend. Your view on life is warped out of shape. Your dad gives you a job for life and you're complaining?' Her incredulous tone said she couldn't believe what she was hearing, her eye roll emphasising the fact before she headed towards the counter to get their order.

Nicci realised she'd made a mistake telling Stacey. Now she was in for a lecture about how easy her life was compared to Stacey's struggle with a monster mortgage, a job that looked like it could disappear any minute and a husband who had turned into a DIY fanatic, and thought having fun was a trip to B&Q.

Joel would understand.

He was the long-term partner of her friend, Louise, and they were expecting a baby together. Although she'd known him for a couple of years, he'd become a close friend when he and Louise moved into a rented cottage in the same village. They kept bumping into each other on dog walks and it wasn't long before they were organising to walk the dogs together.

He was a quiet man, the opposite of his partner, Louise, who was a long-standing member of their social group. It was his love of reading that had endeared him to her. Ethan wasn't interested in fiction, preferring memoirs and self-help books. Joel, on the other hand, read widely and they found they enjoyed the same stories, swapping recommendations and books, if they had physical copies. Talking to him was like having a conversation with a clone of herself, but more interesting. It was undemanding, but engrossing, and after a hectic day, spending time with him, talking books, was exactly what she needed. Total escapism to imaginary worlds.

She trusted his opinion and she longed to talk to him about her dad making her and Ethan directors. Having to postpone her dreams for the sake of others once again. Joel would put it in perspective for her, no judgement, and probably have a few useful suggestions about how she could re-frame things in her mind.

But where was he? A no-show at the wedding, although that was understandable given Louise was in the last stage of pregnancy. It was the fact that he wasn't answering her messages that was bothering her, but that too made sense. The last time they'd met she'd been in a bit of a state, consumed with last-minute nerves about the wedding, and he was probably avoiding her until she'd settled down.

Stacey arrived back at the table with a tray laden with drinks and a sandwich each.

'Have you heard from Joel and Louise at all?' Nicci asked before Stacey could launch into a lecture about how lucky she was. 'They didn't turn up at the wedding and I wondered if everything is okay. I've messaged them but haven't had a reply from either of them.' Stacey always knew what was happening in everyone's lives and if there were problems, she'd have all the details.

'Funny you should ask that. I was round at their house last night.' She leant forward, her voice a conspiratorial whisper. 'Apparently, they had a big bust-up and he said he needed some space to think. She's climbing the walls, freaking out that he's left her.'

'But they're about to have the baby,' Nicci squeaked. Her heart beat a little faster. 'He walked out? Has she heard from him?'

'Not a peep. It's been a week now. But then she didn't expect to hear anything because he asked her to give him some breathing room.'

'Oh dear.' It was all Nicci could think of to say and completely inadequate, but her mind was going at warp speed, thinking about the implications. She took a sip of her coffee. At least that explained his absence. She'd been worried that something more sinister had happened. She stopped her racing thoughts, bringing herself back to the here and now. Lunch with Stacey. Everything was fine. 'Poor Louise,' she added as an afterthought.

'To be honest, I never thought they were a good match.' Stacey gave a dismissive flap of the hand. 'I mean she's so outgoing and he's the exact opposite. He hates parties, doesn't he? But it would be awful for her if he decides to leave.'

Nicci took a bite of her sandwich, chewed slowly as she considered Stacey's words. 'You think that's a possibility?'

Stacey nodded as she stirred sugar into her coffee. 'I do. Perhaps he already has.'

Nicci felt a chill run through her. *Imagine if I never got to see Joel again...* She shook the thought from her head and concentrated on eating while she let the new information sink in. If he was asking for time out from Louise, maybe that's what he needed from her too. She'd have to be patient and wait.

'Louise thinks he's been having an affair, but she wouldn't tell me a name.'

Nicci coughed, afraid she might choke on her sandwich, but managed to recover and swallow it down with a swig of coffee. Louise knew about the dog walks, but had she read more into it? Or had Joel said something? Or was there someone else entirely?

Unease settled at the back of her neck, pulling at the muscles. Stacey continued talking. 'There's no point second-guessing it because we'll probably be wrong. We'll find out eventually and I'm sure Joel will come back once he's had time to see sense.'

Nicci supposed she was right. No point in speculating. Time to change the subject. 'The other person who didn't show at the wedding was Dom. Have you heard anything about him?'

'I know what happened to Dom.' Stacey dabbed at her mouth with her serviette, mopping up the sauce that had dripped out of her prawn sandwich. 'Apparently, he ended up in police custody.' She laughed. 'Drunk and disorderly, can you believe?'

'What?' Nicci frowned. That sounded very unlike Dom. 'When was this?'

Stacey shrugged. 'I don't know exactly, but that's what I heard. I can't remember who told me now. But anyway, nothing to worry about.'

'At least that's those mysteries solved.' Except, there were still a few unanswered questions. She sighed, knowing she'd have to wait.

They were silent for a little while as they ate. Stacey finished first.

'Going back to the situation with your dad.'

'Hmm.' Nicci had hoped she'd forgotten and moved on. She prepared herself for variations on the usual lecture, while she chewed the last of her sandwich.

'I think... As I see it, he's clearly fond of Ethan and he's making plans now before it gets to the stage where he's poorly or something and you need to make alternative arrangements and it's all done in a big rush.' She finished her coffee. 'I mean if he's suggested it, then he's obviously fine with it. You and Ethan running the business together probably makes him think back to when he started it with your mum.' She leant over and squeezed Nicci's hand. 'It doesn't mean you have to do it forever, though. Remember we talked about training up a replacement, didn't we?'

Nicci vaguely remembered that conversation but it was months ago and she'd been so wrapped up in organising the wedding, she'd forgotten about it.

'I think I'm catastrophising, worried he might be planning something awful. You know how low he got after Mum died. Well, he had a big wobble on Sunday. I hope he's not tidying up his affairs because he's thinking—'

'Of course he's not.' Stacey shut her down in an instant. 'I think it's the opposite. It's a lovely wedding present and it just shows how close he is to you and Ethan.'

Nicci hadn't thought about his gesture as a wedding present, but as she considered it, she decided Stacey might be right. It was a comforting take on the situation and much more palatable than her own line of thinking.

She finished her coffee while Stacey started a rant about the cost of wallpaper and Greg's next DIY project, which was their bedroom.

Nicci walked back to her car feeling unsettled. The fact that Louise thought Joel had been having an affair made her stomach churn. Had he mentioned her name? Was that why Louise hadn't been answering her messages? Oh God, she hoped not. But it was the only reason she could think of, and it made her palms sweat just thinking about the fallout from this. If word got out to Ethan... she'd no idea what he would do. Would Louise tell him? It was a distinct possibility because when Louise was riled, she had a tendency to lash out at those around her. She was shaking now, fumbling with her keys.

The truth was... Nicci was in love with Joel.

Yes, she loved Ethan, but not in the way she loved Joel. Ethan was dependable and loyal, a trustworthy companion, fun to be with, but Joel was her soulmate. They had conversations about values and aspirations, things that mattered in life. He was gentle and kind and being with him was like a balm to her soul. Joel's voice soothed her, his words flowed through her, wrapping her in this feeling of oneness with him. She'd never felt so in tune with anyone in her life. It was calm, peaceful, effortless.

She'd been in denial until a couple of weeks ago. *Just friends*, she'd told herself over and over when she found she was grinning as she lay in bed, her mind going over their conversations. They'd never touched. No hugs, no friendly kisses on the cheek. She wasn't sure why this was the case, because she had plenty of men friends that she hugged and kissed. Perhaps she'd instinctively known if there was a physical connection to match their mental connection there would be no going back. They both had commitments. It couldn't happen. And still she knew they were two halves of the same whole.

The pull of him was so strong she'd almost backed out of her wedding. But she knew Joel wasn't available and nothing could come of her feelings. Anyway, she didn't know for definite he felt the same way. Perhaps it was all in her mind. Something for her pre-wedding nerves to clutch onto. A displacement activity. A foolish infatuation.

Her perception of her feelings towards him had changed one evening, not long before the wedding. They'd been putting their dogs back on their leads at the end of the walk when Mack had seen a rabbit and wriggled out of her grasp, bounding back along the path, heading towards the prickly hawthorn hedge where the rabbit had disappeared. Without hesitation, Joel ran after him and managed to grab him before he was out of reach, while she held on to his dog, unable to do anything but watch and hope.

When he brought Mack back, their hands touched as they were swapping dogs, their heads bent low. It was as though he'd lit a touch paper to a firework display inside her chest, her heart suddenly galloping along while doing backflips. She'd glanced at him and caught a look in his eye that made her breath hitch in her throat. Their faces were inches away from each other and she thought, for a moment, he was going to kiss her. But he straightened and mumbled a goodbye before hurrying off back to his house, leaving her wondering what just happened.

Now, having heard about Stacey's conversation with Louise, she wondered if he felt the same way she did. If she was the reason Joel had left.

A tremor of fear ran through her. *What if Louise says something? What if Ethan finds out?*

CHAPTER TEN

Nicci turned on the radio for the short drive back to the industrial estate where the company had its workshop and offices. As she pulled into her parking space, the news came on and she stopped to listen, waiting to see if there was anything about the hit-and-run. It was the third item, and she turned the sound up so she could hear better.

'The police are still looking for information to help identify the victim. Although the patient has now regained consciousness, he remains in intensive care. He is still unable to speak and anyone who may have any information is asked to come forward.'

She sat in the car for a little while, wrestling with her conscience. It was a positive thing that the man had regained consciousness, her worst fears now averted. She hadn't killed anyone. He was getting better. But even though she told herself these things, her body didn't respond. It didn't relax, her heart rate didn't slow, that feeling of dread still weighed heavy in the pit of her stomach. She understood why. There was a chance she knew the person they'd hit. The corner where they'd been standing was a local meeting place, a cut through, on a route taken by late-night dog walkers who lived on their row. People walking back from the pub to the new houses. They all passed that very spot.

She started to cry, tears rolling down her cheeks as sobs wracked her body. All the worries and fears she'd been holding in came bursting out and it was a few minutes before she could force her emotions under control. She grabbed a handful of tissues from the box she kept in the car and tidied herself up, telling herself she had to stay strong. She couldn't have Ethan or her dad finding her in this state. What on earth would she tell them?

It wasn't only the accident that was bothering her. After her conversation with Stacey, she felt uneasy about Joel's silence and the lack of response to her messages.

She could see why he might have asked for space from Louise, but he had no such arrangement with Nicci. He hadn't said he was going away, but he *had* asked if they could meet the night they were over at Stacey's before the wedding. She'd been uncertain how to respond because if she were to meet him that night, it would be after they came home. Which was going to be late. It would be nigh on impossible to think up an excuse for a late dog walk, especially when that was not her routine, preferring to put the dog out in the garden for a pee before they went to bed. Ethan would have been suspicious, asked difficult questions that she wouldn't want to answer. So she'd ignored his message.

It was possible he'd decided to end their friendship, that was something she needed to consider. After all, she was marrying Ethan, he was having a baby with Louise and since that incident the week before, their meetings had been a little awkward. It would make sense to draw a line under the whole thing, so there was no chance of misunderstandings.

Her love for Ethan was steady and strong, something that would stand the test of time. This thing with Joel was a crush, a stupid, foolish crush. Nothing more. She had to put her feelings for him in the past and leave them there. It was lovely being married to Ethan. He would always look after her, and she should focus on looking after him. He didn't deserve a half-hearted bride, not after all the love he'd showered on her and his total commitment to keeping her terrible secret safe.

I've got to know, though.

Her gut was telling her she had to find out the identity of the person in the hospital. Once she knew, she could think about their recovery, support them in any way she could, without implicating herself. A concerned neighbour, helping out. She chewed on a finger nail, knowing that she wouldn't be able to function properly until she had the facts.

She reversed out of her parking space and headed towards the hospital. It was only fifteen minutes away and Ethan wasn't back from his sales calls yet. She wouldn't be long and was confident she could fabricate an errand that she'd had to run to account for her late return from lunch.

Her heart was thumping as she drove. Was this the right thing to do? Would they even let her see the patient at the hospital? She thought through her story, what she would tell them, hoping she could avoid any involvement with the police. That would be a disaster. She was a terrible liar at the best of times, but if they asked her any sort of probing questions, she'd end up telling them the truth.

As each day went by, she was finding it harder to live with what she'd done. It was too big a secret to keep folded inside and it was bursting to be free. One little probe in the right spot and it would all come spewing out. For the sake of this mission, she was a concerned friend, she decided, nothing more.

She pulled into the hospital car park, took a deep breath, and walked into reception, explaining her story to the lady at the desk. Saying she'd heard about the hit-and-run accident and one of her friends seemed to have gone missing. She wanted to check it wasn't him. She kept things as vague as she could, realising this was a bad idea, but she was committed now. The receptionist turned away while she rang the ward, so she couldn't see her face, the conversation murmured. It seemed to be taking a while and when she finally turned back to Nicci, the cheery smile had been replaced with a frown.

'I'm so sorry, the ward has said they can't accept any visitors. They suggest you talk to the police as a matter of urgency.'

Police. She felt nauseous, the contents of her stomach threatening to force their way up her throat, making her hurry out of reception and back to her car. No way could she contact the police, but perhaps the receptionist would tell them she'd been asking anyway. Had she blown their cover by coming here? Panic tightened her chest. Ethan was going to be furious.

I won't tell him, she decided, frantically, looking around the car park for CCTV but there was nothing obvious. By now, her heart was beating so fast she felt it might jump out of her chest, and she got in the car, eager to be on her way back to the workshop.

When she pulled up, Ethan was getting out of his car and he smiled as he walked over to her, bent to give her a kiss. 'Hello, darling. Late lunch?'

She smiled back, her brain frozen, not able to think how best to respond, having to clear her throat before she could speak. 'A catch-up with Stacey.' Her voice sounded odd, strangled. 'Where does the time go?' Thankfully, he didn't seem to notice and held the car door for her as she got out.

They walked over to the office, and he followed her up the stairs. They had two rooms up here, a general office where she, Ethan and her dad all had desks and then there was a meeting room where they could go through plans with clients. There was a big window looking out over the workshop below where they had a production line set up to make the wooden buildings. The whine of saws chewing through wood was a constant soundtrack, along with the punch of the nail gun. Even when the door was firmly shut, the noise was there in the background.

Ethan went to find her dad to discuss an idea for a new client and she pretended to work for the rest of the afternoon but accomplished next to nothing. Her mind was on overdrive, adrenaline making her heart race and her body sweat as she waited for police officers to come thundering up the stairs and arrest her. Never had she been so pleased to see the minute hand tick over to five o'clock.

They weren't the sort of business where people stayed to work late and by ten past everyone was ready to go. Except her dad, who waved them off, saying he was playing around with some plans for a little longer.

He looked happy enough, but she invited him to come round for supper when he'd finished, still worried he wasn't safe to be left on his own. He accepted with a smile and promised not to stay at work too long.

The car she'd been driving earlier was a company pool car, to be used by anyone in the business who had to nip out on errands. She was glad to be able to leave it outside the workshop, not feeling like she was fit to drive, her mind struggling to focus on anything but Joel. Ethan drove them home, a secret smile on his face.

'Good day?' she asked, wondering what was making him so cheerful.

'Yeah, you could say that, Mrs Watts.' She could tell by the way he lingered on her married name that he relished the sound of it and it made her feel mean and unworthy. She told herself she had to do better. Focus on what she had, not what she might have had in a parallel universe. 'Got a few loose ends tied up,' he continued. 'And I'm driving home with my gorgeous wife beside me.' He reached across and squeezed her leg. 'What about you?'

'Same old, same old,' she said, looking out of the window, not wanting him to see her face, which would surely give her away.

Ten minutes later, they were home and she went into the kitchen to start on dinner, switching the TV on as background noise while she cooked. She'd just put the pasta bake in the oven when the local news came on.

'Police have announced that the victim of the recent hit-and-run incident in Cononley has sadly died.'

She grabbed onto the worktop as her legs threatened to give way, not hearing the rest of the report.

Died.

The thought made her feel so weak she had to sit down, not wanting to believe it. Now she had to face up to what had been bothering her since lunch with Stacey. The person she'd hit could be Joel.

She'd tried hard to persuade herself that it couldn't be him but the facts were adding up to make it likely that it was. The person had been standing on the corner where they usually met and in the last message he'd sent to her, he'd asked her to meet him there. That evening.

She pulled out her phone and checked her messages. Nothing new. She was about to send him another, asking him to please confirm he was okay when Ethan's footsteps came pounding down the stairs. She tucked her phone back in her pocket, looked up when he came into the kitchen.

He glanced at her, frowned. 'What is it? You look like you've seen a ghost.'

I killed Joel.

She couldn't say it, because then she'd have to explain why she thought it was him.

'He died,' she said instead. 'The person we hit. It's just been on the news.' She gulped, hardly able to speak the words. 'We're... murderers.'

She hadn't heard the front door open and she was shocked to see her dad walking into the room. 'Who's a murderer?'

CHAPTER ELEVEN

Ethan's heart skipped a beat and he glanced at Nicci, who had a look of horror on her face. He grinned at Pete. 'We were talking about a crime drama we've been watching. Things are hotting up. Final part tonight. It gets Nicci a bit scared, doesn't it, love?'

'Well, if it's good I'll give it a watch myself,' Pete said, taking off his coat and hanging it on a peg by the door. 'Been stuck for decent things on the TV at the moment.'

'Oh... it's um...' His mind had gone blank and he glanced at Nicci, panic fluttering in his chest. 'I think it was on Netflix. Is that right, love?' He knew Pete didn't have Netflix so he'd be safe.

Nicci nodded. 'Yeah, that's right. It's called... um... *Breaking Bad.*' She gave her dad a tight smile. 'You might have heard of it. I think we're up to series six.' She shrugged. 'I don't know, I lose track.' She was gabbling, her voice all breathy and she got up to check the food in the oven.

'Let's go and get comfy,' Ethan said, steering Pete into the lounge, wanting to keep him away from his daughter while she calmed down. 'We'll let Nicci sort out the food, but in the meantime, I wanted to talk to you about the Robertson job over at Grassington.'

There was actually nothing he needed to discuss but Nicci was obviously stressed and he thought it better to give her a bit of time to compose herself. *Phew, that was close.* So the person they hit had died. He could hear himself saying the words in his head, but they weren't sinking in.

Murderers. That's what she'd said. But it was an accident, so that didn't make them murderers, did it? However, their victim being dead would inevitably change the nature of the police enquiry. It would likely ramp up a bit so they would have to be careful.

'So, what's the problem?' Pete said as he lowered himself onto the sofa. 'God my knees are playing up. This damp weather really makes them creak.'

'All those years kneeling on hard floors.'

'That's right. I bet you're glad you gave up the plumbing, aren't you?'

Ethan laughed. 'You're too right. Best decision I ever made. Honestly, after five years of it my knees said enough. And that's with padded trousers. I don't suppose you had those when you started.'

Thankfully, Pete forgot about the original question and they chatted happily about what it used to be like working in the building trade when Pete was an apprentice. It was a subject he loved to share with Ethan, probably because he'd started as an apprentice himself and could relate. At least it bought some time for Ethan's heart rate to get back to normal and when Nicci popped her head in to say supper was ready, he was feeling calm again. Nothing to get spooked about. As long as Nicci could stick to her vows, they'd be okay.

He watched her throughout the meal. She wasn't as stressy now, although she wasn't saying much either, something her dad noticed. 'You okay, love? You're awful quiet.'

She glanced up from her food and grimaced. 'Actually, I've had a headache all day. It doesn't seem to want to go away.'

'Oh dear. Your mum suffered from migraines as well, didn't she?'

Nicci nodded, rubbing at her temples as she looked at the table.

'Why don't you get yourself to bed?' Ethan suggested. 'We'll tidy up, won't we, Pete?'

'That's right. Off you go, love, and I hope you feel better tomorrow. Remember we've got the auditors coming.'

Nicci hung her head, clasping her forehead in one of her hands and Ethan wondered if the mention of the auditors was a bit too much on top of everything else. He knew she'd been worried about them coming. Said it was like having her home-work marked but on a much bigger scale. But he had faith in her. Nicci was efficient at her job, even if she was lacking a bit of confidence in herself.

'Shall I bring you a cup of tea?' Ethan suggested. 'I'm sure that'll help.'

She stood and nodded, giving her dad a kiss on the cheek before plodding up the stairs like she had the weight of the world on her shoulders. *Poor Nicci*, he thought as he went into the kitchen and waited for the kettle to boil. It would be hard for her to hear the person she'd hit had died. Very hard indeed. She was going to need a bit more support in the next few weeks while she came to terms with everything and he would have to keep an eye on her. Make sure she didn't do anything silly. She could be a bit impulsive at times, over-emotional, letting her heart drive her actions.

He liked to think he was more considered, more able to compartmentalise. It was a useful skill to have, being able to put the unpleasant stuff away where he didn't have to think about it. Nicci wasn't like that. She was constantly dredging things up from the past, wanting to go over and over them. He sincerely hoped that wasn't going to happen with this accident. They had to put it behind them and leave it there. Otherwise, they'd go mad.

He made the tea and handed Pete a mug. 'I'll take this up to Nicci. You make yourself comfortable and I'll be right with you.'

'I can't do this,' Nicci hissed when he entered the bedroom. She was pacing the floor, tears streaming down her face, clearly distraught. 'We killed somebody.'

Ethan took a deep breath, put her tea on the bedside table, then went and caught hold of her shoulders, making sure she was looking at him.

'It's awful that he died, but—'

'Yesterday, they said he'd come round. It sounded like he was improving,' Nicci wailed, her voice getting louder. 'I don't know why he suddenly got worse.'

He held his wife to his chest, trying to soothe her while his pulse raced. What if Pete heard all the commotion and came up to find out what was going on?

'Shhh.' He stroked her hair. 'I know, I know. Look, sweetheart, there's nothing we can do to make this better, is there? It's bad that it happened and in honour of the person who's dead, we should vow to never drive when we've had a drink ever again.'

Nicci clung to him, sobbing into his chest. 'I can't bear it.'

'We have to bear it. Think of the consequences. Especially if your dad finds out what happened.' That was an appalling prospect. 'He'll disown us. Our jobs will be gone, reputations out of the window. Prison. Nobody will want to speak to us. We'd have to move away and start again somehow.'

He held her tight, his cheek resting on top of her head, her body shaking as she cried. Patience was the key. He just had to wait this out, let her get all the emotions out of her system. Then they could talk.

'Why don't you sit on the bed? Drink your tea, see if that makes you feel any better. I'll go and chat with your dad until he wants to go home. Then we can have a proper talk about this later, okay?'

She nodded and sank onto the bed, her head bowed, a curtain of hair covering her face. At least she'd stopped sobbing, he thought as he left the room, closing the door behind him.

'Everything okay?' Pete asked when he went back into the lounge. He was looking worried, must have heard Nicci wailing and Ethan had to think fast to come up with a feasible excuse.

'She's not feeling too well and is getting herself worked up about the audit tomorrow. I don't suppose that could be rearranged, could it? I think she could do with a day off.'

Pete looked relieved. 'I can try. Bit short notice but it should be okay. We've got a bit of leeway in terms of deadlines.'

They drank their tea and chatted until Pete declared it was time he went, Ethan relieved to be able to wave him off and close the door behind him. What a tumultuous evening it had been. He felt like he'd been juggling with hand grenades, expecting Nicci to come down at any moment and confess all to her dad. His nerves were shredded and he went into the kitchen and pulled a beer from the fridge, gulping it down in a matter of seconds.

No, that didn't hit the spot. The burning sensation at the back of his brain was still there. He opened the cupboard and pulled out the whisky bottle, pouring himself a generous measure. It wasn't often he drank spirits but he thought the events of the day warranted something to settle his nerves. He leant against the worktop, took a gulp and felt the heat travel down his throat. Another gulp and he could feel the tension starting to ease. He emptied his glass then went upstairs, ready to have that chat with Nicci. They had to protect each other or their lives would not be worth living.

He was so close to achieving his dream, so close to being managing director of a business he was passionate about, having a great relationship, able to afford a bigger house. He'd never wanted anything more in his life and he couldn't let her take that away from him. How could he make Nicci see that silence was the only way forward?

CHAPTER TWELVE

Nicci heard her dad calling his goodbyes, the sound of the front door closing. She'd been sitting on the edge of the bed unable to move, feeling hollow and bereft.

I killed Joel. Who else would have been stood on that corner at that time of night in such atrocious weather? She pulled out her phone to check his last message once again.

> *I need to talk to you. There's something I need to tell you and I want to explain in person. Can you meet tonight, 10 p.m. on the corner?*

Why hadn't she sent a reply, saying no? Had he interpreted her lack of response as a yes? Or maybe he was just hoping she'd come? She thumped the mattress, needing to take her anguish out on something. Then she checked the news site, needing confirmation it was definitely him. But they still hadn't been able to identify the victim. How was she going to get the police to look into Joel's disappearance without implicating herself in some way?

The not knowing was driving her insane, because even

though she thought she was right, she was hoping with every fibre of her being she was wrong. Maybe she could talk to Louise and suggest to her the victim might be Joel. But then she'd ask Nicci why she thought that, because it was a bit of a random suggestion, and that could end up being very awkward.

She buried her hands in her hair and pulled, at a loss to know what to do. At some point Louise would start to wonder where Joel was. But it could be weeks yet, given she thought he'd gone off to think about things and didn't want to be contacted. As Stacey had suggested, if she didn't hear from him, she'd think he'd done a runner and wasn't coming back. But once Louise had the baby, surely she'd expect him to be in touch?

The thump of Ethan's footsteps coming up the stairs startled her out of her thoughts and she instinctively shoved her phone under her pillow. Then pulled it out again. It was time to confront things, not hide them away. She'd done nothing wrong. Nothing at all. She straightened her back, looked at the door, ready for a challenging conversation.

Ethan looked pensive, tired, as he came and sat next to her on the bed, putting an arm round her shoulders. 'How are you feeling now? Any better?'

She turned to him. 'Do you mean have I calmed down?' He met her gaze, and she knew that's exactly what he meant. 'The answer is not really. How can I feel calm when we've killed someone?'

He sighed, and his eyes dropped to their hands as he entwined his fingers with hers. 'It's a hard one to come to terms with, I'll give you that.'

They were silent for a moment, until she took a deep breath and forced herself to say what needed to be said. Her voice was hesitant, a whisper, the words almost impossible to speak out loud. 'I think I... killed Joel.'

His head shot up, a startled expression on his face. 'What? Why would it be Joel?'

She took a deep breath, steadied herself for the inevitable storm. 'Because he'd asked me to meet him on that corner at 10 p.m. He said he had something to tell me. Look.' She showed him the message on her phone.

His eyes took on a hard glint. 'Why, Nicci? Why would he need to meet you in private at that time of night to tell you something? Why not come to the house?'

'I don't know.' Her voice was as weak as her response and she couldn't look at him. 'Stacey said he told Louise he needed space to think. They'd had a big bust-up.'

He let go of her hand and stood up, too restless to keep still.

'And that bust-up wouldn't have been about you and him being such *close* friends by any chance, would it?' He glared at her and she struggled to meet his gaze.

This was so much harder than she'd imagined and when she spoke, she sounded less than convincing. 'If it was, I don't know why it would be a problem. We walked the dogs and talked about books. We were friends. And friends confide in each other.'

'So, he wanted to tell you something that he couldn't say in front of me?' He was getting increasingly agitated, and it was clear from the tone of his voice that he was barely keeping a lid on his anger. 'And what sort of thing would that be, hmm?'

His gaze was intense as he leant towards her and her eyes dropped to her lap where her fingers knotted themselves together. 'I don't know. Something you wouldn't be interested in, probably.'

'Sounds like it might have been something I'd be very interested in, if you ask me.' He straightened up and paced around the room, a hard edge to his voice. 'Three days before our wedding you're having clandestine meetings with another man. How am I supposed to feel about that?'

Nicci hadn't considered Ethan to be a jealous man, and he'd never objected to her going for dog walks with Joel. But then she supposed, there were many occasions where she might have omitted to tell him that Joel would be walking with her. He wasn't aware how close they'd become and if she was being truly honest with herself, she couldn't say she blamed him for his reaction.

Her feelings for Joel had developed in a direction she hadn't anticipated. He wasn't what you'd consider a handsome man. His nose was too large, his mouth a little crooked, his eyes deep-set, giving him a hawkish look. But his soul was beautiful and that's what she loved.

Loved. Past tense.

Tears sprang to her eyes and she squeezed them shut, willing herself not to cry. She had to get through this conversation.

'I'm sorry if it upsets you,' she said eventually. 'But I didn't reply to him. I didn't confirm I'd be there.'

He stopped pacing, looked confused.

'So why do you think the person we hit was Joel then?'

'Because he's gone AWOL.' She took a deep breath and explained it all again. 'Stacey said she was talking to Louise yesterday and apparently, Joel walked out on her a few days ago, telling her not to contact him because he needed space to think.'

'I hope that's not because of you.' Ethan didn't sound quite so angry now. 'I hope you haven't broken them up when she's expecting a baby.'

Could I feel any worse?

'All I did was go for dog walks with him. I have never touched him, held his hand, kissed him or even hugged him. It's all innocent. We're just friends.'

Ethan frowned, the muscles in his jaw tensing. 'Do you think he developed a crush on you?'

She shrugged. 'I don't know. I'm not a mind reader.'

Ethan was a bit calmer now and he came to sit beside her on the bed. 'If it was an innocent friendship, then I'm sorry I got angry. I just... I love you so much.'

'It's okay,' she murmured, knowing if anyone had a crush it was her. Still, at least she'd recognised that and not done anything about it.

He put an arm round her shoulders and pulled her to him. She could feel the warmth of his breath in her hair as he spoke and she sank into him. 'We just have to wait this out. It's the only option. The identity of the person will come out eventually. The main thing is to keep a low profile, not let anyone think we were anywhere near that corner at that particular time. We can't be asking questions, okay?'

She sighed. 'I know. I won't do it again.'

There was a moment's silence. She felt his body tense.

'Won't do what again?'

Her heart lurched. She was shocked she'd said it out loud. But it was time for honesty, so she steeled herself and told him.

'After I'd spoken to Stacey at lunch, she got me thinking about Joel because Louise is going a bit frantic, thinking he's left her. I thought about his last message to me and it made me wonder if he'd been waiting on the corner on the off chance I'd turn up at some point. I wanted to know for certain so I went to the hospital and—'

'You went to the hospital?' Ethan flopped back on the bed, his hand falling from her shoulder to cover his face. He groaned. 'Tell me I heard that wrong.'

She chewed at her lip, her skin prickling with the heat that suffused her body, burning her cheeks. 'I'm sorry, but I did. I thought I'd ask at reception. I told them I might know the person because a friend hadn't been responding and there was a chance he'd been in that area.'

'Oh my God,' Ethan moaned. 'That's it. We're done for now.'

'I don't know,' she gabbled, desperately trying to find a reason why this might not be the case. 'I didn't give my name. And it didn't get any further because when she rang the ward, I think the person must have taken a turn for the worse because she said they weren't accepting visitors and told me to contact the police.'

'CCTV, Nicci. Bloody CCTV!' He groaned again, his hand dropping from his face as he stared at the ceiling. 'The police are going to be all over this. Especially if they still don't know the victim's identity.'

'I'm sorry,' she whispered, feeling stupid. 'I wasn't thinking.'

He closed his eyes. 'I don't understand you, I honestly don't.'

Nicci didn't understand herself either. It had seemed an obvious move to her at the time, to clear up any ambiguity, because she didn't quite believe what Stacey had told her. Now she could see she'd got it wrong. It had been an impulsive, stupid thing to do and she'd put everything at risk, herself and her marriage included.

Ethan slipped into a dazed silence, while Nicci's hands grasped together.

'Okay,' he said eventually, rolling off the bed and walking to the window, leaning against the windowsill, his arms crossed over his chest. 'What's done is done, all we can do is try and not make any more mistakes.'

Nicci nodded, not able to look him in the eye, thoroughly annoyed with herself that she'd messed up and put them both at risk. 'Yes, you're right,' she mumbled. 'But I'm a rubbish liar.'

She heard him walking towards her. 'We're going to make this simple, okay? We did not go that way home, right? If anyone should ask, we went the long way round.'

'But why would we do that? It's another few miles. What was our thinking?'

He paused. 'Umm... the rain was so bad we thought the road might be flooded.'

She nodded. 'Yes. Okay. That makes sense.'

He knelt on the floor in front of her, grabbing both of her hands in his. 'This is really important. Our future is at stake here. And your dad's. And the company's. It would impact so many people if we got caught.' He squeezed her hands as his gaze locked onto hers. She squirmed. 'Remember our vows to each other? I meant my vow with all my heart. Can you say the same? Can I trust you?'

CHAPTER THIRTEEN

Nicci couldn't sleep, her mind galloping down blind alleys and going around in circles as she tried to work out what she should do now. Beside her, Ethan was still, but she wasn't sure he was asleep either. She'd told him he could trust her, but the expression on his face said he wasn't convinced. What was he thinking now?

How could she not love him when he was so committed to them as a couple? It was obvious he adored her and, in truth, she adored him too. If only she could put this infatuation with Joel out of her head. But now she believed she'd killed him, trying to forget about him was a hopeless task.

She had to do what she felt was right, didn't she? But, at the same time, she had to be true to their vows. They were stuck with it, this awful accident, and she was going to have to learn to live with it. The alternative being to destroy her own life and that of everyone around her. In all conscience she couldn't do that.

The vows had been a good thing, she reflected. Till death us do part. It meant that as long as both of them stuck by their promise to take their secret to the grave then they would be safe.

It did mean, though, that her dreams of a teacher training course would have to be put on hold. Because they'd also vowed to support each other and Ethan would definitely think she wasn't being supportive if she deserted the business. The business was as precious to him as a child. A child he was nurturing to the point where it could earn enough money to secure their future. That's what Ethan was thinking about, their future, so why couldn't she?

She was grateful that her mind had latched onto the business, forcing the consequences of the hit-and-run to take a back seat for a little while as she wrestled with this different problem.

Moments later, her mind clicked onto an idea that made her sit bolt upright in bed. That was it! The answer. Stacey was always moaning about her job, envious of Nicci's position. Why didn't she train her up? In fact, now she thought about it, maybe that's what she'd been hinting at over lunch. Stacey could eventually take over and Nicci could finally ease herself out of the business and start working towards the career she actually wanted.

The more she thought about it, the more it made sense. Stacey had worked in lots of admin roles and Nicci was sure she'd done training in the same accountancy software they used in the business. She lay back down, snuggling into her pillow, thankful that at least one of her concerns had been resolved. *Don't think about anything else*, she told herself, as a dark silhouette in the lashing rain tried to invade her thoughts. *Just focus on the job.*

The distraction didn't work and her night, as usual, was interrupted several times by nightmares of the accident. But this time she saw Joel's face pressed against the windscreen before his body flipped over the bonnet out of sight. She woke up screaming, Ethan trying to comfort her, telling her it was a bad dream, it wasn't real.

She lay awake for a long time, her eyes open, not wanting to go back to sleep. Even when she was awake, her mind was obsessed with the accident, wanting to examine every detail. The problem was… she didn't remember every detail because it had happened so quickly and she'd had the panic attack and blacked out. Chinks of what appeared to be memories kept presenting themselves, but when she tried to hold them in place, while she worked out what she was seeing, they faded away. If she'd been hoping to recognise a face, or see something that would identify the mystery figure, then she was disappointed. Just Ethan's shout, the car lurching, that horrible bang.

The next morning, they were in work bright and early, much to her dad's surprise.

'I thought you were poorly,' he said to her when she and Ethan walked into the office and he was already at his desk. 'Ethan said last night he didn't think you'd be in today.'

She gave a feeble smile. In truth, she felt pretty rough after a night of interrupted sleep. It turned out, when you found out you'd killed someone, it wasn't the kind of thought that allowed itself to be silenced. 'I'm not great, Dad. But I have a few things I need to get done before the audit.'

'I've already emailed the auditors, told them we need to rearrange, so at least you don't need to worry about that.' He came and gave her a hug and the comfort of his embrace was almost too much for her tattered emotions. 'You take it easy today and go home when you like. We can cope, can't we, Ethan?'

Ethan nodded, already in work mode and concentrating on his schedule for the day. A few minutes later he hurried downstairs to the shop floor, her dad trotting behind.

She picked up her phone while she was alone in the office, determined to set her plans in motion.

'Stacey,' she said when her friend answered, keeping her

eyes on the figures on the shop floor in case they headed back upstairs and she had to end the call. 'I might have a job opportunity for you if you're interested.'

'Well, good morning to you,' Stacey said, sounding fed up with the day already and not excited by the prospect. 'What sort of a job. Where is it?'

'It's here. At Dad's... I mean our business. I need to train someone up to do my job. I know you've done accounts and I'm sure you'd pick up our invoicing system easily.'

An awkward silence made Nicci squirm.

'Well, that's a really kind thought,' Stacey said, 'but if you're going to be my boss, I think that would be a recipe for ruining a friendship.'

It was not the response Nicci had been hoping for and she tried again, although she recognised Stacey had made a valid point.

'We wouldn't be working together for too long, just long enough for me to show you the ropes. I've been thinking about how I can get myself out of the business so I can go to uni. Dad and Ethan already know you. The trust will be there. You've done the first part of your accountancy exams. Would you at least think about it?'

'Hmmm. I don't know.' Nicci could tell she was wavering and silently urged her to say yes. 'What do your dad and Ethan think?'

'I haven't spoken to them yet. I wanted to sound you out first.'

Stacey sighed. 'Well, it would be better than the crappy admin job I'm doing now.'

Nicci dared to hope she might be able to pull this off. 'It would be a proper rate of pay,' she wheedled. 'Better than you're getting now.'

'Well, I'm on minimum wage, so it couldn't be any worse,' Stacey huffed. 'Not legally, anyway.'

Nicci smiled to herself, sure that Stacey was on the verge of saying yes. 'Leave it with me and I'll get back to you when I've had a chance to talk to Dad and Ethan. It could be fun working together. I get so bored in the office on my own and it would be much more interesting if you were working with me.'

'Okay. But if they say no then I'll be massively offended and never talk to you again, right?'

Another awkward silence, Nicci not sure what to say. She hadn't thought about that possibility.

Stacey laughed. 'You know I'm joking, right?'

Nicci hadn't known, but then Stacey often caught her out like this. 'Of course I knew,' she blustered, a blush creeping into her cheeks. 'I was distracted for a minute, someone knocking at the door. I'll call you later.'

They said their goodbyes and she disconnected, feeling quite elated now she'd got Stacey on board. At least she had something to look forward to and maybe that was the answer in terms of coping with the accident. Because if she was looking forward, she wouldn't be so tempted to look back.

She decided to broach the subject with her dad and Ethan when they came up for their tea break later in the morning, but for now, she had to get on with some work. Her top priority was to get things in order for the auditors. Everything was a bit of a mess and she knew their report would contain a big list of improvements they would like to see. Unfortunately, she still hadn't put in place half the things they'd suggested the previous year and she knew they'd be unhappy about that.

At least she'd have Stacey to help her now. If Ethan and her dad agreed, of course. It wasn't a given and an extra wage would give them all pause for thought. She clamped her jaw tight. Why should she have to do a job she didn't want to do? Give up her dreams because her dad and husband wanted something different? As Stacey kept reminding her, it was time to stop being a people pleaser and with her friend to back her up in the office, she felt she could be much stronger in her views. It was time to lay out what *she* wanted.

Her phone rang a few minutes later. *Louise.* Joel's partner. She refused the call, knowing she couldn't talk to her. Not now. *Maybe never again.* How on earth was she supposed to pretend everything was normal when she knew in her heart what she'd done?

Her phone bleeped to tell her she had a voicemail. She hesitated, then picked it up.

'I don't suppose you've heard anything from Joel, have you?' Louise sounded deflated, her voice small and weak. 'Please call me. There's something I need to ask you.'

Nicci looked at her phone, knowing Louise would think it odd if she didn't respond. They'd known each other since high school and had been in the same friendship group for all their adult lives. She had to ring her back, but what on earth was she going to say?

CHAPTER FOURTEEN

Ethan walked into the office, glanced at Nicci, then went over to her desk, feeling a bit concerned. 'Everything okay, love? You're looking a bit... peaky.'

She looked like she was about to burst into tears, and he couldn't blame her given the situation. They had to tough it out, though, get through it and having a breakdown at work was not the way forward.

'Do you want me to run you home? If you're not feeling brilliant, a restful day might help you feel better.'

'Thank you, but I'm not sure anything would make me feel better.' She took a shuddering breath and he could tell she was on the edge, only just managing to hold it together. He'd come up for his tea break, so he put the kettle on and made her a cup as well, brought it over to her desk, along with a packet of biscuits. He took a sip of his drink, wracking his brains for something to help her through this difficult phase. Because it was just a phase. The fallout from the accident would fade away at some point if they kept their nerve.

'Look, there's something I want to ask you,' she said, 'and I want you to hear me out before you say anything, okay?' He nodded, perching on the edge of her desk, his hand reaching for a biscuit. 'I want some help in the office. Aside from everything else that's happened, I'm not on top of the work and the thought of the auditors coming is freaking me out. I can't get it all done in time.'

Ah, so it was the workload rather than the accident that was bothering her. A wave of relief washed over him. Now that, he could help with. He ate his biscuit while he considered her request. He'd been confident she was on top of her work, but then he didn't have much to do with the office side of things. Pete and Nicci dealt with most of that. He focussed on sales and delivery, the customer side of things.

He supposed the workshop had been a lot busier, and they'd recently recruited a second build crew to reduce the backlog on the orders. And they'd taken on an apprentice. It figured there'd be a knock-on effect in the office.

'Can we afford it?'

She sighed, fiddled with a pen on her desk, spinning it round. 'Well, if I was up to date with the accounts, I'd be able to give you an answer, but I'm a month behind with getting stuff on the system.' She sat up straight, tapped on her keyboard, and opened up a screen, navigating through to a summary page. 'This was where we stood in June. But I'm behind chasing up invoices. Cashflow is okay, though.'

Ethan studied the figures, a bead of unease sitting in his chest. He wasn't sure. But these were the decisions he had to make going forward as managing director. *Not today, though.* Nicci wasn't in the right frame of mind to be making rational decisions and to be frank, neither was he. The news yesterday, that they'd killed someone, had really shaken him and he yearned to push it out of his mind and go and talk to customers who were excited about summer houses or home offices. Do the happy stuff he loved.

He cleared his throat. 'I think it's something we need to

consider. Why don't we talk to your dad about it when he comes up?'

Nicci stared at him and he knew, by her face, she felt he'd let her down.

'I'm not saying no, but we haven't signed the papers yet, have we? We're not officially directors.' He thought it was a valid excuse. 'Technically, it's still your dad's decision.' He was grateful to be able to use this as a get-out clause, knowing she couldn't argue.

'But, in principle, do you think it's a good idea?' she persisted. 'I mean it's not sensible just relying on me. Because that means Dad has to come into the office if I'm off and he doesn't know how half the systems work now we've upgraded. The other thing I've been thinking about... What if something happens to me? I was looking at the recommendations from the last audit and they want us to do a risk assessment. I think having no cover in the office, not only to answer phones and do the admin, but to manage the finances, I think that's a big risk to the company.'

Ethan had never thought about it like that, but she was right. 'Good point.' He nodded. 'That's a very good point.'

Nicci smiled and he bent to give her a kiss, hoping Pete thought the same. It did make a lot of sense as a backup plan.

'I thought I could ask Stacey to help. I mean, we know her, and she's started her accounting exams and—' She stopped mid-sentence, frowned at him. 'What? Don't look so horrified.'

He tried to rearrange his face into a more neutral expression but it proved impossible, the suggestion making him wince like he'd been chewing on a lemon. 'No way can Stacey come and work here. No, absolutely not.'

Nicci frowned, her jaw set. He knew that look and it always spelt trouble. 'Why not? She's been my best friend for ever, Dad knows her and she's great on the phone.'

Ethan shook his head. It was a hard no from him and

nothing was going to make him change his mind. If they were going to get help in the office, they'd go through a proper recruitment process, not just get a friend in.

'I can't believe you've even suggested it,' he countered. 'Do you want your best friend and the rest of Skipton knowing, because that woman does not know what secret means, do you want her knowing everything about our business? How much we get paid? How well we're doing? Because I sure as hell don't.' He shook his head. 'I cannot believe you thought it was a sensible idea...' He read the expression on her face and his shoulders slumped. 'You've already asked her, haven't you?'

Nicci's jaw tightened, a defiant glint in her eye. 'Yes, I have, because if I don't take action to sort out this issue, then you and Dad will put it off. I need help now, the auditors will want to know we've got the risk of my absence covered, and Stacey is available.'

Ethan clutched at the only lifeline he could see. 'She's working. She's already got a job so she isn't available.'

Nicci huffed. 'She hates it, you know she does.' She flapped a hand, dismissing his argument. 'She'll just walk out.'

Ethan gasped. 'And you both think that's okay? It doesn't make her sound like a reliable employee.' But he already knew that about her.

Nicci's chin wobbled. 'After the hit-and-run and how we dealt with that...' She swallowed, and there was a shrillness to her voice as she fought back tears. 'I have no idea what's okay and what isn't. How about you? Are you a fine, upstanding citizen, Ethan? Can you honestly say that?'

Ouch. He held up his hands. She'd got him there. 'Okay, okay, you win. I'm not saying you shouldn't have help, I just don't want it to be Stacey.'

Nicci banged a fist on the desk, making the packet of biscuits roll onto the floor, her frustration with him clear. 'I only want Stacey. I trust her.'

He gave a derisive snort. 'Well, I don't.'

Nicci glared at him for a long moment. 'And why would that be?'

'Because she threatened to tell—' He stopped and pushed himself off the desk. Darn it, she'd got him saying things he didn't want to speak about. Not to anyone. Thank God he'd caught himself in time.

'Go on,' she said, a challenge in her eyes.

'No, it doesn't matter.' He stood, ready to walk away, signalling an end to the conversation.

'I think it does matter,' she insisted, anger flaring. 'What are you saying, Ethan?' She gasped, hands flying to her mouth. 'She doesn't know about the accident, does she? Or... or is it something else?'

It was not always a positive thing to have a perceptive wife, Ethan thought as he started walking towards the door. 'It's nothing, love. Look, I'll go and speak to your dad about it, see what he thinks.'

He closed the door behind him, pausing on the top step for a moment to gather himself, wondering how he could possibly get out of this one. *Bloody Stacey.* She was the last person he wanted working here. It would be like playing with fire, wondering all the time if she was going to spill the beans to Nicci.

He couldn't let it happen, but how the hell was he going to stop it?

CHAPTER FIFTEEN

Nicci stared at the closed door, wondering what he'd been about to say. Stacey knew something that Ethan didn't want her to know. Hmm. Well, that was easily resolved. Nobody could swear Stacey to secrecy; she wasn't that sort of person. There was nothing she enjoyed better than a bit of gossip and she stored it all up, like a squirrel storing nuts for winter.

Even though she was her best friend, Nicci had been selective about which secrets she shared with Stacey from an early age. Ever since Stacey had embarrassed Nicci in front of a boy she'd secretly liked, having foolishly told her about a crush. Well, that wasn't quite true, she hadn't willingly volunteered the information, it was more that Stacey had prised it out of her. Unfortunately, it led to a mortifying series of events and for a while she and Stacey hadn't been speaking. Eventually, her mum had brokered a peace deal, Stacey had apologised and in time it was all forgiven. If not forgotten. Nicci had been a bit wary ever since.

She picked up her phone, called her friend, deciding there was one sure way to sort this out.

'I'd love to come over for supper,' Stacey said, when Nicci

invited her. 'We can sort out start dates for the job and everything.'

'That's exactly what I was thinking,' Nicci said, with a smile. Stacey was jumping ahead but that suited Nicci. This time she was going to get what she wanted, and not only did she want Stacey working in the office, she also wanted to know what secret Ethan was keeping from her. She was optimistic she'd be successful on both counts.

Finally, she felt able to get on with her work and it was lunchtime before she knew it. She'd even made some headway with last month's accounts.

Ethan was often out with customers all day and she had her own lunchtime routine, going to the sandwich van on the estate and meeting up with Dom. He'd let her practise Spanish and at the same time, he'd regale her with anecdotes about Ethan when he was a kid. It seemed he hadn't had an easy time with his parents and through her conversations with Dom, she had come to understand her husband better.

She messaged him.

Lunch and Espanyol, signor?

He was usually quick to respond, but today her phone told her he hadn't even seen her message. When she thought about it, he hadn't been around much since before the wedding, and she'd been a bit concerned about him for a few weeks. He'd been distracted and distant recently, said he had a lot of work on and he'd kept cancelling their lunch dates. He was a private tutor, helping children through their exams but he also taught English to Spanish and Latin American nationals. This was becoming a big part of his workload, and he had contracts with several of the local hospitals in West Yorkshire. He also did translation work for the police and other public services. The workload was unpredictable, he was called into jobs at short notice and sometimes he would be stuck there for hours. It sounded pretty intense, but she knew he had debts he was trying to pay off.

She remembered that Stacey had said he'd been drunk and disorderly, taken into police custody. Perhaps he was lying low for a while after that embarrassment. Or perhaps he was still in police custody? Or did he say he might have to go back to Spain? She had a vague memory of that, but her mind had been unreliable since the accident so she couldn't be sure. She sent another message.

Hope everything is okay with you?

No reply. With a sigh, she picked up her bag and walked to the sandwich van, chose her usual BLT and went back to the office. She'd thought she'd go for a walk but it had started to rain, so she sat at her desk and made a list of all the jobs she did and how she'd like Stacey to help. It would give her some handy prompts in her discussions with Ethan and she'd found it paid to be prepared when you were trying to persuade someone to do something. Especially when they were reluctant. Not that she'd had much success in the past with Ethan, but it was time to get better at being assertive. Stacey could certainly help with that.

It was going to be a tricky evening and she couldn't say she was looking forward to it in the slightest. But 'needs must' as her dad was fond of saying, and she'd just have to grit her teeth, stick to the task and get through it. Another saying of her dad's was 'the hard way is the easy way', which was about doing things properly so you didn't have to go back and do them again. And that's what she was going to do. Be brave and get on with it.

The recent friction between Ethan and Stacey was going to make the conversation harder and she was struggling to under-stand what the root cause of the problem might be. When she and Ethan had first got together, Stacey couldn't say enough good things about him. Then suddenly, relations between them seemed to sour. It wasn't easy when your partner didn't like your best friend and she was the centre of your social group. Thankfully, the others treated it as a joke when the two of them sniped at each other, and the situation was usually diffused by some wisecrack that had them all laughing. It didn't stop her feeling uncomfortable, though.

Nicci thought back to when she'd first noticed the tension. It was five months ago and the only reason she was able to remember was because it was the date of their belated engagement party.

They'd hosted a small gathering of friends and family at their local pub in a private room, booking a meal and dancing afterwards. With hindsight, that was when her love for Ethan was at its height and she couldn't take her eyes off him. Or the gorgeous engagement ring he'd presented her with. He was everything she'd wanted in a man. Good-looking, confident enough in himself to not have to follow the crowd, attentive and sweet, often buying her little gifts and organising surprises.

She remembered at the engagement party, Stacey had cornered her, slurring slightly, because it was the end of the evening. Her eyes were having a bit of trouble focussing on Nicci's face, but she was suddenly earnest. 'Remember it's never too late to change your mind,' she'd said. 'You never know someone. Not properly.' She grabbed Nicci's arm. 'You've got time before the wedding to work out for yourself if this is the right decision or not. But... you just need to be careful.'

Nicci had shrugged it off at the time, put it down to drunkenness. The way she'd said it gave Nicci the impression Stacey just didn't think Ethan was 'the one'. But afterwards she wondered whether this was more of a comment about Stacey's relationship than hers. A warning from her own experience, that she'd thought her husband Greg was right for her until she'd discovered his nerdiness about DIY. She'd dismissed Stacey's warnings as sour grapes, but now she wondered if she'd known something about Ethan. Something she couldn't pass on to Nicci.

To be fair, in her loved-up state, Nicci wouldn't have listened to anyone's warnings about Ethan. She'd liked him from the moment he started work at the firm, watching him through the window as he moved about the workshop, lithe as a cat, sure in what he was doing, always cheerful. She liked that quality in a man, the ability to see the best of every situation and put a positive spin on things.

If Ethan was in the office, working on designs, she'd be stealing glances when she thought he wasn't looking. Occasionally, their eyes would meet and then she'd feel the heat of her blush burning her cheeks. Gradually, they'd started having lunch together. All the while, Nicci tried to keep her distance, because her mum had been a stickler for not mixing business with pleasure and it was ingrained in her psyche. He was a novelty. It was a silly infatuation, nothing more, she told herself. A look but don't touch situation that she would tire of after a while.

Her dad had teased her about Ethan being sweet on her, and she'd sensed he quite liked the idea of them being a couple. Then he was constantly dropping hints, encouraging her to go out with him. So, she did.

Love or lust?

Considering it now, it was probably both. She wasn't sure when she realised the only thing they seemed to talk about these days was the business. He would listen while she talked about her friends and what she'd like to do with her life, like becoming a teacher, but he wouldn't really engage in those discussions. Somehow, he always managed to bring the conversation back to the business and ideas for new product lines and interior design fixes that would save money. That was his passion, his focus and she'd loved that about him too. Because the business was her dad's baby and if Ethan loved it, then it figured that he and her dad would be close, which was an important factor when considering a future husband.

Yes, it was great he was so passionate about his work, but she wished he was more passionate about *her*. It would be fair to say her sex life was not as active as she might have expected at this point in their relationship. His wish to spend time with her tempered by his desire to work extra hours in the business. Or go on trips with his off-roading group. Or go and watch football with his mates. They hardly spent any time together at weekends, and now she came to think of it, that was probably why she'd turned to others for company. Why she'd felt that pull towards other men. Dom was purely a friend. But Joel...

The thought of his name made her shudder. *Don't go there,* she warned herself, aware that she'd get herself all anxious and upset again. Whatever there had been between them, it was over, whether he was alive or dead. It had been ill-fated from the start and she should have stopped her walks with him when she understood what she was feeling.

But somehow there was a disconnect between her head and her heart and her heart had won every time. *Just one more walk,* she'd tell herself. *This will be the last one.* Then, when they were about to part, she'd find herself asking him when she might see him again. And he'd give her that lovely twinkly smile, gazing at her with his gentle brown eyes and her insides would turn to mush. 'Soon,' he'd say. 'I'll see what I can do.'

She was thoroughly confused by her mixed emotions. It was normal to be cross with the person you loved. Normal not to like certain things about them. And Ethan was always lovely to her, when he actually noticed she was there. *Perhaps it's my fault,* she mused. Perhaps it's this thing about being more assertive. Well tonight was the night she was going to put that into practice. One way or another she was going to find out what Stacey and Ethan weren't telling her. That had now jumped up her list of priorities, leap-frogging the need to have help with her work. Because if Stacey was hiding something from her, then she'd have to ask herself how trustworthy she was.

An unwelcome thought squirmed into her head, making her lean back in her chair. Stacey and Ethan. Could there be something going on between them? Is that why his passion had cooled, because he had somebody else? Did Stacey warn her off him because she wanted him for herself? Is that what the antagonism was about? She'd seen it before, people playing at not liking each other to cover up their attraction. The thought took her breath away, her heart racing all of a sudden. *No, he wouldn't.* Ethan wasn't like that, and Stacey was her best friend, her fierce defender most of the time. They both loved her.

But even though she was certain of this fact, she couldn't help searching her mind for evidence that would support her theory, coming up with a list of things. The time they spent apart at weekends would give him plenty of opportunity to meet up with Stacey. The nights he worked late. The trips away off-roading. Lots of opportunities to cover up a relationship.

Are my best friend and my husband having an affair?

CHAPTER SIXTEEN

Later, when she was making a chicken Caesar salad for tea, waiting for Stacey to arrive, she realised that her plan to employ Stacey wasn't going to work. The fact she was even thinking Stacey was capable of having an affair with Ethan told her she didn't trust her. It felt like an epiphany. Surprising, given the number of times Nicci had withheld secrets from her friend because she didn't want her business broadcast all over Skipton.

Intrinsically, she hadn't trusted Stacey for years, but she'd been in denial about that. Telling herself Stacey was her best friend and best friends were trustworthy. She hadn't noticed the contradiction in her own behaviour, never mind Stacey's. Fair play to Ethan, she thought, he'd been right to speak out on that front at least.

All afternoon, she'd been mulling it over in her head, the idea of an affair refusing to go away. She'd been rooting through her memories of the times they'd all been together, unpicking past conversations, observing their behaviour from what she could remember.

When they were at the dinner party before the wedding, she remembered Ethan disappearing for at least half an hour after they'd eaten their main course. The conversation had been lively, everyone tipsy and she hadn't noticed for a while that he was still not back in his seat. Then Stacey had appeared in the kitchen doorway with a fancy dessert in her hands and Ethan had appeared behind her, following her in.

Now *that* was odd. What had he been doing. Or *they*? What had *they* been doing?

The more she thought about it, the more she convinced herself she was on to something. Then she'd talk herself out of it and she'd be right back at the beginning of the circle again. *Stacey is married*, she reasoned. She and Greg were talking about starting a family once they'd finished renovating their house. Was it likely that she'd dump her husband and go through all the hassle of divorce? Or was Ethan a bit of entertainment on the side? Perhaps it had been a one-off thing, a moment of indiscretion that her friend felt obliged to tell her about, but Ethan wanted forgotten? Her head was hurting with all the conflicting theories.

She thought about her own situation with Joel and she had to acknowledge another possibility. Perhaps this was a case of her projecting her own feelings onto Ethan and Stacey. A distraction from her own guilt, making them guilty instead. Perhaps there was nothing going on between them at all. The secret Stacey was keeping might be trivial, nothing to get worked up about. But it mattered to Ethan because he hadn't wanted Nicci to know. She sighed, frustrated, chopping the lettuce with heavy-handed thuds, slamming the knife into the chopping board.

You need to get the facts, not go off into this fantasy world, making things up.

The doorbell rang and she was so startled, the knife clattered from her hand and onto the floor. The thunder of Ethan's footsteps running down the stairs kept her rooted to the spot, as she listened to how he might greet Stacey at the door.

'Oh, it's you,' he said, his voice offhand. 'I thought Nicci might have seen sense and called the whole thing off.'

The tinkle of Stacey's laugh. 'You do not understand what you've got yourself into, do you?'

Hmm. Cryptic.

Silence for a long moment, longer than she would have expected, before she heard the front door close and she snapped back into action, bending to pick the knife up off the floor. She went to the sink to give it a wash before finishing off the salads.

'Hey, lovely,' Stacey cooed as she walked into the kitchen.

Nicci turned, a smile fixed to her face. 'Hiya, I'm just finishing off the food.' She pointed to the wine bottle on the worktop, an empty glass standing next to it. 'Help yourself to a drink, I won't be long.'

'I see you've started without me,' Stacey said, holding up the half-empty bottle before pouring herself a glass.

'It's been a strange sort of a day,' Nicci said with a shrug, sprinkling cubes of chicken over the salads.

Stacey took a gulp of her wine, watching Nicci finishing their plates off with gratings of Parmesan and dressing. 'I've had one of those strange days too. I'm not sure I could spend another minute in that place. God, my boss is a bitch.' She gave a dramatic eye roll. 'Anyway, I've handed in my notice, so thank heavens for small mercies.' She beamed at Nicci. 'Your job offer came at exactly the right time.'

Nicci's heart sank. She'd made it clear when she phoned Stacey that she was sounding her out, hadn't she? And told her she needed to ask Ethan and her dad before anything was finalised. But as usual, Stacey was racing ahead. Unfortunately, now she'd admitted to herself that she didn't trust her friend, there was no way she could have Stacey working in the business. *Christ, this is going to be awkward.* Asking her had been a knee-jerk reaction and she wished she'd waited and spoken to

Ethan first. At the very least, she should have thought it through.

What's got into me?

After the hit-and-run, she was turning into someone she didn't recognise. Impulsive and erratic and inconsistent. But then, knowing someone died because of you was bound to be a life-altering experience, wasn't it? She wondered how Ethan was feeling. They hadn't talked about it since they'd heard the news. Not a word, apart from that conversation promising they'd honour their vows.

'You okay?' Stacey asked. 'Only I've been talking to you and you're staring into space with that bloody great knife in your hand.' She gave a nervous laugh. 'I sort of feel a bit... threatened.'

Nicci had been unaware she'd picked up the knife again and put it down, looking at the salads she'd been creating. 'Sorry, I was miles away.' She glanced at Stacey, gave her an apologetic smile. 'Lots going on at the moment.'

Stacey moved closer, her brow pinched with concern. She put a hand on Nicci's shoulder. 'Do you want to talk about it? A problem shared is a problem halved and all that.'

Nicci shook her head. 'It's nothing. Lots of little things I need to sort out, that's all. It's hard to remember everything.'

Stacey did another eye roll. 'Oh, you're telling me. When did life get so complicated?'

Silence descended, Nicci hurriedly finishing the salads with a sprinkling of chopped herbs while Stacey watched.

'Do you want to go through and I'll bring these?' Nicci said, when she'd finished.

She picked up two of the dishes and followed Stacey into the living room, where their dining table was pushed against the wall. They only used it when they had guests, preferring to eat in the kitchen, and between times it was a handy flat surface which seemed to accumulate all the detritus of everyday life.

She'd cleared everything onto the floor, out of sight, and laid place mats and cutlery, making an effort to dress it up nicely.

Stacey's eyes darted round the room and Nicci realised it was a long time since she'd been in their house. Their lounge was a quarter of the size of Stacey's own living room. In fact, the cottage was a quarter of the size of Stacey's whole house. And as that thought entered her head, she knew it was unlikely Stacey would be leaving her husband anytime soon. Not when she lived in a lovely property and hooking up with Ethan would probably relegate her to this tiny little cottage. It would surely be a deal-breaker for Stacey because she'd never live in a place like this. No, Ethan would have to up his game if he was going to gain her commitment.

She scoffed at herself and her ridiculous line of thought. Honestly, what was going on in her stupid head? There *was* no affair. But if that was the case, what secret was Stacey keeping?

Her heart was racing as she wondered how she was going to backtrack on the promise of giving Stacey a job. Thankfully, Ethan would be there to back her up and he would be delighted with her change of heart. He'd find the words to make it palatable because he always knew exactly what to say. That's what made him such an effective salesman. She'd just have to grab him and have a quick word out of Stacey's earshot.

'You've gone off into dream world again,' Stacey said, making her snap out of her reverie.

'I'm so sorry. I haven't slept well the last few nights and I think it's catching up with me.' She realised the plates were still in her hands and she put them down, went back to the kitchen to get the last one. Ethan had gone back upstairs after letting Stacey in, so she called him, but when he didn't appear she went upstairs to get him, thinking he must have his headphones on and couldn't hear.

The spare bedroom was set up as a home office and he was sitting at the desk, frowning as he scrolled through his phone, his lips pressed into a thin line. He didn't hear her and she watched him for a moment, wondering how she'd got herself into such an horrendous situation. She was a murderer, in love with a man who wasn't her husband, married to a man who was keeping secrets from her. There was no easy way to get out of it. Not with her vows holding her in place.

Till death us do part.

He'd made a point of emphasising that when they were talking the previous evening, and the memory sent a chill down her spine.

'Ethan.'

He looked up and saw her in the doorway, a guilty expression flitting across his face as he stuffed his phone in his pocket. She forgot to speak to him about employing Stacey, her mind fixed on one question: *What secret is he keeping from me?*

CHAPTER SEVENTEEN

When Nicci called his name, Ethan snapped his head up from his phone, turning off the screen and sliding it into his pocket. He could feel a blush suffusing his skin and hoped his wife hadn't noticed. He fixed a smile on his face as he stood, thinking he'd have another look later, see if he could work out what was going on.

He followed her downstairs, Stacey flashing him a sly grin, which Nicci couldn't see as she had her back to her. She was incorrigible and he wondered how he'd ever got himself caught up in this mess. *Stay calm*, he told himself as he pulled out a chair and sat down, making an effort not to meet Stacey's eye.

Nicci had forgotten the wine, so she went back out to the kitchen to get the bottle and a glass for him. He took the opportunity to lean towards Stacey, whispering, 'You promised not to say anything.'

Stacey gave him a wide-eyed look as though butter wouldn't melt in her mouth. 'As if I would,' she whispered. 'A promise is a promise in my book.' Her comment was loaded, her eyebrows raised at the end of the sentence, a little nod to emphasise her point.

He knew what she was getting at, and his unease deepened, made worse when she picked up her wine glass, looking at him over the rim. She was trying not to laugh and he cursed his stupidity. He had to accept responsibility for getting himself in this situation, but it wasn't an easy pill to swallow. She had all the power, and it was a truth he hated with every fibre of his body.

Nicci came back in, poured him a glass of wine and finally sat down. Her body language was spiky and he wondered what was bothering her. Was it because he'd come in and gone straight upstairs? But he'd had no choice, there were things he was trying to sort out, people he needed to speak to without Nicci hearing.

'This looks lovely, darling,' he said, taking a slice of garlic bread, spearing bits of chicken with his fork. Nicci didn't respond to the compliment, ignoring his attempt to spark a conversation, so he decided to leave it there. At least he could zone out while he ate.

His body felt heavy and he was exhausted with it all. Instead of getting their problems resolved, new difficulties kept appearing. It was like playing Whac-a-Mole, a game he'd always been rubbish at. And this was the latest obstacle to him having a happy future. When Nicci had mentioned employing Stacey, he'd thought he might explode. Not just mentioned, insisted. Of all the people she could have picked.

The room fell silent as they ate, the clink of cutlery on china seeming to amplify to a point where it filled his head. He was certain their hidden agendas were the cause; each of them weighing up what they should say to get what they wanted. It was unusual for Stacey to be so quiet, though, and he was hoping he could finish his meal and then dash off on the excuse of having work to do before he was asked to commit to anything.

'Anyway,' Stacey said when she finished eating, putting her

knife and fork neatly together in her dish. 'Can we talk about work now? That's why you invited me here after all.'

Nicci carried on chewing, her eyes on her food. Stacey caught his eye, her hard stare a warning.

He felt beads of sweat breaking out on his brow. It looked like there was no escape. He cleared his throat, aware that Nicci's silence was his cue to answer. 'Yes, I've been thinking about that.'

'So have I,' Nicci said, putting her cutlery down, even though she'd only eaten half her food. She gave him what could only be described as a meaningful glance. He knew what she wanted; she'd made it clear at work earlier. And he knew what Stacey wanted too. He was caught in the middle, helpless.

He was about to speak when Nicci continued.

'I don't think... well, I haven't had a chance to talk to Dad about it, but—'

'It's okay,' Ethan cut her off. 'I spoke to Pete before I left this evening. He says it's our decision. He wants to take a back seat now. Says he wants a rest from decision-making.'

Nicci looked at him as though he'd grown two heads and who could blame her after the resistance he'd put up at work. He smiled at her. 'If you need help, then we'll get you some help.'

'But I don't want to—'

He cut her off again and looked at Stacey. 'The job's all yours. I'm acting managing director now, so ultimately you report to me, but Nicci will sort out your workload on a day-to-day basis. Three months probationary period, which is standard for all employees. We work on a living wage rather than minimum wage for new starters.' His eyes met hers. 'How does that sound?'

She gave a satisfied grin. 'If we can agree to a pay review after the probationary period, then that sounds okay.' She looked at Nicci, then Ethan.

Nicci closed her eyes and sighed before standing to gather the dirty plates. 'You can discuss that with the managing director,' she said, wearily, before heading off to the kitchen.

'What's got into her?' Stacey asked with a frown as she watched Nicci disappear from the room.

'She's not been feeling well the last couple of days. That's what got us thinking about having some help. We wouldn't manage at all if she was off work.' He picked up his wine and downed the remaining half a glass. 'Apparently the auditors listed it in their recommendations last year and they're coming back next week, so we've got to get it sorted.'

Stacey gave a nod, accepting his explanation. 'So, it's definitely a permanent position?'

He hesitated, realising she'd given him a way out of the arrangement. 'As long as your performance is up to requirements.'

'I can guarantee my performance will be stellar,' she said, giving him a wink. She stood and dabbed at her mouth with a napkin, picking up empty glasses and the remains of the garlic bread. 'I'll go and help my co-worker sort out the dishes.' And with that she disappeared into the kitchen.

Ethan puffed out a breath. That had been awkward, but it was done now. He hoped it didn't turn out to be the worst decision of his life, because although it had been a bit hairy since the accident, things had been working out just fine. If Stacey didn't keep her word, though, his whole world could come tumbling down.

He remained at the table, gazing into space, his mind full of all the what ifs and maybes. He was still sitting there when Stacey made her excuses and left a little while later, walking out the door with a spring in her step, clearly delighted.

. . .

He moved to the sofa, switched on the TV, thinking he could catch the end of the football match if he was lucky. He was fully immersed in the action when Nicci marched in and switched off the TV, standing in front of him, pointing the remote at him like she'd like to switch him off too.

'What did you have to go and do that for?' she asked, throwing the remote onto the coffee table, before folding her arms across her chest, a deep frown creasing her brow. 'Why didn't you talk to me first and confirm what we were going to do before making a job offer?'

Ethan was confused. Nicci had been so adamant she wanted Stacey to come and work for them when she'd raised the subject earlier. He'd thought the two women had played a pincer movement on him, forcing him into a decision he honestly hadn't wanted to make. He'd been so sure he'd done the right thing for Nicci, but apparently not by the look on her face. He was so befuddled he couldn't even work out what he wanted to say.

'Don't look so gormless,' she snapped, annoyance twisting her mouth. 'You were right. It's not a good idea employing Stacey. For all the reasons you said.'

He realised his jaw had dropped and he snapped his mouth shut. 'I don't... understand.'

She huffed. 'No, I'm sure you don't. But it looks like we're committed now.'

He sighed, closed his eyes. Today had been tortuous and he wanted it to end. To wake up in the morning and discover none of it had been real. It seemed he couldn't do right for doing wrong.

'She can work her three months then we can legitimately fire her,' she suggested, obviously trying to make the best of a situation she had initiated but had decided she no longer wanted. He gritted his teeth. Why hadn't she listened to him in the first place? But then by the time she'd talked to him about it, she'd already spoken to Stacey, so it was more or less a done deal.

'Not if her performance is satisfactory,' he pointed out, remembering Stacey's comment to him earlier when he'd been thinking along the same lines.

Nicci gave him a stare that would burn holes in stainless steel. 'Believe me, if I'm assessing her, I can guarantee her performance will be well below par.'

He shook his head, unable to fathom this change of heart. 'What's got into you? I only asked her because you were so adamant you needed help and she was the only person you would work with.'

What could Stacey have done to get Nicci so riled up against her, he wondered, especially when Stacey herself seemed oblivious to the fact there was a problem? *Bloody women*, he thought, raking his hand through his hair. *They're impossible.*

She glared at him for a long moment, then gave a derisive snort. 'I know,' she said, her eyes narrowed as she pointed a finger at him. 'I know exactly what game you're playing.'

His mouth dropped open again, not sure what the heck she was talking about. Then he watched her stalk out of the room, heard her feet stomping up the stairs. The bedroom door slammed behind her with such force it made him jump. A bead of unease lodged in his chest.

What does she know?

CHAPTER EIGHTEEN

Nicci sat on the bed listening to the sounds from the football match filtering up through the ceiling. There was definitely something going on between him and Stacey. She'd heard them whispering when she went to get the wine. Maybe the idea of them having an affair wasn't so stupid after all? After half an hour she thought she might implode if she didn't confront Ethan and find out exactly what was going on.

She stomped back downstairs, picked up the remote and turned the TV off for a second time.

Ethan glared at her, grabbed the remote from her hand and turned it back on again. 'There's only six minutes of injury time left,' he snapped.

'I need to talk to you,' she insisted, reaching for the remote, but he'd kept it in his hand and lifted it out of her grasp.

'Five minutes,' he said, eyes on the screen. 'Go and make a cup of tea or something and then it'll be finished. I've had a hell of a day, sweetheart, and I would love to watch the end of this match.' He turned to her, his eyes blazing. 'Please.'

She was not going to be that woman who trotted into the kitchen and put the kettle on at her husband's request. Those days were over. She sat down, arms folded and waited. They were going to have this out tonight whether Ethan wanted to or not because her suspicions were driving her mad.

After what seemed like an eternity, the final whistle blew and Ethan turned the TV off, his eyes still staring at the screen. 'Are you going to tell me what's going on with you?' he asked, his voice so much calmer than she felt. 'I did exactly what you *demanded*.' He emphasised the last word before he turned to meet her stare.

She wavered slightly because what he'd said was true. But that was before she'd worked out something underhand was going on.

'Are you having an affair with Stacey?' She paused, surprised that she'd just come out with it, but determined to press on. 'That's what all this animosity between you two is about, isn't it?' She jabbed a finger at him, hardly able to contain her anger at the betrayal. 'It's a smokescreen. Fake. That's why you changed your mind about employing her, isn't it? It's what she wants so it's what *you* want.' She gave an annoyed huff. '*She* talked you round, didn't she?'

Ethan laughed. He actually laughed, and that was it, her emotional dam burst and before she knew what she was doing she was on him, pounding him with her fists, before he managed to throw her off. She landed on the sofa and he staggered to his feet, backing away from her with his hand outstretched as protection.

'Christ, Nicci. What the hell do you think you're doing?'

She was breathing hard, feeling feral, an urgent need to attack again. And it wasn't only about him and Stacey keeping secrets from her, it was a release for all the trauma of the past week.

'Nicci! I'm not having an affair with Stacey,' he shouted. 'Absolutely, definitely not.' She could see red weals rising on his cheek where she'd hit him. 'What the hell has got into you?'

She sprang to her feet and stood in front of him, fists clenched by her side, puffing like a bull about to charge. 'I'm not sure I believe a single word you say, to be honest. You said she threatened to tell. Tell what? What else am I supposed to think?'

He took a deep breath, held his hands up in surrender. 'The animosity between me and Stacey is real. I can assure you of that. I don't like her.' She caught a glint of steel in his eyes and her anger started to melt away, replaced by confusion. 'I really don't like her. I think she takes you for granted and treats you like a sort of pet rather than a friend. You're always running around after her. It makes me sick to see you treated like that.'

He sounded like he meant what he was saying and it made her pause, consider his words. Did Stacey treat her like that? Did she believe his dislike for her was genuine?

'If you hate her so much and despise the way she treats me... why on earth did you give her a job?'

He glared at her. She glared back. She thought it was a fair question.

'Because this morning, you practically begged me to do it. I thought about it all day and then I thought, if it will make my wife happy then I can deal with it.' He shrugged. 'I don't know what else to say.'

'That's why you gave her a job? Really?'

He nodded. 'Yep. No way on earth I'd choose her for the role. But if that's what you want, then I'm happy for you to have her as your assistant.'

She shook her head and slumped onto the sofa, all the fight going out of her, leaving her feeling limp and washed out. 'It's not what I want, though. I thought about it after we'd chatted and decided you were right.' She sighed, not sure what she wanted. 'Why didn't you speak to me first?'

He came and sat next to her. 'Oh, love, I'm sorry if I've done the wrong thing.' He reached for her and she hesitated before sinking into him as he put his arms around her and pulled her close, confused that she'd got it so wrong.

'I heard you whispering when I went to get the wine.'

Ethan tensed. 'I was just telling her that you were a bit out of sorts. She'd sussed you weren't quite yourself.'

That could also be true, she acknowledged.

'Let's not fight, love. Things are hard enough as it is and we need to stay strong.' He squeezed her shoulder, leant down for a kiss. 'I know things have been tough since the accident. I wanted to do something to support you.' He kissed her again. 'And let me say this now. Stacey is the last person on earth I would ever hook up with.'

He was so adamant, his shock at the suggestion so genuine, she believed him.

She thought about her relationship with Stacey. Did she behave like her pet? She'd have to consider that, she decided, but in her heart, she already knew the answer was yes. It was ironic that the person who told her she should stop being a people pleaser was the one she tried hardest to please. But then she supposed that had been the nature of their relationship from the start. Stacey had been her first friend at high school. A scary place for Nicci and she'd found comfort hiding behind Stacey's confident demeanour. It had suited her at the time, but now she understood things had to change.

She could feel her cheeks redden and she hid her face in Ethan's chest. She'd just made a complete idiot of herself. Humiliating didn't even begin to cover it.

'I suppose I'm going to be her boss,' she mumbled, wondering how to put this right. 'Well, we both are, so if she steps out of line, we can let her go.'

Ethan nodded. 'That depends if you want to risk losing her as a friend, doesn't it?'

At this point, Nicci wasn't sure how she felt about Stacey now her eyes had been opened to the nature of their friendship.

'We could always go back to her and say we've had a bit of a financial hit,' Ethan suggested. 'Tell her we don't think we can afford it at the moment.'

Nicci shook her head. 'She's handed in her notice. I don't think that would be fair.'

Ethan's breath blew through her hair. 'I suppose you're right.' He bent to kiss her again, tender and gentle. 'Well at least we know where we stand now, don't we?'

And Nicci thought she did, all her concerns forgotten, their lives back on an even keel.

Later, when they'd gone up to bed, and Ethan was in the bathroom, she lay there, looking at the photograph that hung on the wall at the end of the bed. Her dad had taken it at the engagement do, an unguarded moment when she and Ethan were dancing, laughing, looking into each other's eyes. Their expressions shone with love and she felt a warm glow in her heart, reminded of how good they were together. It was the accident that had thrown them, but they could get back to that place, be those people in the photo again.

The ringing of his phone broke into her thoughts. It was unusual for him to have a call so late at night. She deliberated with herself for a moment, asked whether it would be right to check who was calling. Then decided at this time of night it could be an emergency. He'd left his phone on his bedside table and she leant over, looked at the screen. It was Stacey.

Now what would she be doing ringing him at this time of night, and why did she have his number?

CHAPTER NINETEEN

Nicci let the call go to voicemail and decided not to say anything. She shouldn't have been looking at who was calling and knew she'd only get denials again. Her mind dissected the events of the evening, examining Ethan's behaviour. He'd sounded so convincing when he said he didn't like Stacey. Had he completely fooled her?

Earlier, when she'd been lying in bed after their make-up sex, she'd been full of desire for her husband. He was so gentle with her, so keen to please, and her heart had filled with tenderness. At that moment she'd convinced herself she'd done the right thing by marrying him. This was love, wasn't it? She had to put her infatuation with Joel out of her mind, forget her silly theories about the reason for his absence, and quash her imaginings about Ethan having an affair with Stacey, because that question had been answered.

And then his phone had rung and she understood that the question hadn't been answered at all. However, maybe she'd asked the wrong question in the first place. If he wasn't having an affair with her, something else must be going on. But what?

For the life of her she couldn't work it out. If she asked him, straight out, what was going on with him and Stacey she knew she'd get a big, fat nothing. And, however unconvincing his answer may be, he'd stick to it. Until she understood what the deal was between them, her suspicions would drive her crazy but she couldn't confront either of them until she had some hard evidence. She'd have to catch them unawares, and that would involve watching and waiting.

Ideally, she would be able to look at Ethan and Stacey's phone records, because that's where the evidence would lie, but they both used fingerprint access so there was no chance of that happening. *Hmm, this is going to take a bit of thought.*

It was a while before she fell into a fitful sleep, her mind taking her back to the moment before the accident. The rain lashed against the windscreen once more, the shape in the darkness, Ethan shouting at her to watch out, the steering wheel jerking to the left. Then that terrible noise.

She woke in a cold sweat, whimpering, feeling there was something she was missing. Some part of the sequence of events wasn't making sense and that's why her mind kept going back to it. Searching for the answer to a question she kept asking herself. How could the accident have happened? Ethan said it was a lapse in concentration, like she was falling asleep, but she didn't remember feeling sleepy. In fact, she'd been running on adrenaline, conflicted between the life she was planning with Ethan and her feelings for Joel.

She got up and went downstairs to make herself a cup of hot milk, hoping it would help her get back to sleep, but still her mind was locked on the puzzle she couldn't solve. She tossed and turned for the rest of the night.

The next morning, she woke feeling groggy and stumbled through her morning routine, knowing she couldn't live like this. The lack of sleep was starting to have a serious impact on her mental health and even a morning walk with Mack didn't freshen her up like it normally would. But there were no easy answers, nothing she could think of that could settle her mind.

She went into work with Ethan and the news came on the radio as they were pulling into the parking lot of the workshop. He turned it up. 'Police working on the identity of the hit-and-run victim are again appealing to the public for their help.' The report gave details of the location of the accident and the time and date and gave a number to ring with information.

Ethan turned to her, his mouth pressed in a thin line. 'Remember our vows,' he said, taking her hand. 'Please promise me you won't do anything silly.'

She gazed out of the window, her heart telling her that not owning up to the accident was very wrong, especially when it impacted on her friends. 'Louise is frantic,' she said, remembering her voicemail. 'What if I suggest to her that she needs to make sure this person isn't Joel?'

Ethan pulled a face, clearly horrified by the idea.

'But she'll ask you why you think it might be him, won't she?' He shook his head, squeezed her hand. 'Honestly, I don't think we should say anything to anyone. The best thing is to keep our heads down, go about our business as usual and it will all blow over.'

'But there is a perfectly innocent reason why I think it might be Joel. That's the corner where we always used to meet when we were going to walk the dogs.'

Ethan raised an eyebrow. 'Is it? I didn't know that.'

Nicci tensed. 'I'm pretty sure I told you.'

Ethan shook his head. 'I'm pretty sure you didn't.'

Unease swirled in her stomach. 'Why are you looking at me like that?' Her cheeks burned and she couldn't look at him, didn't even wait for his answer. She pulled her hand from his grasp and got out of the car, hurrying inside and up the stairs to the office, finding her dad at his desk.

He looked up and frowned, stopped what he was doing. 'You okay, love? You're looking a bit... flustered.'

She gave him a smile, flapped a hand, dismissing his concerns. 'Oh, it's nothing.'

But it was something. A very big something and she wasn't sure how much longer she could hold her emotions in check. She could accept that her crush on Joel had been ill-advised. What was harder to accept was the fact she might have killed him. Even worse that she'd left Louise not knowing what had happened to her partner, especially when she was about to have his baby.

Her dad stood and came to give her a hug, which Nicci gratefully accepted, sinking into him as she hugged him back. She savoured the moment, thinking that the number of times they could do this might be limited, because if he knew about the hit-and-run, he wouldn't want to touch her ever again. This connection, this love between them would be lost forever and she couldn't risk that. Ethan was right, again. They had to stay silent.

After a few moments she felt composed enough to pull away. 'You're in early,' she said as she walked over to her desk.

'I'm working on a project for Ethan. I'm nearly there with it.'

'That's great, but I don't suppose he expects you to work the same hours he does. I thought you were going to start taking it easy?'

Her dad laughed. 'We're cut from the same cloth, me and Ethan. I couldn't take it easy if I wanted to. But you and Ethan taking over has lifted all the pressure off me, so I can just enjoy myself.' His eyes sparkled and he sat back in his chair with a satisfied sigh. 'I'm so happy you two are married. Your mum would be so pleased. You know that, don't you? She would have loved him the same way I do. I can't tell you how lucky I feel to be able to hand the firm over to such a safe pair of hands.'

Nicci chewed at her lip, aware that an opportunity had been presented to her, a conversation opening up where she could tell her dad how she felt about working in the business. Was now the right time? She gritted her teeth, told herself to be brave and put the people pleaser in her away. It was an opportunity to point her life in the direction *she* wanted, not the direction everyone else wanted. Although she loved her dad without question, she was well aware that he regularly played on her kindness to get the outcome he wanted. In fact, that's what he was doing now.

'I'm happy you feel like that, Dad, but I'm honestly not sure I'm doing a brilliant job. I mean, I muddle through, but I'm not on top of things like I should be. And it's so stressful feeling like I'm firefighting all the time.'

The smile dropped from her dad's face. 'I'm sure it's just the stress of the wedding. All that organising, I'm not surprised it's been hard to keep up.' His faced changed then, eyebrows raising like he'd remembered something. 'By the way the auditors rang just before you came in. They can't come for a couple of weeks now due to annual leave.'

Nicci felt herself sag with relief and she sank into her chair, did a celebratory spin, making her dad laugh. 'Well, that's good news.'

'And Ethan tells me Stacey is coming to help out, so that should take the pressure off.'

'Yes, but—'

'That husband of yours was telling me how special it is to be running the business with you beside him.' He beamed at her. 'So many positive things coming together at the moment... after the shock of your mum's death, I feel it was meant to be.'

Christ, this is hard, she thought, but pushed on because if she didn't say it now when would she ever tell him that the business was not for her? It wasn't her passion. It was her prison.

'I know, but I don't really...'

Her voice fizzled out. There was no point in trying to tell him. It was as though he couldn't hear her. He wasn't even looking at her now. He was gazing through the window at the lads starting to get to work on the shop floor.

'You've made me so happy and proud. This business was as much your mum's as it is mine and it's lovely to think it will live on through you.' He laughed. 'You know, some days, I look over and see you at the desk there and I think for a moment it's your mum. It might sound daft but it gives me a lot of comfort.'

He turned and walked over to her and planted a kiss on her cheek. 'You keep me sane, do you know that? You keep me going, give me a reason to live. God knows what would happen if you weren't here.'

What could she say? She said nothing, just looked at her desk and the pile of paperwork left over from the day before and a lead weight landed in her gut.

He left the office then and went down to speak to Ethan about whatever it was they were working on, while she closed her eyes and told herself she'd get another chance to tell him. At some point, she would, but he was so insistent on seeing things his way, she was going to have to be stronger, more persistent.

That little exercise in asserting myself didn't go well. More practice, she told herself, *that's all I need.*

She rang Stacey.

'Hey, lovely,' Stacey said, all cheery. 'I was going to give you a call.' There was a pause, her voice lowering. 'Was it me or was there a bit of an atmosphere between you and Ethan last night. Honestly, it felt a bit... awkward.'

Nicci gritted her teeth. *Awkward because of you*, she thought to herself. 'Sorry about that. We've sorted it out now. Just a misunderstanding.'

'That's good. I suppose it will take you guys a little while to settle into being married. Even though you've lived together for a few months, marriage is a big step, isn't it? That commitment.'

She was silent for a moment. 'I'm not gonna lie, I found it quite scary, wondering if I'd made the worst mistake of my life.' She laughed, as though she'd made a joke.

Here we go again, Nicci thought. Stacey transferring her own emotions onto my relationship. At least she'd got that right. Perhaps it wasn't going to be as hard as she'd thought to find out what Stacey was up to with Ethan. It was a question of being vigilant.

'I was ringing to see if you'd thought about a start date. I know you said you'd handed in your notice.'

'Monday. I can start on Monday.' Stacey sounded excited. Upbeat. 'It's going to be fun working together, isn't it?'

Fun was not the word Nicci would have used. She gave a satisfied smile, thinking that Stacey wouldn't be having much fun when she found out what Nicci had planned for her.

CHAPTER TWENTY

The morning was lost in a blur of figures and phone calls. When it was almost lunchtime, the phone rang again and she told herself she'd answer it and then stop for something to eat.

'Nicci, I'm so glad I caught you.' It was Louise, calling on the business landline, and Nicci closed her eyes, unable to hide the sigh of despair. Louise was the last person she wanted to talk to and she felt bad for not returning her call, but hadn't been able to bring herself to do it. She took a deep breath, gathered herself together. At least she wasn't talking to her face to face because then it would be impossible to hide her emotions. There was that small mercy to be thankful for.

'Louise, I'm so sorry. I got your message but it's been chaos here and I forgot to ring you back. I'm trying to get ready for the auditors and I've such a lot to catch up on.'

'No, that's okay.' The snippy tone of her voice made it clear it wasn't okay and Nicci knew she hadn't been a good friend. Especially when Louise was in such a vulnerable situation. She'd been a coward, not ringing her back, and she was ashamed of herself.

'I was just wondering, though,' Louise carried on, 'because

you and Joel were *such* close friends...' There was a bitterness in her voice and Nicci tensed. It was obvious she was trying to make a point. 'I thought you might have heard from him by now.'

Nicci hesitated, her heart telling her exactly what she should do, her head telling her she couldn't. She swallowed. 'No, I haven't heard a thing.'

'Are you sure?' It was clear from the tone of her voice Louise thought she was lying.

'Absolutely sure,' Nicci said, confidently, because it was true. But the fact she hadn't heard from him made her more certain that Joel was the man lying dead in the hospital morgue.

Louise was quiet, only the sound of her breathing rasping down the line. She was obviously worked up and emotional and Nicci's heart went out to her. Sweat gathered under her arms, heart pounding in her chest, as she fought the urge to suggest he might have been in an accident.

'He told me, you know?'

Nicci tensed, rubbing the back of her neck, trying to erase the prickle of unease. 'Told you what?'

'That he... he was in love with you.' Louise broke down, her sobs making it impossible for her to talk.

Nicci gasped, horrified for a whole variety of reasons. *He was in love with me?* The knowledge made her heart skip a beat. So, she hadn't been imagining the connection between them. But why did he tell Louise when he knew there was nowhere for their relationship to go? He knew Nicci was marrying Ethan and telling Louise something as shocking as that had been cruel. But not as cruel as the terrible thump of the car hitting a body, the judder as they ran over the person they'd hit. Then not admitting what they'd done.

'No, no, no, I think you've got that wrong,' Nicci said, trying to tear her mind away from the images.

Louise launched into a tirade of swear words, calling her all the names under the sun and Nicci knew there would be no reasoning with her. She put the phone down, her elbows on the desk, her head in her hands, fingers digging into her scalp.

If Joel loved me, if he'd told Louise, then surely he would have been in touch with me. Unless, and this was the only conclusion she could draw, unless he was dead.

She closed her eyes, took herself back to the night they were driving home. Rain lashing against the windscreen, the wipers hardly able to keep up. Her hands had been gripping the steering wheel so tightly it felt like they were glued in place. She knew she shouldn't be driving, but it wasn't far, the back road was quiet, nobody would know.

Ethan sat beside her, hanging on to the leather strap that hung from the ceiling as they drove round the corners on the twisty lane, discussing wedding arrangements and who was picking up the flowers. She hadn't taken her eyes off the road for a second, though, and there... yes, she *did* see somebody. She'd noticed a dark figure standing on the corner and she knew it must be Joel because he'd messaged her earlier saying he wanted to meet her there.

Something shifted in her mind's eye. By admitting to herself that she'd seen him, the cloak of denial was lifted and everything seemed to sharpen up. She tried to relax, wanting the images to stay, wanting to be sure exactly what had happened. She heard Ethan's voice shouting at her to watch out, but she wasn't sure what she was supposed to be watching out for. There were no other vehicles, nothing except the figure. Then his hand grabbing the steering wheel and yanking it to the left, making the car veer off the road.

Somehow, they'd come to a halt. Had Ethan pulled on the handbrake? She couldn't remember. Could only feel the panic of not being able to breathe, her throat closing, her chest not moving. It was a blank from that moment to the point at which Ethan carried her into their home.

Her hands covered her mouth, eyes flying open as she understood what had happened. If Ethan hadn't grabbed the wheel, she wouldn't have hit Joel. He wasn't standing on the road, he was standing on the corner and there was no reason for her to go near him, the road veering round to the right.

This was the missing bit of information, the extra clarity her mind had been searching for. Now she'd found it, though, her world seemed to have tipped on its axis, leaving her feeling dazed, confused. Uneasy. Why *had* Ethan grabbed the wheel? She picked over every detail again in her mind, but came to the same conclusion.

One thing was certain. This was Ethan's doing. He'd deliberately steered them *towards* the figure, not away from them. There was no doubt in her mind it was intentional. Ethan had wanted that person dead.

CHAPTER TWENTY-ONE

Ethan whistled as he walked up the steps to the office, happy with his morning's work. It was Friday lunchtime and at this point in the week, he liked to review where he was up to with everything. He was looking forward to spending the afternoon tying up loose ends, sorting out the work schedule for the week to come, and making sure clients were up to date with progress on their jobs.

He opened the door to see Nicci slumped over her desk, her head buried in her hands. He could hear her sniffing. *Oh God, what's happened now?*

'Hey, sweetheart, what's wrong?' he asked as he dashed over to her, crouching by her side, his hand on her back. He felt her body tense at his touch.

It was a moment before she responded, raising her head to show a tear-stained face, her nose red, her eyes puffy. She opened her mouth to speak, then closed it again. The look she gave him would have turned fire to ice. 'I've remembered,' she said. 'I know what happened when the car hit Joel.'

His heart fluttered, going from slow and steady to a flat-out gallop in a matter of seconds. He glanced at the door, listened for footsteps coming up the stairs. He couldn't let anyone see her in this state, or overhear what she might be about to say. Fortunately, all was quiet.

'I'm not sure what you mean,' he said, trying to make his voice soothing, but he could hear the vibration of panic in his words.

She was still staring at him, with a look on her face he'd never seen before. Disdain? Dislike? Whatever it was, it was making him feel uncomfortable.

'I think you know exactly what I mean.' She shrugged his hand off her back and stood, walking away from him and perching on the edge of Pete's desk. 'You pulled the steering wheel out of my hands. You pulled it to the left, which meant we were headed straight for that person. You made us hit them on purpose, didn't you?'

'What? That's crazy! You were the one driving, I was hanging on for dear life when you swerved. It was nothing to do with me. I tried to stop you from hitting him.'

He glanced towards the door again, but it remained shut. They were alone for now, although Pete would probably come up at some point to tidy his desk before he clocked off for the weekend. His hands were slick with sweat, his body flushed with the heat of panic. This was not a conversation they should be having in the office.

Her frown deepened, eyes narrowing. 'It's clear in my mind now. I know you grabbed the wheel.'

He nodded. 'Yes, I did. I grabbed the wheel to try and steer you away from him but it was too late at that point.' He walked towards her but she held out a hand to stop him. He leant against her desk, facing her, their feet almost touching. 'Look, I do know how to drive that car when it's swerving out of control. It happens all the time when we're off-roading. Me and Dom take turns as driver, so I know how to do it when I'm in the passenger seat as well.' He shook his head, his voice gentle. 'I think you've got it wrong. You're misremembering and I can understand why, now the person you hit is dead and the guilt is strong. But believe me, I feel it too.' He folded his arms across his chest. 'Anyway, why would I want to deliberately hurt anyone?'

'It was Joel you hit and you were jealous of our friendship.' Her head gave a little nod when she finished speaking, her arms tightening round her chest, eyes burning with rage.

He frowned. 'That's just not true. I never minded you going for walks with him. I have no problems with you having male friends. You know that.' He waited for her response but she stayed silent, still glaring at him. 'Look, I'm the guy who rescues spiders out of the bath. I don't kill anything. And I definitely would never deliberately kill a person. Why would I throw away everything I've worked for, our relationship?' He shook his head. 'No, love. I'm not that man. You know you've had this before after panic attacks... Your memory is playing tricks on you.'

Nicci blinked at him with red-ringed eyes before dropping her gaze to the floor.

'I need you to believe me,' he said, his hands clutching the edge of the desk. 'Our relationship, the business, it's not going to work if you have it in your head that I deliberately made you run someone over.'

Nicci stayed silent for what seemed like an hour but was probably a few seconds.

'Okay,' she mumbled, eventually. 'I suppose I believe you. Like you said, it's probably my guilty conscience looking for a way out. For someone else to blame.'

'Sweetheart, I know it's hard, but you have to remind yourself it was an accident. You weren't driving like a crazy person, they were just stood in a stupid place on a night like that, in the dark. It was an accident, nothing more.'

'Louise just rang. She still hasn't heard anything.' She heaved in a big breath, wiped at her eyes with her hands. 'I want to tell her to call the police. I want her to be able to go and identify the body, so she knows for sure what's happened to Joel.'

Her eyes met his and he desperately wanted to look away but knew that would be a mistake. Their lives depended on him talking her down from the state she'd got herself into.

'She's about to have their baby for God's sake and she thinks he's walked out and left her.' She sniffed, then her body was shuddering with sobs and he leant over and grabbed the box of tissues she kept on her desk, passed it to her.

'It's a tough situation for everyone,' he said. 'But let's think this through, sweetheart. If you suggest to Louise that she talks to the police about the unidentified body, that will get both her and them wondering.' He had her attention now, the sobs starting to subside. 'Louise will wonder why you thought to suggest it, but also, she will know that you and Joel used to meet on that corner when you took the dogs for walks together. She will probably mention that to the police. Who will then come and investigate us.'

'Oh God,' she muttered, closing her eyes. 'It's too awful. I can't take the not knowing.' She blew her nose, wiped her eyes and her cheeks. 'Is there any way we can find out if it's Joel or not?'

He thought for a moment, then his eyes widened as an idea popped into his head. 'I know. Crimestoppers. We could make an anonymous call.'

Her eyes blinked open, her voice weak with relief. 'Yes, that's it. I'll ring them now.' She reached past him for her phone, which was on her desk, but he grabbed it first, holding it out of her reach.

'Careful. I know they say it's anonymous, but I have my

doubts about that. It might be better to ring from a public phone, then there's no way of tracing it back to us.'

She nodded and turned, looked like she was going to head out of the office and go and find a phone right there and then. He pulled her back, folded her into a hug, but she was so tense it felt like he was holding a plank of wood.

'It's okay, sweetheart. You're in no fit state to go anywhere. I'll do it. I'll go into Keighley then it's not too close to home.' He gave her a gentle kiss. 'Let me make you a cup of tea. You just need to sit and rest for a little while until you're feeling a bit better.'

'Thank you,' she said, pushing away from him and plonking herself in her seat, pulling a fresh handful of tissues from the box while he went and made her a cup of tea. Her voice cracked as she murmured, 'I'm not sure how much more of this I can take.'

'I know, love. I know how difficult it is. He was my friend too.' He put the tea on her desk, but she didn't register its existence, her eyes staring into the distance. 'The thing is, we don't know for sure it was him, do we? It's only a theory of yours, so I think you're right about putting his name forward and getting that checked out. Then we'll know for certain and at least that's one thing we can put to bed. There's a chance you might be wrong.'

He put an arm round her shoulders. 'I want you to remember we're in this together and I'll do whatever it takes to protect you. I love you, sweetheart.' He bent and kissed her before heading down the stairs and outside to his car. The sooner he sorted this out the better because he wasn't sure how much more of this he could take either.

It was all about acceptance. Accepting that things happened that couldn't be changed. Accepting mistakes and moving on from them without beating yourself up all the time. Accepting that actions had consequences and not always the ones you might have anticipated. You had to let the universe do what it was going to do and work with it. That was his philosophy. No regrets, because they ate away at you. Learn and move on. That's what he aimed to do. Now if only he could take his own advice...

CHAPTER TWENTY-TWO

Nicci had never been more delighted for it to be five o'clock on a Friday and time to go home. It had been a tumultuous week and without the wedding arrangements to distract her from the hit-and-run, she'd been obsessing over it. At least the police had Joel's name now, so hopefully Louise might get some definite news, and through her, they would too. Or hear it on a news bulletin. Either way the uncertainty would be gone.

She was grateful to Ethan for calming her down and taking control of the situation. He was right, as usual. It was her mind playing tricks on her, wasn't it? Once again, he was proving himself to be a valuable person to have around in a crisis. It had been the same on the night of the accident when she'd had a panic attack. He'd not put a foot wrong and sorted her out then as well. Perhaps their marriage could work after all.

Stacey, whispered her mind.

Ah yes. Her positivity about Ethan started to crumble round the edges. There was still that, wasn't there?

If only she could discover what Stacey was up to. But she could start working on that on Monday and in the meantime, what she needed was a full weekend of relaxation, to try and switch her mind off from the terrible thing she'd done.

The house could stay dirty, the cupboards might be empty, but the freezer was well stocked and she decided she would get outside and enjoy the nice weather. Unfortunately, the football season was starting that weekend and she knew Ethan had arranged to meet up with his mates the following day. After the accident, she couldn't face seeing any of their friends, which left her dad as the only option for company.

'What are you up to this weekend?' she asked as she watched him tidying everything off his desk, ready to go home.

'I thought I'd do a spot of fishing. I haven't been out for ages and the weather's supposed to be nice.' He looked at her then, a hopeful gleam in his eye. 'I don't suppose you fancy coming with me, do you? Be like old times.'

Nicci beamed at him. 'I would love to.'

And that was the truth. Hours of peace and quiet by the river, watching the dragonflies flitting over the surface of the water, listening to the birdsong, the splash and gurgle of the water, random chatter with her dad. It was about as stress-free as a day could get. It would be like being a child again and that was exactly what she needed. An escape from her life, even if it was only for a few hours.

She remembered many a Saturday up early with her dad when she was young, right up until her late teenage years. It was a way to spend some quality time with him, given he worked such long hours during the week. With all the stresses of recent days, she yearned for that peaceful alone time now and thought it might be the perfect way to settle her over-wrought emotions.

'Shall I pick you up then, love? I was going to go early, but I don't know...'

'Early is fine, Dad. I'll put us a picnic together, shall I? And Mack can come too. He'll love a day by the river.'

Her dad laughed. 'A proper family day out.' He finished clearing his desk with a smile on his face and if nothing else positive had happened that week, Nicci knew she'd made him happy.

Ethan was quiet on the drive home. It felt like the hit-and-run had initially pulled them together, then as time went on it had driven a wedge between them. She didn't have the energy to talk about it with him, not right now, but if she could untangle her own feelings, it would be easier. A day fishing with her dad would give her some breathing space to work out what had happened that night and what *she* wanted to do about it.

The next day, the sun was shining and there was a gentle breeze ruffling the leaves on the alder trees, which lined the riverbank. Nicci lay on her back, her head resting on her fleece jacket. Mack was curled up at her side and her dad was thigh deep in the river, fly fishing for trout. Nicci was his helper, and if he caught anything, she would get the landing net, take the hook out of the fish's mouth, then snap the required picture before her dad returned it to the water.

She watched the clouds drifting across the sky, wishing she could turn back time. If she had told Ethan a week before the wedding that she was having second thoughts and didn't want to go through with it, would Joel still be alive? Had she been that unsure? She'd been conflicted, she knew that. Part of her thought the attraction of Joel was the fact he was the opposite of Ethan. He flowed through life much like the river, never trying to swim against the current, but going with it.

He said it was the Tao philosophy and he'd read to her from the *Tao Te Ching*, a wonderful little book of Eastern philosophical verses, and they spent many a dog walk discussing what they thought the cryptic poems might mean. It had intrigued her. *He* had intrigued her and he'd opened a door to some interesting thoughts. Life didn't have to be all about earning money. It could be about enjoying what you had. Making do, being happy with the little pleasures that every day brought.

It felt so much less stressful than Ethan's constant drive to be bigger and better. To achieve. To have all the things he didn't yet have. The house, for example. She loved their little cottage, found it cosy and friendly. Ethan, on the other hand, wanted somewhere bigger, and had come to dislike where they lived. Granted it was a squeeze with the two of them, but something else would come along when they needed it. To be honest, Ethan could be exhausting. His mind was always onto the next thing he wanted rather than enjoying what he had. Thinking about it now, she realised it made her feel she wasn't quite enough.

They say opposites attract and she thought that was probably how she and Ethan could be described. He did have a gentle side to him, though. He could be thoughtful and caring and she loved that about him.

I do love him, don't I?

She didn't love the fact he'd been adamant they shouldn't own up to the accident. She also didn't love the fact he'd talked her into making those vows as part of their wedding ceremony. They were tied together by their crime now, whether she liked it or not. And their crime had escalated from an unreported accident to death by dangerous driving. She was also feeling uneasy about the way he'd persuaded her she was wrong about him pulling the wheel and hitting the person intentionally. Okay, maybe it *was* her guilty conscience putting images into her head, she had to consider that as a possibility. But he'd been so dismissive, so patronising, it didn't sit right with her and she wasn't convinced she believed him.

Joel loved me. A fact. Something she could hold onto.

Her stomach knotted as the thought grew in her mind, spreading like ink on blotting paper until it was the only thing she could see. If only she'd known. Would she have gone ahead with marrying Ethan if he'd told her? Perhaps that's what he'd wanted to say on the night he died. That's why he'd wanted to meet her. But they were in an impossible situation, both of them stuck in their own lives. Nothing good could have come of their union, because she would always have the guilt of making Louise a single parent. Not to mention the impact it would have had on her dad. He would have been distraught.

The only positive thing she could do at the moment was to ensure Louise got closure by making certain she knew the unidentified victim was Joel. *Hmm. No time like the present.* She sat up, took a deep breath, pulled her phone from her pocket and checked her dad was still out of earshot before she rang.

'Hello,' Louise said, sounding distinctly unfriendly. 'What do *you* want?'

Nicci was thrown by her hostile tone, but gathered herself and made herself speak. 'I wanted to make sure you're okay after our chat yesterday. See if there have been any... developments.'

'Hah. What's it to you?' Louise spat the words down the phone. 'With your shiny new husband and everything to look forward to. I'm not sure I even want to speak to you.'

Nicci was regretting her decision to call but steeled herself, determined to carry on. This was clearly going to be more awkward than she'd thought, but she had to put the record straight. 'Look, Louise, what you said the other day... About Joel being in love with me. I didn't know. Honestly, I didn't know that's how he felt.'

Silence.

After a few seconds she found she couldn't bear it, had to say something to fill the void. 'Obviously we enjoyed each other's company, but that's as far as it was ever going to go. We were friends.' She sounded defensive, but that's how Louise was making her feel. Like she'd done something wrong when she knew she hadn't.

'You bloody liar,' Louise snarled. 'You could at least give me some respect and be honest with me.'

'But that's the truth. Really... I didn't know.'

'I saw the message he sent you.'

Nicci frowned. 'What message?'

'The night he left. He sent you a message. Telling you he was in love with you.'

Nicci couldn't speak for a moment and when she finally did, she stumbled over her words. 'What? No, no, he didn't. I didn't get a message like that from him.' She wouldn't have forgotten something as huge as that. Not when it was something she'd been yearning to hear, confirmation that her feelings were reciprocated. 'The last message I had from him, he asked me to meet him, but we were going to Stacey's, so I didn't get a chance to reply.'

'I'm not talking about that message,' Louise snapped. 'I'm talking about the one after that. He sent another one.'

Nicci scrolled through her phone, just to make sure, and found her last chat with Joel. 'Honestly, if he did send me another message, I didn't get it.'

Louise gave a derisive snort. 'Well, you would say that, wouldn't you? I don't believe you.'

'But it's the truth.'

This wasn't going well at all and Nicci had no idea how to turn things round.

'You are a lying, deceitful bitch,' Louise shouted. 'I can't believe we were ever friends and I don't want to hear from you ever again, do you hear me?' The venom in her voice shocked Nicci to the core. 'I'm blocking you right now. Then I'm going to tell Ethan to watch out for Joel and let him know what you two have been up to. You think you can have it all, don't you? Married to Ethan and Joel as a bit on the side. You make me sick.'

'No, Louise, please, don't...' The line went dead. She'd ended the call.

CHAPTER TWENTY-THREE

Nicci blew out a long breath, so disturbed by the conversation, and the hate in Louise's voice, she was shaking. But one thing was very clear: Louise still thought Joel was alive. Which made Nicci wonder if Ethan had made that call to Crimestoppers or if he'd just been saying he would to placate her. Because if he'd made the call, the police would have asked Louise to go and identify the body and that hadn't happened. Another black mark against Ethan. They were starting to add up.

She lay back down, trying to regain the calm she'd felt before the phone call, letting her breathing slow until her pulse returned to normal. Mack snuggled next to her again, gave her arm a little lick. She glanced over to where her dad was still fishing, flicking the line on the water with practised ease. Everything was okay, nothing to get worked up about.

At least that's what she'd like to think.

Whatever she told herself, though, she knew there was plenty to get worked up about. If she'd received Joel's second message, would it have changed things? A sudden surge of emotion forced a sob from her chest and she knew that was her answer. Of course it would have changed things.

Her body felt weighed down with a terrible sadness and she allowed the tears to fall. It was all academic now. There was no going back and Louise's vitriol would spread to the rest of their friendship group, she was sure of that. But she had to wonder what had happened to that message from Joel and why it wasn't showing on her phone.

Was Louise telling the truth? And how did she even know about the messages?

She wiped her face with the back of her hand as she took her mind back through their conversation. Did she say she'd *seen* the message? In which case she must have been looking through Joel's phone. That was sneaky and wrong, but wouldn't she do the same if she suspected an affair? The answer was a definite yes, given the opportunity and knowledge of the password.

Assuming Louise was telling the truth and Joel had sent her the message, the next mystery was why hadn't she seen it? The only conclusion to be drawn was it had been deleted from her phone. And the most likely person to have done that was... Ethan.

It was possible. Ethan knew the passcode because Nicci had needed him to unlock her phone for her in the past. But why delete it? Why not keep it as evidence and confront her about it? Her mouth twisted in frustration; her theory not making sense. Maybe it was a technological blip, and nobody had deleted anything. She had to be careful about jumping to conclusions, had to limit the number of times she threw accusations at Ethan, only for him to come up with a perfectly feasible explanation.

She got to her feet, stretched out her limbs, wishing she could stretch out her mind in the same way and untangle her knotted thoughts. The most immediate issue to address was Ethan not calling Crimestoppers. Her spirits sank a little lower. She'd trusted him to do that but it was clear he hadn't. Presumably he'd thought it was too risky and the police would work out who'd called them.

After everything Louise had said to her, and the obvious pain she was in, Nicci felt she owed it to her to make the call. And if Ethan wasn't willing to do it, then she'd do it herself. She shouted to her dad that she was going to go for a walk, then headed to the public phone box in the village half a mile away.

Her call was answered on the second ring, taking her by surprise. 'Hello, Crimestoppers, my name is Neil. How can I help you today?'

'I... um...' She hesitated, her heart racing, wondering if this was the right thing to do. *You owe it to Louise.* She cleared her throat. 'I want to report a missing person.'

'I'm afraid that's not what we're here for. We're here for information about crimes. You need to go to the police about that.'

'No, no, that's not the whole story.' She thought he was going to end the call and was desperate to keep him on the line now she'd got this far. 'I think he's been the victim of a hit-and-run. The one that happened about ten days ago. Near Skipton. The reports say they haven't identified the body but... I think I know who it is.'

The operator was silent for a moment. 'And you can't go to the police?'

'No.' Her voice was firm, leaving him in no doubt it was not an option.

'Okay. Well, I can pass on an anonymous tip-off, if that would help?'

'Thank you. That would be very helpful.'

She gave Joel's details and slammed the phone down, eager to be away from the phone box and the village and any eyes that may be watching her. It had been risky doing this. Too risky, and she could see why Ethan hadn't done it in the end. He'd bottled out, pure and simple, but she had a stronger motivation to go through with it.

She could try kidding herself that she'd done this for Louise, but she knew, in her heart, she'd done it for herself. Not knowing what had happened to someone you love was the worst feeling in the world, the feeling of being in limbo, floating between two different worlds – one where the person was alive and one where they weren't. You ended up living no life at all, existing in a waiting room, not able to think or function or even feed yourself properly. It was no way to live and she was glad she'd been brave. At least now she'd know.

Trudging back along the riverbank, her spirits sank to a new low. She'd been dishonest with everyone, including herself, but making it right was going to take some careful thought, otherwise her whole world would implode. There were people she couldn't face hurting, number one on that list being her dad. His mental health was so fragile, she constantly worried about him. If her actions pushed him over the edge, how would she live with herself?

He was wading out of the water when she returned to his fishing spot, a glum look on his face. 'Nothing's biting.' He started gathering his things together. 'I think I'll try further down, in that deep pool past the bridge.'

She mustered a smile and gathered the picnic blanket and the cool box with their lunch and drinks in. 'Okay, let's do it.'

He gazed at her, head cocked to one side. 'Are you okay, love?'

She didn't reply, unable to think of a single truthful thing to say that wouldn't cause him to be upset. He wanted her to be happy and she definitely wasn't.

'I sense something is troubling you. And I'll be honest, I'm a little concerned that you're here fishing with your dad only a week after getting married.' There was a note of indignation in his voice. Frustration maybe. 'What's Ethan doing?'

She grimaced, understood exactly the point he was making and there was nothing she could do to sugar-coat the truth. 'I told you. It's the start of the football season. Tradition says he has to go round to Mike's house with the lads, drink a case of beer and shout at the TV for most of the day.' She laughed, but it sounded hollow.

Her dad tutted as he picked up the rest of his fishing gear and they started walking towards the bridge. 'I'll be having a word with him on Monday. It's no way for a newly married man to behave. Honestly, your mum would have had my guts for garters if I'd done that.'

'Yeah, well me and Mum are very different.'

He huffed. 'You're not wrong there.'

She had the feeling he was disappointed, that she'd let him down in some way. For the first time, she realised he did this a lot, comparing her to her mum and making the point that she didn't quite shape up, or not listening when she tried to tell him they were different people. How had she not noticed it before? She supposed he used it as a way to motivate her to do better, but she was starting to understand how he controlled her with his words and she really didn't like it. Even if he didn't mean to, he was comparing Nicci to an impossibly perfect model of her mum.

'I would have done anything for that woman,' he continued, unaware of her upset. 'Honestly, I just wanted to be with her. All the time. That's why we started the business together, so we could spend more time with each other. I know it doesn't work for everyone, but it was perfect for us.' He glanced at her and she saw his chin wobble, his voice cracking. 'We had such a lovely life.'

Nicci stopped walking, pulling her dad into a hug. His hurt was her hurt and however much she might not like the way he spoke to her sometimes, her love for him was solid. 'We'll always have each other, Dad. And we've got our memories, haven't we?'

He nodded and pulled away, carried on walking to his next fishing spot while he sniffed his tears away.

Nicci knew for certain that her relationship with Ethan was nothing like the relationship her mum and dad had enjoyed. Her dad had made a pertinent point which had hit its target. Why had she settled for a relationship where she wasn't as important as a few football games? When had she decided it was okay to be second best? And for the love of God, what had made her promise Ethan she would never tell anyone their secret?

It was killing her, knowing what she'd done. Eating away at all the values she'd held dear. At some point, if she was going to be true to herself, she was going to have to confess. Face up to her crime, accept the punishment and start her life again when she came out of prison.

She wanted to be a person her dad would be proud of and although he'd hate the fact she'd killed someone when she was drink driving, he would respect the fact she'd owned up to it and done her time. He probably wasn't as mentally fragile as he liked to make her think and he'd manage. He'd have to. This was her life, she had to live it her way and she couldn't live with the guilt. Even if she'd been slow to confess, at least, in the end, she would have done the right thing.

So that was the nub of it, she realised. All her thinking over the course of the day had actually led her to an answer. She'd become someone she didn't want to be, talked into doing things she didn't want to do and it was time for her to make a change. A big change.

CHAPTER TWENTY-FOUR

'You're very quiet,' Ethan said as they were driving into work on Monday. Nicci sat in the passenger seat, her hands wrapped together, wondering how she was going to face Stacey and act normally given her suspicions.

'Lots to think about,' she said, watching the scenery go by rather than looking at her husband. Her dad had got her thinking with his comments and he was right. What newly married man would prioritise watching football on TV with his mates over spending time with his wife? Especially when they hadn't even had a honeymoon. Perhaps Ethan wasn't as committed to their marriage as he liked to make out?

'Are you mad at me for watching footy all weekend?' Ethan said, seeming to read her mind as he turned off the ignition. He chuckled. 'The lads said I'd be in trouble, but I told them you weren't like that.' She turned to face him, and he gave her a disarming smile. 'Or are you still mad at me for giving Stacey the job when you'd changed your mind, but didn't tell me?'

There he was, blaming her for their lack of communication, making light of a serious situation, like she was being silly. She felt herself tense, a pithy response stuck on her tongue. Now wasn't the time for a fight. He was a handsome man, she thought as she gazed at him, but she wasn't feeling any warmth towards him. Nothing at all. No, that was a lie. She had a heavy, sinking sort of feeling in the pit of her stomach. Dismay, she thought.

'I'm fine, honestly. I'm not mad at you, just got a lot on my mind,' she lied. There was no way she could tell him she'd phoned Crimestoppers and had been waiting for a knock on the door from the police ever since. But it hadn't happened yet and there'd been no up-dates on the news about the hit-and-run. The media seemed to have lost interest in the story and she wondered if they would even report it when they did find out the identity of the victim. It could be ages before she knew for definite it was Joel.

'Are you getting out of the car?' Ethan asked, dipping his head inside the vehicle. She'd been so lost in her thoughts she hadn't heard him open the door. 'Stacey's here.'

She looked up to see her friend's silver BMW slide to a halt next to them, Stacey giving her a little wave. *Get a grip*, she told herself. There was an agenda to get through, a list of critical actions to do and things she had to discover before she made decisions that would change not only the rest of her life, but the lives of those closest to her. She had to get it right, be alert, tuned in.

She took a deep breath and gave Stacey a full wattage smile before getting out of the car. Her friend gave her a hug, which Nicci tried to return with equal enthusiasm. Out of the corner of her eye, she caught Ethan looking at them, his expression hard, tight-lipped and she wondered what he was thinking. It didn't look like he was pleased to see Stacey at all. If there was something going on between them, a relationship, he was hiding it well. She filed that thought away to study later.

'Hi, Ethan,' Stacey said, a cheery note to her voice.

'Morning,' Ethan replied, before turning and heading into the building.

'He's grumpy,' Stacey said, hooking her bag over her shoulder as she watched his back disappear through the door. 'I hope he's not going to be the employer from hell.' She nudged Nicci and laughed.

'He's got a tricky job on this morning, that's all.'

Nicci opened the door and let Stacey in ahead of her. She knew where she was going as she had visited Nicci here many times over the years and she ran up the stairs, obviously keen to get started. Nicci plodded after her, with limbs as heavy as lead.

'This is going to be so cool,' Stacey said as she walked into the office and made a beeline for the big window looking out over the shop floor. 'Thank you so much for giving me the job. I don't know how much longer I could have stuck my last one. I was at the stage where not only did I hate the work but I hated everyone I worked with.' She laughed. 'It was awful.'

'Well, I hope you like it here,' Nicci said, sitting at her desk and turning on the screen, wondering if it was the people and the job that were the problem or Stacey herself. 'Why don't you pull that spare desk over here, then it will be easier for us both to keep track of what we're doing.'

Ten minutes later, they were all set up, Stacey had made them coffee and Nicci was ready to start. 'I thought we'd begin with the ordering system. I'll show you how we do it and then I'll watch while you have a go before I let you get on with it yourself, while I sort out this list of things for the auditors.'

Stacey frowned, looked confused. 'I thought I was doing accounts? I don't know anything about ordering.'

Nicci gave a patient smile. 'I'm going to show you. Don't worry, it's very straightforward.'

'But what if I make a mistake?'

Nicci opened the system and pulled up the list of materials for the next job. 'I'll be watching you; it'll be fine.'

Stacey shook her head. 'No, I'm sorry, I think it would be better if I started with something I'm already familiar with. So, let's put the ordering to one side for now and start with invoices.'

Stacey had only been in the office for twenty minutes and already Nicci's patience was running thin. She hadn't slept properly for over a week, her mind was exhausted with thinking about the accident and what she should do about Ethan's behaviour, not to mention Stacey's involvement with her husband in some shape or form. She'd had enough. It was time to put one of those big changes in place. Time to stand up for herself against Stacey for once.

'You know what? I don't think this was a great idea. I'm sorry, Stacey, it's not going to work if you won't do exactly what I'm asking you to do.'

Stacey's jaw dropped. 'What do you mean?'

'I'm sorry but you can't work here with that attitude towards me.'

'Are you firing me before I've even started?' Her eyes were wide, voice incredulous.

'Well, you haven't officially started, have you? We haven't got a contract of employment signed. I was going to do that this afternoon, but—'

Stacey pushed her chair back, no longer listening and headed for the door, slamming it behind her. Nicci could hear her heels clacking down the stairs and waited for the external door to slam as well, but it didn't. She got out of her chair, considered calling her back but decided against it when she noticed that she'd left her handbag. She'd have to come back up anyway.

Christ, this was such a bad idea. In the past, she would have let Stacey push her into doing what she wanted. There would have been no resistance and she couldn't believe she'd been that person. There was no way Stacey was getting involved with the accounts because, like Ethan had said, the whole of Skipton would get to know their financial affairs. *What a mess.* She sat back down and started writing herself a to-do list for the day.

A few minutes later, footsteps thumped up the stairs and the door opened to reveal Ethan, Stacey hot on his heels.

He stood with his hands on his hips, Stacey peering over his shoulder. He looked as weary as she felt. 'Nicci, can you please show Stacey how the accounts work. That's what we've employed her to do. We have a verbal contract and we need to honour it. I said we'd have her contract of employment ready this afternoon if you could sort that out.'

Stacey walked round him into the office looking smug as he disappeared back downstairs.

She sat next to Nicci and smiled at her as though nothing had happened. 'Right then, let's get started.'

Nicci was finding it hard to speak and she got up, her eyes looking for an escape, thinking she would explode if she didn't get out of that office. 'Okay. I'll just nip to the toilet, then we'll do what the boss says.'

She hurried downstairs and into the workshop.

'Ethan!' she shouted, over the whine of the saw. 'Can I have a word?'

It was time for him to give her answers. Her first question being, *why are you choosing Stacey over me?*

CHAPTER TWENTY-FIVE

Ethan stifled a groan and turned away from the plans he'd spread out on the table. He wanted to get on with this job, hide himself away down here for a while and forget about Stacey and his wife. Forget about everything.

If only people could behave in a rational manner, he thought, life would be so much easier. He threw his pen down and walked over to where Nicci was standing, hustling her out of the door and outside the building. Taking her arm, he led her round the back, where nobody could see or hear them.

'What is it now?' He threw his hands up in frustration. 'You wanted her to work here. I asked her. Then you decided that wasn't what you wanted. Now you've fired her before she's even started.' He glared at her. 'What the hell is going on with you?'

Nicci's rage notched up another level. 'I'd like to know what's going on with you actually. Why would you side with Stacey over me? I've asked her to learn the ordering system but she has insisted she should start with accounts.' She jabbed a finger at his chest. '*You* were the one who didn't want her going near the accounts because you were worried about our financial situation being broadcast all over Skipton. Anyway, I could see she wasn't going to listen to me.' She gave a frustrated huff. 'It was you who pointed out the way she treats me and I see it now. It's never going to work with me as her boss.' Her jaw was set, chin jutting out and he could tell she was seething. 'She doesn't listen, so I tell her it's not going to work. Then she trots down to speak to you and suddenly she gets to do exactly what she wants.' She glared at him, hands on her hips and he thought he'd never seen her quite so angry.

He'd been counting on her behaving to type, basically doing what she was told, but recently something had happened. A rebellion. Or an awakening. Or maybe a combination of the two but her timing was the worst it could possibly be. Unease swirled in his gut.

'We have a verbal contract,' he said as calmly as he could manage. 'She has a voice recording of me giving her the job. And unless you want to be hauled in front of an employment tribunal, you can't fire her before you've given her a chance.' He slapped his forehead with his palm, beyond frustrated. 'I mean it hasn't been half an hour yet.' He glared at her; she glared back. 'Be reasonable,' he pleaded.

'A voice recording? You're kidding me.' Nicci looked flabbergasted, her frown deepening.

He nodded. 'That's what she told me and I believe her. We have no choice but to play by the rules.' He gave a frustrated sigh. 'Now please can I get back to what I was doing?'

He didn't wait for an answer but stalked off, hoping she would believe his lie about a voice recording and toe the line. He wasn't sure what was happening with his wife but he sure as hell didn't like it. Typical for her to decide to grow a pair of balls at the exact moment he needed her to behave the way she always had.

Of course he hadn't wanted to back Stacey over his wife, but he'd had no choice. None at all because she had this threat she could dangle in front of him all the time. He'd been stupid giving in to her demands the first time, all those weeks ago. And now she was becoming dangerous, because she was getting too bold. At some point, she'd be careless, then Nicci would find out and that would blow his marriage apart. Disaster. All his careful planning, all the groundwork, all the effort for nothing. But keeping it together was starting to feel like an impossible task.

What could he do, though, stuck as he was between a rock and a hard place?

He gritted his teeth. Then smiled as an idea took shape in his mind. Yes, that was it. He gave a jubilant fist pump, delighted that he now knew exactly how he was going to get rid of at least one of the complications in his life.

CHAPTER TWENTY-SIX

Reluctantly, Nicci started to show Stacey the finance system. However, she limited her access so she could only input data at this stage and not look at the reports. At least she had the power to do that, even if she didn't have the power to get Stacey to do what she was told. She hadn't told Stacey what she'd done and she wondered how long it would be before she said something. It would be interesting to find out. Because Stacey had an agenda, one that involved her husband, and Nicci was determined to discover exactly what it was.

She watched her friend, thinking it was like she was seeing her without a filter for the first time. It was the filter she'd viewed everyone in her life through, the one that made her feel second best, always striving to do what people wanted so she would be liked, loved and accepted. After the accident, though, none of that mattered. What she wanted was the truth, to be honest in her approach to life and how she lived it. How strange, she thought, that she hadn't been able to see things so clearly before. Weird that it took such a traumatic experience to shake the veil from her eyes.

Stacey was behaving as if nothing untoward had happened,

all chirpy and chatty, offering to go and make coffees and get the sandwiches at lunchtime. Nicci was glad to see her leave the office for a little while and as soon as she'd gone, she got up from her desk to stretch her legs. Ethan appeared in the doorway.

'How's it going now? Has it calmed down?'

Nicci met her husband's gaze, thinking, it's now or never. This was her chance to ask the question that had been burning a hole in her brain.

'Tell me honestly. What's going on between you and Stacey?'

Ethan's gaze didn't waver, his expression blank.

When he didn't immediately respond, she carried on, finding she had quite a lot to say, her voice sharp with anger. 'I'm not stupid. I can see that you don't like her and yet you're letting her walk all over me. What does she have on you?'

Still no response, although his expression had changed, and the way he'd stuffed his hands in his pockets told her he was uncomfortable.

'We should have told her it was a mistake offering her the job before she even had the chance to walk in the door. But you did a U-turn, and tried to pin that on me.' She held up her hands. 'I don't understand. Please, enlighten me.'

Ethan's lips were pressed together so hard they'd practically disappeared. He was obviously having a debate with himself, unsure whether to tell her the truth or not. 'Okay,' he said eventually. His body visibly sagged and he sat on the edge of the desk, his eyes on the floor. 'She's blackmailing me. She saw something.'

It took a few seconds for the words to register because it was so unexpected. Nicci's hand flew to her mouth. 'Oh my God, no. She saw the accident?'

Ethan shrugged, still not looking at her, his words guarded. 'I don't know exactly what she saw or how she got the information, but she knows too much.'

Nicci felt the office start to sway and she closed her eyes, leant against the wall, unable to rid herself of the feeling she was falling. No wonder Stacey had been so keen to work on the accounts. Once she knew how much money was in reserves, her demands would escalate. *Christ, can things possibly get any worse?*

'Why didn't you tell me?'

'Because I didn't think you'd believe me. She's your best friend and you've always defended her.' He gave her a sheepish look. 'I thought I could handle it. But she keeps coming back for more.'

'Of course she does. That's what blackmailers always do.' Their eyes locked. Nicci couldn't believe he'd been so stupid as to give Stacey money, but maybe he'd thought he had no choice. *He was protecting me.* And what would she have done in his shoes? She sighed, went and sat next to him on the edge of the desk. 'So, what's your plan?'

He gave another shrug, looking utterly defeated. 'I wasn't thinking straight when I paid her the first time. I was still in a bit of a state about the accident.' He pushed off the desk and stood, his hands jingling the loose change in his pockets. 'Leave it with me.' He reached for her, rubbed her shoulder. 'I promise, I'll get it sorted. I've had an idea, so I need a little time to give that a go. And in the meantime, if you could try and get along with her that would really help.'

Nicci nodded, not sure how she was supposed to get along with someone who was blackmailing them. She was seeing a side to Stacey she'd never imagined could exist and she thought back over their friendship, wondering how she'd never seen it before.

Stacey had always been keen on *things*, she supposed, as she mulled this over while waiting for her to come back with their lunch. Greg was not a natural match for her but his family were loaded so that provided an obvious attraction. He'd trained as a chartered surveyor and had recently been made a partner in his parents' estate agency business. The money was the pull for Stacey, not him. She got bored easily, liked to play games with people, often said she was joking when Nicci suspected that she wasn't. She realised now there was a nasty side to her that Nicci had chosen to ignore, gloss over, in her haste to be friends with the magnet of their social circle.

It was all adding together to create a very different picture of the person she was now sharing an office with. She could prove to be a dangerous enemy and Nicci shivered as a chill ran through her. How on earth were they going to deal with this?

Somehow, she muddled through the afternoon, pretending everything was normal, but she knew there was a limit to how many times she could manage that feat. To say it was an ordeal would be an understatement. Tortuous would be a better word. Especially when Stacey kept asking about parts of the accounting system that weren't working on her computer and Nicci had to fudge it, pretend it was temperamental and she'd get it sorted.

Later that night, when she was lying in bed, staring at the ceiling, the answer came to her. There were three options.

If they did nothing, Stacey would bleed the business dry and at some point, they wouldn't be able to meet her demands and she'd let the authorities know what had happened anyway. It would destroy everything her parents had worked towards and would destroy her dad. He was innocent in all of this and didn't deserve such a cruel twist of fate. So that wasn't an option.

She *could* let Ethan come up with a plan, but it was his decision-making that had led them to this point. She didn't trust him to get it right, so that wasn't an option either.

The third option was the only one worth considering,

because if she was looking at damage limitation, it was the best choice. Nicci would have to own up to the police, then Stacey would have nothing to blackmail them about and the business and her dad would be safe.

It was the same answer she'd come to a few times now from several different directions, only her timescale had shrunk. She'd thought she'd train Stacey as her replacement before she confessed, so she didn't leave the business in the lurch. However, thinking about it now, any qualified admin person would be able to pick up her role and her dad would just have to recruit someone, or use an agency for the time being. There were several possibilities but she'd been too frazzled to see them. Hopefully by confessing and doing the right thing, the business wouldn't be too badly tarnished by her crime and the damage could be contained.

She could see now that all she'd been doing over the past week or so was procrastinating, putting obstacles in the way so she didn't have to face her destiny. Avoidance tactics. But she was done with all that, done with making excuses, she just had to get on with it, however hard it was going to be.

Tomorrow *had* to be the day. One more night at home, in her own bed. Then it was time to hand herself in.

CHAPTER TWENTY-SEVEN

Nicci was up before Ethan, nervous about the day ahead and keen to prepare him before she went and confessed. She rang her dad, who was an early riser.

'Hello, love,' he said, sounding a bit puzzled. 'This is a nice surprise... Everything okay?'

'I wanted to say... I love you very much.' Her voice hitched in her throat. 'And I'm sorry I messed up.'

'Wait, what are you talking about? What's going on?' He sounded worried and she knew she couldn't tell him, knew she would break down and be unable to speak. Ethan would have to explain it to him later.

'Nothing for you to worry about,' she lied, giving a laugh that sounded false even to her own ears. 'I'm having...' She gulped, steadied herself. 'I just want you to know that you'll always be my hero and I wanted to thank you for everything you've ever done for me. You really are the best dad ever.'

There was a stunned silence.

'That's lovely,' he said, carefully. 'But have I forgotten it's my birthday or something? What am I missing here?'

'Nothing,' she said, her voice thick with emotion. 'I wanted you to know, that's all. Anyway, I better go.'

'Okay, love. Well... I'll see you later, then.'

'Yep,' she said, knowing that it would be the last time, because after that she'd be in police custody. She disconnected, her hand shaking as she sank into a chair.

'Who was that?' Ethan asked as he walked into the kitchen. If they ever received a phone call this early in the morning it was usually about work.

'Just Dad. I wanted a quick word. Nothing important.' *How the lies were flowing this morning*, she thought, but then she might as well get them all out there before she had to tell the police the truth.

She watched as Ethan put two slices of bread into the toaster, his back to her as he gathered margarine and jam, ready for his usual breakfast.

'I've worked out how to stop Stacey,' she said, in a sudden flurry of words.

He turned towards her, eyebrows raised. 'You have? Well, that's great. I've had some thoughts myself.' He sighed and returned his attention to the toaster. 'I don't think it's going to be easy.'

'No, it's not.' She took a deep breath, forced herself on. 'I'm going to hand myself in to the police.'

'What?' He spun around to look at her and she could swear she could actually see the blood draining from his face, his complexion going pale.

He opened his mouth to speak but she held up a hand to stop him. 'I know it sounds drastic, but hear me out.' She explained her thinking and how it was the only real solution.

'No, no, no. You can't do that.' He rushed over to her, knelt on the floor in front of her, grabbing her hands. His eyes were wild, searching her face. 'You can't be serious.'

'I'm deadly serious, but I'm not going to implicate you at all. I'll admit I was driving but I'll say you weren't in the car at that stage. You were feeling sick and had decided to walk. Then it's all on me, no question. I'll say I didn't tell you what had happened.'

He hung his head, ignoring the sound of the toast popping up. His grip on her hands tightened and she winced as she waited for him to say something. Finally, he looked up, and when she caught his eye, she could see the sheen of tears. He clearly didn't want to lose her. Her heart clenched, but she knew she had to do this. It was her only route to peace of mind. It was the only way she'd be able to live with herself. And it was the only way to stop Stacey in her tracks.

Of course there would be collateral damage to the business, her father and Ethan, but that damage had already been done. It was only a matter of time until the truth came out and it would look better from every angle if she voluntarily confessed.

'Please don't do it,' he begged. 'Please think again.'

She shook her head. 'No, I've been considering it for days. Thought about all the different options and honesty is the only way. I can't live with the lie, can't live with myself knowing I've killed someone. Yes, it'll be hard in the short-term but in the long run it's the best solution. And then Stacey will have nothing over us.'

'No, sweetheart. I don't agree.' There was a desperation in his voice, his words gushing out of him like a river in a storm. 'What would this do to your dad? It would kill him. And even if it doesn't kill him, it will kill the business, which is our livelihood. He might have to sell the house to repay debts. He could be left penniless. Is that what you want? Just so you can have a clear conscience?'

Nicci wasn't going to be swayed. It had been hard enough getting to this point and she wasn't ready to back down. 'It's not only about me.'

'But that's how you're looking at it.' He put his hands on her shoulders, his eyes locked on to hers. 'We made a vow, remember?' His fingers dug into her flesh. 'We promised never to say or do anything that would harm the other. I can't lose you. If you confess it will destroy me. Is that what you want?'

Her calm deserted her and she dissolved into tears. 'No, I don't want to destroy you, or Dad or anyone. But it's the only way.'

'No, it's not the only way,' he shouted. 'It's not!' He was so frustrated with her, he was shaking her as he spoke, as if he was trying to rattle some sense into her brain. 'Confessing will ruin so many people's lives, can't you see? That's why it can't just be *your* decision. It has to be *our* decision.' He seemed to realise what he was doing then and let her go, sitting back on his heels, one hand raking through his hair. 'I'm asking you to give me a chance. I want you to give me until the end of the week to sort out the Stacey issue. Then we can talk again, see how you feel.'

The weight of her guilt pressed down on her. Not only for the accident, but the damage she would do by confessing. Still, she knew she'd looked at every scenario and her solution was the only way forward she could see. She couldn't agree with him, but couldn't say no either.

'Look, let's think about this,' he continued. 'How will your confession change things for the better, eh? The person will still be dead, won't they? That can't be undone.'

She thought about his question for a long moment, but still had no words to explain why he was wrong.

'Their loved ones will still get compensation if you don't confess. The only thing that will change is you. You will feel you've done the right thing. But is that enough to pay for the destruction your confession will cause? So many innocent people who will lose their livelihoods, their lives ruined because you can't cope with the guilt. And the person you will hurt the most is your father. Is that what you want? To break his heart.'

Finally, she found her voice.

'Of course that's not what I want, but nothing about your predictions is certain. In fact, you're wrong about one thing. If I confess it *will* change things for the better because Stacey will have nothing to blackmail you about.'

He looked confused for a moment, then shook his head.

'People like Stacey never let go once they've got their claws into you. This is not the solution.' He reached for her hands again, his eyes pleading with her. 'It isn't.'

He gazed at her until she had to look away, unable to stand the intensity any longer.

'Please give me a chance to deal with the Stacey situation. Please.'

'Okay.' She nodded, unable to resist. It was only fair, she decided, to give him a chance, although it wouldn't salve her conscience and her heart told her it wouldn't make a difference to her decision. It was a postponement, not a cancellation, but he didn't need to know that. She was too tired to fight.

He got up and made his breakfast, wolfing it down while she was unable to think about eating anything. She felt separate from her body, different parts of her psyche in open combat with each other, like boxers circling in the ring, looking for a weak spot, a place to land the killer punch. Is this what her life was going to be like now?

Perhaps Ethan was right and confessing *was* a selfish act on her part. It wouldn't help Louise because she already blamed Nicci for Joel deserting her. She'd wait, she decided and see if Ethan could sort out the Stacey blackmail situation.

If he could remove her from the business that would be one less complication to think about. Unfortunately, it was likely to get messy, that was her gut instinct, given Stacey's nature. What on earth could he be planning?

CHAPTER TWENTY-EIGHT

Ethan arrived at work feeling jittery, his hands shaking like he'd drunk half a dozen cups of coffee when he hadn't even managed one yet this morning. Adrenaline was giving him a buzz all on its own now he'd come up with an idea he thought might work.

'You're looking pleased with yourself,' Nicci commented as he pulled into the car park and he rearranged his features into a more suitable expression.

'I was thinking about our wedding and how wonderful it was,' he said, giving her a meaningful look, which he hoped she understood. *We made vows, binding vows.* How could she not see that confessing was not compatible with her promises? He'd make her understand though and he now knew exactly how he was going to do that.

He turned to her. 'I know it's been a stressful time for you. And I do understand about you wanting to do what you see as the right thing.' He leant over and gave her a gentle kiss. 'I love you, sweetheart. Always and forever.' Was that too much? Perhaps he'd over-cooked it a bit because she looked surprised, eyeing him with a suspicious glint in her eye.

It was a moment before she muttered, 'Love you too,' and got out of the car before disappearing inside.

Stacey arrived then, with that smirk on her face which seemed to always appear whenever she saw him. Like she knew a secret, *his* secret, which, of course, she did. He gave her a wide grin, like he hadn't a care in the world and watched her follow Nicci inside the building. With nobody around to see what he was doing, he pulled his phone out of his pocket and started making some calls.

The one person he wanted to speak to still wasn't answering, but there was nothing he could do about that. He'd obviously well and truly pissed them off this time, a situation that had been unavoidable in the greater scheme of things, but if he could talk to them and explain, surely they'd understand. He gave an irritated tut and made some more calls, determined not to let it bother him too much. Focus on what needs doing today, he told himself. Everything else will sort itself out in time.

Pete turned up a little while later, but Ethan had already found out what he needed to know by then and was ready to put his plans aside for the day while he got on with some real work. He stepped out of the car and grinned at his father-in-law. Pete wasn't smiling, though, instead he looked troubled. He walked over to Ethan, his shoulders stooped like he was carrying a heavy load.

'I'm glad I've caught you on your own.' He took Ethan's arm and led him away from the building, glancing over his shoulder. 'I had a strange phone call from Nicci this morning and I'm worried about her.'

Ethan's heart flipped. *Please tell me she didn't confess to her dad.* He swallowed, nervous. 'Really?' he squeaked, then cleared his throat. 'What did she say?'

Pete frowned, his lips pursed while he thought for a moment. 'It wasn't so much what she said, but the fact that she's never made that type of call to me before. You know, all emotional.' He grimaced, his frown deepening, etching grooves onto his forehead. 'In a way, it felt like... a goodbye.'

Ethan suppressed a gasp, realising how close he'd been to Nicci handing herself in. He had to find a way to convince her that his way was the only way, that their vows were the core of what mattered.

He sighed and put a hand on Pete's shoulder, gave it a comforting squeeze. 'To be honest, she's been a bit emotional since the wedding. I think all the organising and then knowing the auditors are coming has put her under too much pressure.'

Pete nodded. 'I did wonder if that was it. And it's a shame you guys weren't able to go off on honeymoon and have a bit of time out to relax, like most couples.'

Ethan nodded. 'I know... with hindsight, I should have sorted out the workload so a break was possible, but it's been mad busy, hasn't it? And I always feel in this business, you never know when the orders are going to dry up. Make hay while the sun shines and all that.' He sighed. 'I thought it would be okay to wait a few months until we hit the quiet period.' He looked at the ground, rocked back on his heels. 'You know... I was wondering how you'd feel... if I booked Nicci a spa day tomorrow? I know it's midweek, but I'm sure Stacey could hold the fort for a day. I was thinking about getting her a massage booked, and a nice lunch and a facial. You know, a lovely relaxing day. See if that helps.'

Pete smiled at him, but it didn't quite reach his eyes, his voice leaden with doubt. 'That's a great idea to cheer her up, but I'm not sure it'll fix the problem. I was worried about her at the weekend when she came fishing with me. Hardly uttered a peep all day, just staring into the distance, not hearing me when I was talking to her. I thought she must have something on her mind.' He looked Ethan in the eye. 'Apart from the auditors, do you know of anything else that might be worrying her?'

Ethan was caught unawares by the directness of the question. He tried to maintain eye contact, keep his voice steady while his heart leapt up his throat. 'Not off the top of my head, no.'

Pete looked at him for a lot longer than was comfortable, and Ethan was wondering if he could see the lie in his eyes.

'I'm going to come right out and say it, lad... I'm disappointed that you put watching football over spending time with your new wife. How do think that makes her feel, eh?'

Ethan cringed, feeling himself shrivel under Pete's stony gaze. 'Yeah, you're right, I made a mistake there. And I have apologised to her. I promise I'll make up for it.'

'Make sure you do,' Pete said, in a tone that demanded compliance. Finally, his eyes moved to look at the workshop. 'I'll see if I can have a quiet word with her later, but in the meantime, I think your idea of a spa day is an excellent one. Hopefully she'll feel a bit more relaxed after that, even if it doesn't get rid of her worries.'

Feeling like he'd been given a dressing down, Ethan steered the conversation towards work and the latest sales enquiry, knowing he was going to have to try and keep Pete away from Nicci at all costs. It would only take a bit of sympathy and some gentle questioning to get the truth out of her. 'I don't suppose you'd like to come and look at this new job with me, would you? It's not the easiest bit of land to build on. Quite a slope and I wanted your opinion on whether it's feasible.'

Ethan knew it was feasible. But the client and Pete didn't know that. 'And I've got another call today you might be interested in coming along to. It's for a granny annex and I know you've been working on designs for our "Elder Spaces" range. We can test out your thinking against what the client wants, see if the specification needs tweaking.'

Pete's face cracked into a happy grin and Ethan knew he'd said the right thing. 'I'd love that. I haven't been out to see customers for ages since you took over that side of things. As long as we're back for lunch. I'll just make sure the lads know what they're doing in the workshop then I'll be right with you.'

Ethan gave a sigh of relief and made a hasty phone call, setting up the visit he'd told Pete about and rearranging a couple of others to accommodate the change in plans. Thankfully the clients were happy to shift their appointments about, but his heart was racing by the time he'd finished and he felt he'd done a day's work before he'd started.

He leant against the car door, taking some calming breaths. Running on adrenaline was not to be recommended, he decided, feeling his stomach griping, the taste of acid at the back of his throat. It'll be worth it in the end, he reminded himself. Don't forget the big picture. No pain, no gain. Nothing good ever came easy.

He had a whole string of positive thinking mottos he'd collected over the years which usually set him right. But today his brain wasn't working and his mind flipped to images of police stations and cold cells and jangling keys. *That's not my future*, he promised himself, shutting down his imagination. As long as he could keep Nicci quiet, he'd be fine.

But first, he needed to attend to the issue with Stacey. That was his top priority.

Telling Nicci about the blackmail had been a difficult decision, but had turned out to be the right one, even if she'd misunderstood what Stacey had seen. In fact, it had been a blessing in disguise, and it served his purposes well to let that confusion stay. In the long run, it wouldn't make a difference, not if this idea of his worked out.

He smiled to himself and made one final call before Pete returned and they were ready to set off. Tomorrow was going to be a better day, he thought as he drove out of the car park. A day when at least one of his problems would cease to exist.

CHAPTER TWENTY-NINE

The next morning, Nicci lay back in her reclining chair, while the beautician applied a face mask, her body glowing after the most wonderful hot stones massage. She'd never had a spa day in her life before, but now she was wondering why on earth she hadn't. This was utter bliss.

The massage had smoothed the knots in her shoulders to nothing, the tightness in her neck had eased, her lower back pain had been rubbed away and even her legs felt wonderful and light. One of the treatments had even soothed her hands and she now felt like they were floating. Once the face mask had done its stuff, she would have a face massage to make her skin glow.

It had been so thoughtful of Ethan to organise this treat for her and her feelings for him shone a little brighter. He was the only one who understood the dilemma she faced and she felt this gift from him was an acknowledgement that what he was asking her to do wasn't easy. His way of trying to help her get through this week at the very least, until he'd had time to sort out the Stacey blackmailing situation.

She'd been trying not to think about the fallout from the

accident, because she knew it would only make her tense and defeat the object of the day. But now she was quiet and still, her brain locked on to the Stacey situation and wouldn't let go. If only there was a massage that would soothe her mind.

When Ethan had told her about the spa day, her first reaction had been to say no. How could she leave Stacey in charge when she was a danger to all of them? But Ethan had talked it through with her and suggested she limit Stacey's remit for the day to answering the phone, running any errands and tackling the backlog of filing that was sitting on Nicci's desk. None of that would involve seeing sensitive financial information.

Eventually, he'd talked her round because a day off being pampered seemed like a lovely idea. Especially when her dad rang up to make sure she was going, telling her she deserved it and insisting she take the day off. There was no doubt she needed time away from her life, because she felt like she was wobbling on the edge of a precipice, her heart constantly racing, her mind unable to concentrate. Hopefully, this would help her to settle down and maybe get a proper night's sleep.

Unfortunately, although her body was relaxed and pliant, her brain still refused to rest. Instead, she was fixating on the issue of blackmail and how to stop someone from asking for more and more money when they knew a secret. A big secret. A criminal secret. When the stakes were too high to risk them sharing what you'd done, you kept on paying until they'd bled you dry. And then what? What was to stop them from calling the police and telling them what they knew?

Nothing. There was nothing to stop them. So that's how the Stacey situation would play out and she'd have Nicci and Ethan squirming like the maggots on her dad's fishing hook. Ethan was being optimistic if he thought he was going to sort it out by the end of the week. So, in reality, it was a stay of execution for her rather than a solution. She was still going to have to go with Plan A and hand herself in. Better enjoy today to the max then, she told herself, finally managing to push Stacey out of her mind.

That lasted for all of five minutes before she was back in her head, sitting there with that stupid grin on her face. It was weird how they'd been so close for all those years, but now she'd shown her true colours, Nicci couldn't imagine how they'd ever been friends.

She supposed their friendship had become a habit.

They were friends at school, so they carried on being friends afterwards, especially when most of their group went off to university. They were the only two who'd stayed at home, which brought them closer. Even when Stacey had gone down to London for a few years, she came home often, dragging Nicci off to Leeds for nights out that she wouldn't have dared to do on her own. Going to see bands. Night clubs. Most of it had been fun at the time, but since Stacey had married Greg, she was happy not to be doing those things any more.

Perhaps this happened to a lot of friendships that started at school. You outgrew each other when you matured, no longer having much in common when you'd made your own decisions about which direction your life was going in. Stacey had certainly turned out to be different from the person she'd thought she was and, as she lay in the treatment room, she tortured herself for a while, wondering how much Ethan had paid her, whether there was anything left in their savings account.

The moment she'd had that thought, her phone rang. She glanced at the screen. 'Talk of the devil,' she muttered to herself, seeing it was Stacey on the line. She refused the call.

A few minutes later her phone rang again. She was expecting it to be Stacey, but it was the local garage. They looked after the company vehicles, so she decided she better speak to them.

'Hello, Nicci. I'm so sorry to bother you on your day off but we're having problems getting hold of anyone. Can you tell your dad his car's ready, please? He dropped it off this morning. Tell him we've put a new starter motor in.'

'Yeah, no problem. I'll do that now.'

She rang her dad, but he wasn't answering. She frowned at her phone. That was odd. Her dad always answered, even if he was in the middle of a conversation with someone, he'd always excuse himself and answer his phone. She rang Ethan instead, thinking he could pass the message on but his phone went straight to voicemail.

Now she was worried, a sick feeling in her stomach. Where was everyone? It was possible Ethan could be out of range if he was up in the Yorkshire Dales doing sales calls. Her dad, though, should be at the workshop. She rang Stacey.

'Oh, thank God,' Stacey gasped, when she answered. 'Thank God you called back.'

Her panicked tone sent a feeling of dread seeping into Nicci's bones and she hardly dared ask, 'What's going on?'

'Something awful has happened,' Stacey said and Nicci's heart began to race.

CHAPTER THIRTY

Stacey's voice was hesitant and hard to hear. Nicci put her phone on speaker, confused as to what might have happened to get her so worked up.

'It's... it's your dad.' Stacey gulped and Nicci realised she was crying. Her panic ramped up a few notches. Stacey was not a crier, so whatever had happened was bad.

'What about Dad?' Nicci's chest was tight, fear squeezing the breath from her lungs.

'I'm so sorry...' She sniffled. 'He's had an accident. A car accident.'

Nicci sat up, her heart racing even faster, knowing she had to go. Right now, she had to go to him. 'Where is he? Is he in Airedale?' That was the local hospital, only a short drive away, but if he'd been out on site he could have been taken to a different location.

'I think so. I think that's what they said.' Stacey sounded flustered, unsure. 'It's hard to take it in.' She sniffed again and Nicci heard her blow her nose, her voice thick with tears. 'I'm so glad I got hold of you. I thought you must have switched off your phone when I couldn't get through straight away.' She paused to blow her nose again. 'The police traced the car back to here, so they rang the office, but they didn't want to tell me much. And I can't get hold of Ethan.'

Nicci was already hurrying towards the changing rooms, clutching the towel to her chest to stop it falling, not caring that her face was still plastered in gunk. 'I'm on my way,' she said before ending the call.

She stumbled into the changing rooms and leant against the wall, her legs threatening to buckle as the enormity of what she'd been told started to register. She'd seen her dad that morning before Ethan dropped her at the spa and he'd given her a hug and a kiss, told her she deserved a treat. 'I love you, sweetie.' Those had been his last words to her and she'd returned the sentiment. She couldn't bear the thought of him being hurt.

Sandy, the beautician, popped her head round the door, a puzzled look on her face. 'I came to finish your facial and you'd disappeared.' She laughed. Then frowned, concern in her eyes as she noticed Nicci's distress. She came into the room, closed the door behind her. 'Is everything... okay?'

'My dad... he's had an accident...' Nicci was gasping, could hardly speak, the threat of a panic attack looming. She remembered her breathing exercises, the way she'd been taught by her therapist to stop things from escalating, and she started the routine with Sandy rubbing her shoulder and trying to tell her she'd be okay. It was funny how the touch of another person could calm her, the knowledge that she wasn't alone allowing her to focus on her breathing patterns until she could finally speak.

'I've... I've got to go.' That was all she managed to say before bursting into tears, sobs wracking her body as she covered her face with her hands.

She felt an arm round her shoulders, guiding her to a seat. 'Here, let me help you.' Sandy's voice was calm, soothing. 'We'll get you tidied up and ready to go in no time.' She scuttled out of the room, coming back moments later with damp cloths to wipe off the face pack. 'Is someone coming to get you?' she asked as she wiped. 'Do you need a taxi? Can I get that organised for you?'

Nicci couldn't think, her brain stuck on the words 'a car accident'. Another one. She pictured her dad, her lovely, kind dad trapped in mangled wreckage, frightened and alone, writhing in pain. Fresh sobs made her shoulders heave and Sandy stopped what she was doing, her eyebrows pinched together in sympathy. 'Oh, hun, I'm so sorry this is happening to you. But it might not be as bad as you think. Come on, let's get you cleaned up and out of here.'

A few minutes later, she'd finished Nicci's face and left her to get changed while she went and rang for a taxi. Nicci found getting dressed a struggle, rushing too much, arms getting tangled in sleeves, clothes inside out, legs stuck in her skinny jeans. It was like she'd regressed to being a toddler, not in control of her limbs.

Finally, she was ready and called Ethan to make sure he knew what was happening, but his phone went straight to voice-mail. *Where is he?* Just when she needed him, he'd gone AWOL. But reception out in the Dales could be patchy, so it probably wasn't his fault. She left him a message, then sat tapping her phone against her chin as she wondered what to do. Stacey hadn't seemed certain of her facts in terms of which hospital her dad had been taken to, so she called the police, and they confirmed he'd been taken to Airedale Hospital. They couldn't tell her anything else, but at least she knew where to go.

Sandy came back a few minutes later, bringing a glass of water, because a massage could make you feel a bit light-headed and water would help flush out the toxins, she explained. Nicci gulped it down, then hurried outside to the waiting taxi.

'You okay, love?' the driver asked, looking at her in the rear-view mirror as he pulled into the main road.

Nicci sniffed, 'No. No, I'm not.' There was no point saying she was fine when that clearly wasn't the case. She swallowed, thought she might burst into tears again, her voice cracking. 'Just get me to Airedale as fast as you can, please. It's my dad, he's...'

Unable to finish the sentence without breaking down, she lay her head back against the headrest, her eyes fixed on the windscreen, willing the car to go faster, for them to be there. *At least it's not far*, she reassured herself. *It won't take long.*

Twenty minutes later, they were pulling up outside the Accident & Emergency Department and she paid her fare and dashed inside. It was impossible not to think about the last time she was here, coming to see the hit-and-run victim. *It's karma*, a little voice whispered inside her head. *What goes around comes around and this is your punishment. An eye for an eye, a tooth for a tooth.* She gave a silent scream, unable to bear her own thoughts.

Please let him be okay.

Her teeth gripped her bottom lip, keeping the tears at bay as she waited at the reception desk to find out where her dad was being treated. She scanned the rows of people waiting to be seen, hoping that Ethan would be sitting there, but he wasn't. Frowning, she called him again, but still it went to voicemail, so she left another message, her eyes watching the door, hoping he'd come rushing through any minute. *He'd want to be here.* She knew that with absolute certainty, because Ethan loved her dad more than his biological father. He'd actually told her that and she knew he'd be on his way as soon as he was able to pick up her messages. But it didn't stop her from feeling terrified, shaken and alone.

Finally, it was her turn and she was told to take a seat and someone would come out and see her. What seemed like an eternity passed before a middle-aged woman in a white coat and short, greying hair, called her name.

'Hello, I'm Doctor Babatunde,' she said, her expression grim. 'I've been looking after your father.'

She showed Nicci into a side room fitted out with four chairs surrounding a low coffee table, a box of tissues sitting in the middle. She closed the door and a weight dropped into Nicci's gut. She was shaking, her face already crumpling because this was the place where they brought relatives to give them bad news. She could sense it without a word being said.

'Have a seat,' the doctor said and Nicci perched on the edge of the chair, while the doctor sat opposite.

'I'm so sorry, but your father succumbed to his injuries a short while ago.' The doctor's voice was deep and mellow, a velvet cushion to deliver the terrible news she'd imparted.

'Dead?' It was a struggle for Nicci to speak, her voice thin and reedy, sounding nothing like herself. 'Are you telling me he's dead? He can't be!'

The doctor's eyes held hers with a compassionate gaze. 'It was a very bad accident, and I promise you we did everything we could for him.' The doctor stood and came and sat beside her, cupped Nicci's hand in both of hers. 'If it's any comfort, I can tell you he wasn't in pain when he passed away. He was unconscious when the emergency services got to him, and I don't think he would have known anything about it. He never regained consciousness while he was in our care and he slipped away very peacefully.'

Nicci bowed her head, jagged breaths ripping through her as the tears came. The doctor pulled a handful of tissues from the box on the coffee table, passed them to her. 'Can I get you anything? A cup of tea maybe to help with the shock?'

'I saw him this morning,' Nicci said, gulping. 'How can he be dead?'

The doctor rubbed her back as Nicci howled in anguish, not

able to keep her emotions in check as the enormity of the news finally struck home. 'It's okay. Let it all out. It's a terrible shock when a loved one dies in an accident. It's so sudden, sometimes it takes a little while for your brain to catch up and come to term with the news.'

A few minutes later, she squeezed Nicci's shoulder and stood. 'I'll get you that cup of tea. And please, take your time, as long as you need.' She turned to look at Nicci as she reached for the door handle. 'Is there someone we can ring to be with you?'

'My husband...' Nicci gulped, struggling to get the words out. 'He should be on his way. I haven't been able to speak to him, but I've left messages.' She glanced at the doctor. 'Can I... Can I see him? My dad?' The urge to be with him was overwhelming, to see with her own eyes that what the doctor was saying was actually true. Then maybe she'd believe it.

Doctor Babatunde winced. 'I'm not sure that's a good idea. You have to understand... There was a fire. His face...' Her voice tailed off and Nicci was grateful to be spared the details, her mind already visualising what had happened.

She whimpered, not wanting the terrible images in her head. 'I want to hold his hand. Say goodbye.' Nicci caught her eye. 'Please, let me say goodbye.'

The doctor shook her head. 'I'm afraid his injuries...' She pressed her lips together. 'No, it's really not possible. Not now. Honestly, if I thought it would be beneficial to you there would be no problem.' She came back to Nicci and sank into the seat beside her, patted her knee. 'Keep your lovely memories from this morning. Don't let them be tainted, because I can tell you, the last image you have of your loved one matters.' She looked certain about her words. 'That image will stay with you forever.'

Nicci's tears finally came to a shuddering halt and she dabbed at her eyes, blew her nose.

'Let me get you that cup of tea,' the doctor said, as she stood again, ready to leave. 'And like I said, take your time. There's no need to rush.'

'I wonder... Can you see if my husband's here yet? He should be on his way.'

Doctor Babatunde nodded. 'I'll ask for you.'

She left the room, closed the door and Nicci was alone with her thoughts until a nurse brought in a cup of tea and a couple of biscuits, making sure she was okay before leaving again. Being alone was too much, though, her mind creating a mental image of her dad's final moments that was too terrible to bear. She needed voices to distract her, to take her away from her thoughts.

She rang Stacey and told her the bad news.

'Oh, Nicci, I'm so sorry. I've been sitting here praying for things to be okay.' She sighed. 'Your dad was such a lovely man. Always so kind and thoughtful.' There was a moment of silence before she spoke again, her voice wavering. 'I can't stop thinking about it because... it should have been me in that car. It should have been *me*.'

Nicci frowned. 'What do you mean, it should have been you?'

'Well, when Ethan came back from dropping you off, he asked me to run an errand, deliver some bits to the lads on site. Something vital they'd forgotten to take with them. Told me to take the pool car. Then he zoomed off to do his sales calls or whatever it is he's been doing today. Anyway, I was about to set off when your dad stopped me. He wanted to use the pool car because his car was playing up this morning and he'd had to take it to the garage. They didn't have a courtesy car available but he'd said it was okay because he knew you weren't here today and the pool car would be free.'

Nicci felt her skin prickle, something slotting into place in her brain while Stacey had been talking.

'So, I said fine,' Stacey continued. 'I'd use mine. It wasn't like I had far to go.' Her voice wavered. 'But he said he'd drop the stuff off for me as he was going that way, no need for me to go out at all.' Nicci heard a sniffle. 'The police said he missed a bend, went straight into a tree. It sounds like something went wrong with the car. A fault like the steering or the brakes or something.' Nicci could hear her blowing her nose again. 'That's why I said... It could have been me.'

Nicci didn't realise Stacey had stopped talking, Ethan's voice in her head, pleading with her, saying he'd had an idea. He knew how to stop the blackmail if she gave him to the end of the week.

Had he done this?

As that thought crept into her head, like an unwanted guest, he walked through the door.

CHAPTER THIRTY-ONE

Ethan rushed over to Nicci, out of breath like he'd been running. 'What's happened? I got your messages about Pete having an accident.' He looked dishevelled, his face red and blotchy. 'Is he okay?'

She gazed at him, unable to reply, the reality too awful to put into words. Through her shock, Nicci's mind zeroed in on the one thing that was really bothering her about this whole situation. The pool car had only recently had its annual service. She knew this because she'd organised it. The car was only a couple of years old. It was in perfect working order and when she'd used it just the other day there'd been no hint of a problem. There was absolutely nothing wrong with it, no reason for anything to fail. If the accident had been caused by a problem with the brakes or steering, then it was because the car had been tampered with. And she had a strong suspicion she was looking at the culprit.

Her heart was pounding, terrified by the place her mind had taken her. If she was correct, Ethan had tried to kill Stacey but had killed her father instead. Ethan, her husband, was a killer. A cold-hearted murderer.

A rush of adrenaline sent her brain spinning, collecting all the bad things that had happened and presenting them to her in high-definition clarity.

It made her think about the hit-and-run in a different light, sweeping his excuses away like the rubbish they were. He *had* pulled the wheel out of her hands; her memory was correct. He'd sent the car veering to the left, crashing into Joel and killing him.

She glared at him, an icy chill suffusing her body as her mind jumped from what had actually happened to what might have happened and what could happen in the future. A swirling loop of thoughts that led to the question: *if he's capable of trying to kill Stacey, am I in danger too?* She shivered, wrapping her arms round her chest, feeling lost, alone and very, very scared.

'Nicci!' He was sitting beside her, his hand on her shoulder, giving her a shake. 'Nicci, come on, speak to me.'

She snapped out of her thoughts, her heart racing, bewildered by the day's events and the consequences that would change her life. *Be careful*, she warned herself, not sure what she was going to do now, wondering how she could best keep herself safe. *How can I continue to live with this man?*

If he thought she would go to the police and confess about the hit-and-run, would she end up having an accident too? She was a danger to him, to the life he wanted, just as much as Stacey had been. She jerked her body away from him, his hand dropping from her shoulder.

'He's dead,' she said, not trying to break the news gently, or make it easy for him, her voice cold and hard. She looked at him, her heart filled with loathing, rage thrumming through her veins.

Ethan grabbed at his hair, rocking backwards and forwards in his seat as he let out an anguished moan. 'No, no, no!' He looked genuinely distraught, but she could feel no empathy for him, none at all. It was as if her heart had turned to stone, untouched by his feelings, his emotional needs. All of a sudden, what Ethan wanted didn't matter anymore.

The door opened and a nurse came in holding a folder.

'I'm so sorry for your loss,' she said, gently, her eyes moving from Nicci to Ethan as she sat opposite them, her face a picture of sympathy. 'I know this is a difficult time and we want to help you as much as we can.' She handed the folder to Nicci. 'This tells you all the things that will happen now your loved one has passed away. Things for you to do, useful phone numbers and so on.'

'I want to see him,' Nicci said, putting the folder on the coffee table, not ready for the next step. 'But the doctor said I couldn't. Because of his injuries.'

Ethan put an arm round her shoulders, pulled her close and it was all she could do to stop herself shaking him off. The last thing she wanted was to cause a scene, though, and she had to work out how she wanted to play things with Ethan in order to keep herself safe. Now was not the time for confrontation. Now was the time to say goodbye to her lovely dad.

'Ah yes, well the situation has changed slightly. The police just rang through to say they need a formal identification, which I can organise for you.'

Nicci felt herself wilting with relief. She didn't think she'd believe he was dead until she saw him, and whatever the doctor said, she needed that confirmation.

'Thank you. I really...' Her chin started to crumple and she struggled to finish her sentence. 'I need to see him.'

'Of course you do,' the nurse said. 'I absolutely understand. I'll go and see if I can sort that now for you. I'm sure the police will be happy you've agreed to do the identification. At least this way you can get on with organising the funeral.'

She left the room, closing the door behind her. Nicci eased herself out of Ethan's arms and stood, pacing the floor, arms clasped round her chest like protective armour. Once she'd seen her father then she could think about other things, but for now that felt like the only thing that mattered.

'I'm so sorry,' Ethan said, his eyes brimming with tears. 'So very sorry. You know how much I loved Pete.' He shook his head and mumbled, 'I can't believe it.'

'Me neither,' she snapped.

Nicci was so angry she pressed her lips tight, not wanting to speak for fear of saying something she might regret. She didn't trust her thoughts right now, aware that grief could colour her thinking. She needed to talk to Stacey again, make sure she had her facts straight before she confronted Ethan. Was there still a chance she'd got this wrong? She wanted there to be.

You're doing it again, she scolded herself. Second-guessing, not trusting what you think. Not wanting to face the truth. He was the one who'd got things wrong. He thought he was getting rid of Stacey and ended up killing her poor, innocent father instead. The man who'd given Ethan a chance in the first place, who he'd trusted to become managing director of his business only a few days ago.

The more she thought about the injustice of it all, the more furious she became.

He gave her a puzzled look. 'I know you're grieving but we shouldn't get angry with each other. Now's the time to pull together. I'm here for you, to help you through this.'

'Hmm,' she said, turning her back on him, studying the paintings on the walls. Copies of Monet's Water Lilies, scenes of peace and calm. The opposite of how she was feeling. However much she wanted to behave like nothing was wrong between them, she was finding it impossible.

She turned to look at him and her jaw tightened. In that moment, she understood things would never be the same again.

. . .

A few minutes later, the nurse came back and told her she could do the formal identification and sit with her dad for a little while, if she was ready.

Ethan stood, to go with her, but she couldn't bear the thought of his crocodile tears anywhere near her father. She swallowed, remembering she had to keep things neutral to protect herself. She put a hand on his arm. 'Would you mind if I go alone? I just need to have a few moments with him.'

Ethan looked unsure, then nodded. 'Okay. If that's what you want. I'll wait here.' He sat back down, his eyes following her as she left.

The nurse led Nicci through the A&E Department and into a side room. A body lay flat on the bed, covered by a white sheet. They had covered his face, as well, but his left hand was laid on his stomach.

She knew straight away it was him. Recognised the distinctive wedding ring with a band of Celtic knots running all the way round it. The scar by the base of his thumb where he'd cut himself badly with the circular saw. The black fingernail, where he'd hit himself with a hammer the previous week. She didn't need to see his face and after the conversation with Doctor Babatunde, she realised she was right. She wanted to remember him how he'd been that morning when she'd seen him. A big smile on his face, wrapping her in a hug, kissing her cheek.

'It's him,' she said to the nurse. 'It's definitely my dad. I recognise the ring and that scar on his hand.'

'Okay, we were hoping that would be the case. I'll pass that on.' She put a hand on her shoulder. 'I'll leave you alone for a little while. You take however long you need.'

Once Nicci was alone, she moved closer to touch his hand, snatching her own hand back when she felt how cold his skin was. He'd gone. Her dad was really gone.

'Bye, Dad,' she whispered, tentatively stroking the back of

his hand with her fingers. 'I love you so much. You know that, don't you?'

It no longer mattered what would happen to her, or the business, or what Stacey might say or do. Nicci knew this whole chain of events had started with something *she* had done. She had to bear some of the responsibility, but not all of it.

It had started with her being talked into driving home by Ethan. Because he had an agenda, a plan. He must have seen the message from Joel. He was the one who'd deleted it because he didn't want her to change her mind about the wedding. He'd deliberately killed Joel and now his actions had killed her father. His death was down to Ethan alone.

She gritted her teeth as the rage gathered in her chest, filling her up until she wanted to scream. 'I promise this will not go unpunished,' she said, her teeth clenched tight. 'He'll pay for this.'

CHAPTER THIRTY-TWO

Ethan sat in the waiting room, his elbows resting on his knees, head in his hands, feeling desolate and hollowed out. Pete, his beloved mentor, friend and father-in-law was dead. It hurt, but what hurt even more was the fact that Stacey was still alive.

Bloody Stacey. He rued the day he'd given in to her blackmail. Honestly, thinking about it now, he should have laughed it off, told her she was wrong, she hadn't seen what she thought she had. He could have said it had been a joke, a celebration, an accident. He could have made up any number of things to explain what she'd seen.

But then... she had pictures, didn't she, so it hadn't been that simple. If she'd shown those to Nicci before the wedding, the whole thing would have been called off. The end of his dreams and Stacey knew it. Thank goodness Nicci had jumped to conclusions and thought Stacey was blackmailing him about the accident. It was inevitable that she would know the truth at some point, or maybe... the way things were going, it might be better if she never knew.

The thought shocked him for a moment, but he understood, in his heart, that his intuition was right. It was something he now had to consider if he was to rescue his plans and achieve the goals he'd worked so hard for.

A knock on the door made him look up and a nurse came in with two cups of tea, which brought his mind back to the matter in hand: Pete's death. It truly was a game changer, altering the whole dynamics of his world. He'd miss the man, really miss him. Tears pricked at his eyes, and he sniffed, grabbed a tissue from the box on the coffee table and blew his nose, telling himself now was not the time to get all sentimental, there would be time for that later. Right now, his priority was to stay strong and calm and get this show back on the road as fast as he possibly could.

He ripped open a couple of sugar sachets and stirred them into his drink, sat back in his seat and took a sip. The hot, sweet tea spread a warmth through his body and he took another sip, trying to relax. He'd been running on adrenaline for the whole day and his neck and shoulders felt tense and sore. He rubbed at them with a hand while he slowly drank.

Now, let's think this through.

As soon as he'd picked up the messages from Stacey and Nicci, he'd rung the police for more information, checking the facts, finding out what they knew, trying to get a feel for the theory they were working on and what hospital Pete was in. Yes, that had been the right thing to do. He wiped a sweaty palm on his jeans, his leg jigging up and down, making his tea slop over the edges of the cup. Had he asked too many questions?

Well, there was nothing he could do about that now. Thinking back over the conversation, the officer he'd spoken to had been extremely helpful, nothing he could detect, as he played back their conversation in his mind, to suggest he was suspicious of foul play in any way.

The police hadn't established the cause of the accident for definite and it was perfectly possible the garage had messed up when the car had been in for a service a couple of weeks ago. In reality, lots of things could have caused Pete to lose control and hit the tree when you thought about it. Something as simple as a cat running across the road, a pheasant flapping in front of him. Maybe they would never know for certain and the police would be happy to leave it at that.

Having reassured himself about the accident, he realised the thing that was bothering him now was Nicci's reaction. The way she'd looked at him was alarming, to say the least, hatred in her eyes. Yes, pure hatred. And it made him think, even though the police were treating it as an accident, she believed this was *his* doing. *Now why would she think that?*

Had Stacey said something? It was the only possibility that made sense. He gritted his teeth. That woman, the source of all his woes. Had she told Nicci she was the one who should have been in the car?

He finished off his tea, put the cup down, thinking that his biggest worry was what Nicci might do next. Would her father's death tip her over the edge? Would this push her to confess their secret to the police?

She didn't seem to understand that the whole point of a vow was that it was binding. A promise that you were bound to keep. To her, it seemed that was not the case. He picked up a biscuit and popped it into his mouth. Unfortunately, she was not the team player he'd thought she would be. He let out a heartfelt sigh, thoroughly exhausted with it all. It wasn't supposed to be like this.

Still, every cloud had a silver lining and this one was actually quite huge. Everything that belonged to Pete would now belong to Nicci. Including Pete's four-bedroom house, newly renovated, sitting above the town with amazing views and beautiful landscaped gardens. It must be worth well over half a million and by legal definition, as Nicci's husband, it would now be half his as well. Same with the business.

Things were moving forward faster than he could have

imagined and alongside the grief, he felt a bud of excitement starting to blossom. He pulled out his phone and sent Dom a message, asking if they could meet, telling him he had news. He waited for a reply but none came and after a few minutes, he stuffed his phone back in his pocket. *Let him stew on that for a bit*, he thought with a smile. He'd come around, especially when Ethan gave him an update.

He was thinking about how great it would be to move out of the pokey little cottage and move into Pete's place when the door opened and Nicci came into the room. Her face was puffy and red, eyes bloodshot, a bunch of tissues clasped to her nose. She closed the door behind her and leant on it, her eyes meeting his with a glare that would turn living creatures into stone.

'You've got some explaining to do,' she said, the tone of her voice making his blood run cold.

CHAPTER THIRTY-THREE

Nicci glowered at him, sitting there looking like nothing had happened. She wished that looks could actually kill because by now her husband would be dead and although it wouldn't bring her father back, she might feel like justice had been done. Nothing would heal this hole in her heart, though, not even revenge and that thought sent a blast of fury blowing through her body.

'You killed him,' she snarled from between clenched teeth as she walked towards him. 'You did, didn't you?'

Ethan's eyes grew wide. 'What? What are you talking about?' he stammered, looking genuinely shocked. 'It was an accident. That's what the police told me.'

He was good, but his act didn't fool her. She sneered at him. 'That's what they *think* happened. That's what it looks like on the face of it. But they don't know the truth, do they?' She walked closer, her finger jabbing the air as she spoke. How she wished it could be a dagger spearing him through the heart, causing him as much pain as he must have caused her father.

'Stacey told me about the pool car and you sending her on an errand to take some spurious thing to the lads.' She gave a derisive huff. 'You've never sent me out on an errand like that, ever, and neither did Dad.' She glared at him, and he blinked a few times, trying to maintain eye contact, but she could see it was a struggle. 'It was a made-up mission so she would drive the pool car, wasn't it? Because you'd tampered with the damned thing in some way.'

'Oh, come on,' Ethan scoffed, standing up and moving away from her before she came within striking distance, putting the chairs and the coffee table between them. He was looking a little worried now, his hands holding on to the back of one of the chairs. 'Where's this coming from? That's just fanciful. This is grief talking, love. You're lashing out at me because you're hurting so much, and I understand. I really do. Anyway, why would I do that when there was a chance other people would use the car?'

His attempt to talk her down infuriated her even more, her hands clenched into fists by her side. 'Because you thought nobody else would be using the car today. You wanted it to be Stacey who was hurt in an accident to stop her blackmailing you. But you didn't know Dad's car was in the garage, did you? He had problems getting it started this morning. He needed to use the pool car and told Stacey he'd run the errand for her.'

Was it her imagination or had Ethan gone pale? He'd also gone very quiet.

Her anger flared brighter, burning in her chest. The more she went through the story, the more it made sense. Watching the expression change on Ethan's face, noticing the lost look in his eyes, like he had no idea what to say next, made her sure she was right. 'Why would you take a risk like that? Look what you've done!'

Nicci thought, if she was a bull, she'd be pawing the ground and steam would be flaring from her nostrils. She wanted to charge, to hurt him, to throw him to the ground and stomp all over him.

He shook his head, frowning. 'I am not a killer.' His voice had an icy tone she'd never heard before, his eyes narrowed. 'You are the one who's killed someone, or has that slipped your memory?'

She gasped, as if he'd caught one of the verbal daggers she'd thrown at him and fired it straight back at her. It struck its target, a pain stabbing at her heart as she acknowledged the truth. But then a voice in her head reminded her what had happened that night. She could see his hand on the steering wheel, could feel him pulling the car to the left.

It was him.

She'd made a stupid decision to drive, but she wasn't a killer at all. He was and he was trying to distract her from the truth. But she was poking a bear with a stick and needed to think more carefully about where she was going with her barrage of accusations. Yes, she was hurt and angry, but she had to think about self-preservation. If she was right, and she was ninety per cent sure she was, Ethan was dangerous.

'How dare you accuse me of something like that,' he carried on, hurt raising his voice. 'Your dad's crash was an accident. Perhaps he had a medical incident. A heart attack or a stroke or an aneurysm.' He sounded convincing, his hands flying through the air to emphasise his point. 'We don't know yet what actually killed him and won't until after the post-mortem.'

She had to accept this was true. Could it have been an accident? Had she taken Stacey's theory and run with it when it was not proven? Her resolve started to waver.

He moved towards her, his voice softening. 'Your dad might have swerved to avoid something in the road. We don't know, do we?' His eyes were pleading with her to at least accept there might be alternative explanations. 'You're making assumptions and that's a dangerous thing to do.' Was that a hint of a threat in his voice?

His face relaxed. 'I don't want us to argue, sweetheart. I

want to support you.' His body seemed to sag, all the fight going out of him. 'I know this has been a terrible shock for you but you've got to remember he was like a father to me as well.' He tapped his chest. 'I'm feeling this too. I loved your dad, I'd never do anything to harm him, and you know that's the truth.'

His words settled around him like a protective shield, making her stop and think.

He was right that they didn't actually know what had caused the accident and wouldn't until the police had finished investigating. Neither did they know the cause of death yet. Was she jumping to conclusions? Was this Stacey stirring things up again? Because, when she actually stopped to think about it, she only had her version of events. Only had *her* slant on what had happened, and Nicci realised Stacey's conclusions had coloured her own thinking.

Ethan moved closer, and she offered no resistance when he pulled her into an embrace. She needed comfort, she needed to be held and there was nobody else she could turn to. For now, at least, she decided to pretend it was all okay, if only to give herself some respite, a calm before the inevitable storm.

With nothing left to do at the hospital, they drove home in silence. There was little to say until Ethan asked if he should get a takeaway for tea and she shrugged, not caring about food, even though hunger gnawed at her belly. He left her at the cottage, while he went into town to pick up a meal.

She dropped her bag on the floor and flopped onto the sofa, sitting in a daze, her eyes staring out of the window. Instinctively, Mack seemed to sense something was wrong and he came to sit next to her, offering little licks of comfort. She jumped when her phone rang and she pulled it out of her bag, wondering if Ethan had forgotten her order. But it was Stacey. She hesitated, then decided to answer.

'I'm so glad I got you,' Stacey said. Then whispered, 'Is Ethan with you?'

'No, he's gone to get food.' Nicci's voice was dull, monotone, which was exactly how she felt, like a limp rag that had been washed too many times.

'That's perfect.' She heard the rattle of Stacey's sigh in her ear. 'The thing is... I can't stop thinking about what happened today. And what might have happened if I'd been the one driving.' Her voice was gaspy and Nicci could tell she was scared. 'I'm freaking out here. Not just for me, but for you too.'

Nicci adjusted her position on the sofa, got more comfortable, trying to work out how much she actually trusted her friend.

'I'll be honest,' Stacey continued. 'I'm worried about you being alone with Ethan. Do you want to come and stay with us for a while? Greg's finished decorating one of the guest rooms and I'm sure you'd be comfortable there. Let yourself be looked after.'

Nicci realised she had no energy left for tact. She was exhausted and empty and the last thing she was going to do was her usual trick of pandering to Stacey's whims. She felt something had shifted in her psyche now her dad was dead and she could never be the same person again.

'That's okay, I'm fine,' she said, more abrupt than she should have been, but she was in no mood for Stacey telling her what was best for her any more.

She knows your secret, she reminded herself with a jolt. But then she realised she no longer cared. Her dad dying had given her a different perspective. She wanted him to be proud, not ashamed, of his daughter. Thankfully, he'd died unaware, but to honour his memory, she was more determined than ever to tell the truth.

'I don't think you've understood what I've told you.' Stacey's voice was shrill, indignant. 'It's probably the shock. But Ethan tried to kill me today. Are you hearing what I'm saying? He. Tried. To. Kill. Me.' She said the last sentence slowly, emphasising each word. 'That actually happened.'

Nicci hesitated, then decided to go for it. This was her chance. 'Stacey, I'm puzzled,' she said, with feigned innocence. 'I don't understand why you think Ethan would want to kill you. It's a pretty big accusation, don't you think?' She wondered if Stacey would tell her that she'd been blackmailing him, was curious to find out. 'As far as I'm aware, the police believe it was an accident.' She paused to let that sink in. 'Have you told the police what you think happened?' Rhetorical question. Of course she hadn't because then she'd have to explain what motive Ethan might have to kill her. She wasn't going to confess to blackmail, Nicci was sure of it.

There was a deafening silence before Stacey spoke. 'Look, there's something I need to tell you.' She gave another big sigh. 'I should have told you this a while ago. I was going to, but... Remember I tried to warn you off Ethan but you wouldn't listen?'

You didn't try very hard, Nicci thought, but stayed quiet, waiting for Stacey to carry on.

'I saw something.'

Nicci knew what was coming next and anger flared in her chest. What friend would think blackmail was the answer to anything?

'I know you did,' Nicci snapped. 'And I also know you've been blackmailing Ethan about it.'

'He told you?' whispered Stacey, clearly shocked.

'He did.' For once, Nicci felt she had the upper hand.

'He told you about... the kiss?'

CHAPTER THIRTY-FOUR

Nicci frowned, confused by Stacey's comment. 'What kiss?' She'd thought they'd been talking about the accident.

'Ethan and Dom. I saw them kissing.' Nicci's brain froze, hardly able to take it in. 'And I mean proper full on, tongues down throats sort of kissing. They were by the canal, sitting on a bench and I almost walked past without noticing, but then Dom was wearing that Hawaiian print shirt of his, and I did a double take. I didn't know he was gay, so I was trying to work out who his boyfriend was, and I couldn't believe it when I saw it was Ethan.'

'No.' Nicci's head felt like it had been shrink-wrapped, a tightness squeezing her skull. It was preposterous. Ethan was an alpha male, one of the lads. Stacey must have been mistaken.

'Yes.' Stacey was emphatic. 'I'm one hundred per cent certain it was Ethan and Dom. Honestly, I know it's hard to take in, but that's what I saw.'

Nicci wondered if this was another attempt at manipulation, although she was struggling to work out what the goal might be. A moment later her phone pinged. A message.

'Have a look at the video I just sent.'

She swallowed, but clicked on the message, her mouth dropping open as she watched the short clip. Once. Then twice. By the third time, she had to admit there was no mistaking what was happening. 'Bloody hell,' she whispered, her world turned on its head, a starburst of emotions firing through her body. Anger, dismay, the raw hurt of betrayal. Everything she thought she knew about her husband was wrong. Completely and utterly wrong.

'Exactly what I thought too.'

Nicci heard a car door slam and glanced out of the window to see Ethan walking up the path. 'He's back. I've got to go. But... thanks for telling me.'

'I want you to know I did it for you. The blackmail.' Stacey was gabbling, trying to get her words out before Nicci ended the call. 'I wanted to make him leave you. I wanted to break him for what he was doing. Honestly, I promise that's the truth.'

'But... why didn't you tell me? Then I would have left him.'

Nicci hung up, leaving no time to hear Stacey's answer, her brain scrambled by what she'd just learnt.

The door opened and her husband walked in.

CHAPTER THIRTY-FIVE

Ethan seemed to be watching her the whole time they were eating, not saying much, but every time she glanced at him, his eyes were on her. Observing. Taking note. The air crackled with tension and things unsaid. Her skin crawled when she thought about her conversation with Stacey. Had Ethan been putting on an act the whole time, this romance with her fake? It astounded her that anyone could be that devious and manipulative. Being completely dishonest, while fooling her into falling in love with him? What sort of person was able to do that?

A dangerous one. A psychopath. A killer.

Fear shut down the normal functions of her body, sending adrenaline shooting through her veins, making her heart pound and her muscles tense. She found she couldn't speak, not even to answer perfunctory questions about the practicalities of going to work and how they would manage without her dad. She just nodded at his suggestion that they should close for a week as a mark of respect, feeling restless and anxious, trapped in this small room with a man who constantly lied. A husband she no longer recognised. A devious, manipulative man who clearly had an agenda. Although she couldn't quite put her finger on what that might be.

Eventually, she threw down the fork she'd been using to swirl chow mein around her plate, deciding she couldn't possibly eat anything. The urge to leave was overwhelming, her eyes constantly drawn to the front door, wanting to be on the other side of it. But she didn't want to alert him to her nervousness, to the fact her view of him had changed.

She stood, Ethan's eyes still tracking her every move.

'Not hungry, love?'

'I'm... too upset,' she stammered, unsure what she wanted to do or where she wanted to go. There was always Stacey's house as a refuge, she reminded herself, the offer had been made. But as soon as the thought popped into her head, she knew it wasn't an option. If Stacey thought blackmailing Ethan was the sort of thing a friend would do, instead of just telling her what was going on, then she clearly had a warped moral compass. No, Stacey had seen an opportunity to make some easy money, that was the truth of it.

In the end, she grabbed the dog lead and called Mack. 'I need a bit of fresh air. A bit of alone time.' She headed out of the door before Ethan could stop her, hurrying down the road in case he tried to catch up. She kept glancing over her shoulder, half walking, half running as Mack panted along beside her, trying to keep pace. Her breath rasped in her throat, her heart pounding, the feeling she was in danger magnified now she had a different context for everything that had happened.

What was Ethan's goal though? That was the question she couldn't yet answer, because if she knew that, she'd know whether he was a threat to her or not.

Without thinking where she was going, she found herself on the corner of the lane, the place where she used to meet with Joel. The place where she'd killed him. She stopped, unable to go any further, as if there was an invisible barrier keeping her in place. It was the first time she'd been back this way since the accident. The first time she'd had a chance to come to terms with what had happened.

If only she'd seen Joel's message before it had been deleted. If only she'd listened to her gut instinct and run down the aisle and out of the church before she'd said her vows.

Gingerly, she stepped forward, leant her back against the dry-stone wall and studied the road, finding no trace of the terrible thing she'd done. This was the place where Joel would have been waiting for her, and she wondered if she could channel the essence of him, feel his presence. Oh, how she missed him. A sob caught in her throat and she closed her eyes, weary beyond words. This was where it had all started, where the mayhem had begun. Just two weeks ago, but it felt like a lifetime.

And in that time, she'd married a man who was apparently in love with another man. A man who'd tried to kill her friend and had succeeded in killing her father. He was also responsible for Joel's death. She was certain of that now, her memory crystal clear. Ethan had deliberately run into him and now she knew about Joel's last message to her she also knew why. He'd seen him as a threat to the wedding. A threat to the future that Ethan was working towards with his scheming and lies.

'Joel,' she whispered, as tears tracked down her cheeks. 'Why didn't I follow my heart instead of my head?'

Mack looked up at her and whined, pulling on the lead as he tried to get her to move, to carry on with their walk.

She pushed herself off the wall and followed her dog on their regular route, round the fields and along the river, doing a circuit back to where they started. Her mind wandered, and she wasn't taking much notice of her surroundings. It had started to drizzle, a fine mist of water droplets hanging in the air, tickling her skin, blurring her surroundings. She didn't care that she was getting wet, didn't care about anything much at all.

How could she have let Ethan fool her so completely? And Dom, come to that. He'd become her friend too. But she realised it was likely their first meeting wasn't a chance encounter at all. He'd probably engineered it so he could legitimately worm his way into their lives. And their regular lunch dates weren't about spending time with her, or helping her with her Spanish, they were a cover for coming to see Ethan. Now she thought about it, he always went to have a chat with him when he walked Nicci back to the office. Sometimes, Ethan would give him a lift somewhere. Or at least that's what he'd said he was doing. And how often did he go over to Dom's to watch football, or go on off-roading excursions with him? Excuses, that's all they were, a pretence to spend time with his lover.

She felt stupid, really, really stupid, wondering again what Ethan stood to gain from this charade.

Then it hit her. A moment of clarity that made it all so obvious.

The business.

He didn't want to marry *Nicci.* He wanted to marry into the family business. It was, after all, Ethan's passion. It was all he thought about most of the time, the subject of most of their conversations, the thing that bound Ethan and her dad together.

She stopped walking as her thoughts hurried along a clear line of logic. Now her dad was dead, the business would be hers. But Ethan was a director. The managing director. Her dad had lived long enough to get that all signed and now Nicci and Ethan were joint owners.

If Nicci should die, he would have everything to himself. Her dad's house, the business, the money. He could move Dom in when the dust had settled. That's what he'd been doing, creating a future for him and his lover.

It was all so clear, like she'd opened up a map and suddenly knew exactly where she was. Why hadn't she seen it before? And if Stacey was right about him trying to kill her, as far-fetched as it sounded, she had to think she might be in danger herself. Hadn't she told him she intended to go to the police and confess? That act alone could ruin the business he loved and make him a criminal too for not reporting the accident. He would see her as a threat.

Am I next?

She shivered, glanced over her shoulder, a creeping sensation at the back of her neck, sure there was someone behind her, that she was being followed. The walk they were doing was a quiet route and there was nobody else around. Nobody to hear if someone came up behind her and pushed her into the river, or hit her over the head. Nobody to stop her from being killed.

Unease swirled in her stomach and she hurried on, picking up her pace so she was jogging and speed-walking along the path, slipping and sliding on the uneven surface, trying to get back to a place where there might be other people, where she might be safe.

Dusk was falling, the drizzle forming a dense mist now, muffling sound, making it impossible to see far in front of her face. At last, she reached the road, and she bent over, heaving in gulps of air before she was able to carry on.

'Nicci! Nicci, stop.' She turned, saw a tall figure lurching towards her out of the mist and realised Ethan must have followed her. Now why would he do that? Her mind was full of death and accidents, lies and betrayal, and she could think of no valid reason at all.

She set off at a sprint. But Mack cut across in front of her, trying to run back the way they'd come, obviously recognising that Ethan was behind them. She felt the lead wrap round her legs and before she could do anything, her feet went from under her, and she landed with a thud on the hard ground.

Silence, thick and ominous, filled her ears, the feeling of shock that happens the first few seconds after a fall. Then she could hear her breathing, heavy and laboured.

Her heart raced, but she couldn't move, couldn't escape. She was winded, her cheek throbbing where she'd landed on the hard surface, her arm twisted underneath her. The pain was intense and, when she tried to move, a thousand knives seemed to be stabbing into her wrist making her cry out.

I've got to move, got to get away from him.

But she couldn't, the pain was too much, making her think she might pass out. She could hear his footsteps getting closer, and desperation brought her the strength to struggle on to her knees. Her heart thundered in her chest as she tried to get to her feet, but she was too slow. A hand clasped her shoulder, and she screamed, certain in her heart this was where her life ended. Her death staged as another tragic accident.

CHAPTER THIRTY-SIX

Her eyes were closed, and she was sobbing, waiting for oblivion, for the end of her misery. The hand released its grip from her shoulder, then stroked the tears from her cheek.

'Hey, Nicci, it's okay. It's me,' the man said, crouching beside her, his breath fluttering against her face. 'Joel.'

She howled into the tarmac, sure it was Ethan playing tricks on her, a final cruelty. Mocking her. Joel couldn't be alive. But when she felt a hand rubbing her back, heard him trying to soothe her, she realised it wasn't Ethan's voice. It definitely *was* Joel.

Her heart skipped, and she desperately wanted to believe it, but she was wary. *Is this happening in my head?* Was she hallucinating again, wanting what could never be? She forced her eyes to open, blinking, her vision still blurry with tears. She gasped when she saw Joel's familiar face, his brow creased with concern, those lovely brown eyes fixed on hers and for a moment, she found herself drowning in his gaze.

She reached out and touched his face, could feel the warmth of his skin, the rasp of stubble beneath her fingers, and the relief that he was real drained all the energy from her body.

Laughing and crying at the same time, she clung to him, the pain masked by euphoria. Her mind repeating, *he's alive,* over and over again.

He helped her to her feet, holding her steady while she found her balance. She held on to the wall, wincing as gravity pulled at her damaged wrist.

'I thought... I thought you were dead.' She gazed at him, still finding it hard to believe this wasn't the case.

'What?' He frowned, clearly puzzled. 'Why would I be... dead? I only went away for a couple of weeks.' To her, it felt like a lifetime since the accident.

They were both very confused now, Nicci wondering, if it wasn't Joel they'd hit that night, who else it might be. They perched on the wall next to each other, Mack sitting beside her, while she told Joel everything that had happened. The hit-and-run two weeks ago, her dad dying in a car crash earlier that day. Her suspicions about Ethan.

When she'd finished, he gave a low whistle. 'Wow, that's a lot to take in.'

'I know. I can't believe Ethan pulled the steering wheel out of my hands, deliberately trying to hit you.' She sighed. 'Louise told me you'd sent me a message, but I didn't see it. I think Ethan must have deleted it before I had a chance to read it. That's my theory. Anyway, the point, is... he saw you as a threat. He didn't want anything stopping the wedding, so in a fit of madness, because that's what it must have been, he decided to take you out of the picture.'

'But he killed somebody else.'

She sighed, appalled that her husband had taken an innocent life. 'That's right. The police haven't been able to identify the body yet. I rang in an anonymous tip-off that I thought it was you, but there's been nothing on the news since.'

Joel shook his head, incredulous. 'I wouldn't have thought

him capable of something like that. I mean, he's always been friendly towards me. No sign of any problems at all.'

Nicci huffed, cradling her damaged wrist against her chest. 'Yeah, well I've found out that my husband is not the person he makes out to be. Stacey is convinced the car crash that killed Dad wasn't an accident and she was the intended target.'

Her dad's death was so fresh and raw, the mere mention of his name was enough to trigger her and she had to take a few moments to wrestle her emotions under control before carrying on. 'I thought you were Ethan chasing after me. I have this terrible feeling I'm going to be next. Because if he gets rid of me, he'll have the business to himself and Dad's house. Everything. That's his goal, I'm sure of it. I know he's always been keen to show his father he was wrong to throw him out. That's why he's so driven, determined to be a big success. Dom was telling me how abusive his dad was to him when he was a teenager and I think the need to prove himself has consumed him.'

Joel was quiet and she wondered what he was thinking, whether he was about to run as far away from her as possible now he understood that being anywhere near her was a death wish. She kept stealing glances at him, still finding it hard to believe that he was real. When he finally spoke, he turned to her with a puzzled frown.

'I'm still not sure why you thought it was me who was killed in the accident, though.'

'Because you asked me to meet you here at ten that night. I know I didn't reply, but I assumed you'd just come anyway.'

He shook his head. 'I wouldn't turn up without you saying it was okay.'

Nicci whimpered, unable to process what he was telling her because the ache in her wrist was getting worse by the minute and when she tried to make it more comfortable, every movement sent needles of pain up her arm.

'Hey, are you okay? Can I do anything to help?'

'I fell on my wrist. I think...' She gritted her teeth. 'I think it's broken.'

He looked sheepish. 'I feel so bad for frightening you. I shouldn't have followed you like that, but I had to see you.'

'Don't be daft, it's not your fault. I'm so on edge after everything that's happened today, anything would have made me jumpy.'

'I'd been waiting around the corner from your house, hoping I might catch you when you took Mack out, so we'd have a chance to talk.' He sighed. 'But talking can wait, I need to get you home.'

Nicci sucked in a horrified breath. 'No! No, I can't go home. Ethan's there. It's not safe.' She wondered if he'd even been listening. If he believed her.

He slapped his forehead with the heel of his hand. 'Sorry, I wasn't thinking. I feel a bit punch-drunk with everything you've told me. It's not sunk in.' He pointed in the opposite direction. 'I can take you to the hospital. My car's parked in the lay-by round the corner.'

Relief washed over her as she thanked him and she grabbed his arm for support, stumbled to his car, feeling light-headed with the pain.

He opened the door for her and helped her with the seat belt before climbing into the driver's seat and starting the car. She was aware of his proximity, wanting to reach out and touch him, reassure herself that she wasn't dreaming. She kept stealing glances at him, her heart pounding, her body telling her there was no doubt she had feelings for this man. Deep feelings.

'Have you been to see Louise?' she asked, her mind immediately presenting her with the barrier to a relationship with Joel. 'She's been so worried about you. We all have.'

He stopped at the junction to the main road and waited until he'd pulled out into the traffic before he answered. 'Yes, I've seen her. We've had a long talk and she understands that if

I stay with her, it will be for all the wrong reasons.' His voice was calm and measured and tinged with sadness. 'I've told her I want to be part of our baby's life and I'll help her financially, but I don't love her the way I should.' He glanced at Nicci and she could see the sorrow in his eyes, could tell this had not been an easy thing for him to do.

Her heart started beating faster, possibilities unfolding in her mind, and she wondered about the message Louise had said she'd seen. The one that Joel had sent to Nicci telling her that he loved her. Was she making that up, or had Louise really said it? She bit her lip, unsure how she could possibly ask him. At the last minute, she lost her nerve and stuck with the conversation about Louise instead. 'She was very angry with me when you disappeared. She thought I knew where you were, even though I didn't.'

'I've told her you don't feel the same way I do.' His voice was flat, defeated and he was looking straight ahead as he said it, like he couldn't bring himself to look at her. 'I made it clear it was me making the moves, so she understands that now. It's okay.' He pressed his lips together. 'I must have misread the situation and I'm sorry if I've caused bad feeling between you two.' He glanced at her. 'I know you've been friends for a long time.'

'I told you, I never got your last message. But Louise had read it. She told me that you said...' She swallowed, hardly able to say the words in case she was wrong. 'You said you loved me,' she whispered. 'And I've realised, since you've been away, that I love you too.'

He pulled into a lay-by and stopped the car, so he could look at her properly, his eyes shining, searching her face.

They gazed at each other for a long moment before their heads slowly bent together for a first, lingering kiss. A kiss that felt different to any she'd ever known because she'd yearned for this to happen, but thought it never would when she believed Joel to be dead.

Finally, they pulled away from each other, Joel grinning, like he'd been given the best present ever.

'I can't believe it,' he said, shaking his head. 'I just...' He laughed, lost for words.

Nicci winced, the throbbing in her wrist intensifying.

'Do you think we could talk as we drive?' she asked. 'I need to get some pain relief.'

'Sorry, sorry.' He laughed again, all giddy now as he started the engine, heading to the hospital.

'Why didn't you answer my messages?' she asked, a little while later, thinking she'd wasted a lot of energy grieving for a man who was still alive.

'Stupidly, I went to the pub to drown my sorrows and my phone was stolen. Then I decided it was fate giving me some time out on my own to think about things.' He frowned. 'Is that why you were convinced I was dead? Because I didn't answer?'

She grimaced, thinking it wasn't his fault. 'It didn't help.'

They were silent then until they arrived at the hospital and she was relieved to find it was relatively quiet and the wait for orthopaedics wasn't too long. It was only when the painkillers they gave her started to work and she was having her wrist set in place that she wondered if Joel had fully understood what she'd told him about the accident. Had he registered the fact that she'd killed someone while drink driving?

She thought back to her garbled version of events, her relief that he wasn't dead making it hard to focus on what she was trying to say. Making her rush the story. Did she leave bits out? It was a lot to take in for anyone and a sudden heat rushed through her body as her brain posed a question she didn't want to answer.

When it did sink in, when he understood what had happened that night, would he still love her?

CHAPTER THIRTY-SEVEN

Nicci watched the doctor gently wrap her arm in layers of cotton and then a fibreglass material, her mind pondering her situation.

She loved Joel. Of that she was sure now she'd seen him again and shared a first magical kiss. She was also sure she was frightened of Ethan, and quite certain, having spoken to Stacey, that Ethan had something to do with her dad's death. He may have been trying to stop Stacey's blackmail, but he'd hit the jackpot when he killed her father by mistake, as he stood to get exactly what he wanted – the business and the house he'd admired so much.

Thinking about it now, over all the time she'd known him, there had been lots of conversations about her dad rattling around in that big house on his own. He'd even suggested building her dad an annex in the garden so they could move into the house when they started a family and he could move out to his own little space. His argument had been persuasive, repeated several times, usually when she'd come back from a mercy mission to her dad's, sorting him out after an emotional wobble. His reasoning was that her dad would always have the company he craved, he'd be much happier with them on the doorstep, and they would have the space they needed. She'd always slapped down the suggestion, telling him it was her dad's decision, not theirs, and he was to suggest no such thing to him.

Then there were the conversations about taking on more responsibility, lightening the load for her dad, letting him have an easier time of it. All of it couched in terms of helping when, in reality, his intention was all about taking control.

If Nicci happened to die, Ethan would have it all. Mission achieved.

Fear trickled down her spine, cold and dank, making her shiver. As far as she could see, the only way to stop this situation from progressing to a terrible conclusion was to tell the police.

She sighed, annoyed with herself for going round the same old circle so many times. If she'd only confessed earlier, her dad would still be alive. But something had been stopping her from actually doing it, like an invisible arm holding her back every time she tried to move forward. Fear, she supposed. Fear of what it would mean for her, losing her friends, her job, the life she knew, how she would cope in prison. How she would ever face people again. The shame would be crippling, but living a lie would be worse, and if Ethan thought she was a danger to his plans, then she might not have a life at all.

At least she knew she hadn't killed Joel now. But as soon as that happy thought flitted into her mind, she was reminded that *someone* had been standing on that corner. Someone had died and Ethan had been desperate for them to cover it up.

It was time for honesty, whatever Joel might think of her. She would have to suck it up and live with the consequences. No more lies. Maybe if she went through it all again with Joel, made sure he understood exactly what had happened, that might give her the push she needed to do what was right. If he agreed to go to the police station with her, would that give her the confidence to finally confess?

She couldn't talk about it now, though. Not in the waiting room where other people might hear. Later, she promised herself, definitely later.

'How are you feeling?' he asked when she emerged from the treatment room, her wrist and arm in plaster, secured with a sling to help alleviate the pain.

'Sore and tired,' she murmured, suddenly overwhelmed by everything. Her cheek was burning where she'd hit the tarmac, a big graze stinging like crazy and her wrist was throbbing, despite the painkillers she'd been given.

'I'm not sure where to take you now,' he said as they walked down corridors to the car park. 'I haven't sorted out a place to stay yet. Obviously, I can't stay with Louise, so I was going to sleep in the car tonight.' He glanced at her. 'Can I take you to a hotel or something if you're sure you don't want to go home?'

Nicci thought about Stacey's invitation again, but knew she couldn't face the inevitable interrogation, not to mention the questions that were still unanswered about her rationale for blackmail. Some friend she'd turned out to be. She yearned for peace and quiet but wasn't sure where she might find it.

Too much had happened too quickly and her emotions were swirling around like a grade four hurricane. What she needed was a shelter from the storm, somewhere she could process her grief and confusion and anger. She knew exactly where to go.

'You don't need to sleep in your car. We can go to my dad's.' Her breath hitched in her throat at the mention of his name. 'I need to... come to terms with his death, start saying goodbye.' She couldn't look at him, not without bursting into tears. Instead, she stared straight ahead, her jaw locked tight.

'Okay,' Joel said carefully. 'If that's what you want.'

She nodded, her teeth digging into her bottom lip to keep her emotions in check. It was exactly what she wanted. She'd feel close to her dad in his house, her old home, surrounded by familiar things, stuff she'd grown up with. It was what she needed to keep herself grounded. And now she'd got Joel back, she was reluctant to lose sight of him again.

They drove in silence for the rest of the journey, apart from Nicci giving directions. Her family home had been an old farmhouse, ramshackle and run-down when her parents bought it when they first got married. It stood on the edge of Skipton at the top of a narrow lane that was dotted with detached properties, some of them now smallholdings, some of them old farmworkers' cottages.

The views were stunning, stretching out over the valley at the front and up to a gritstone edge that marked the start of the moors above. Over the years, they had completely renovated the place and although it still looked like a traditional stone farmhouse from the outside, the inside was modern and comfortable, fitted out with her mum's interior design flair and her father's carpentry skills. Her parents were in every inch of this house, as they had done the renovation work themselves, and she thought she'd feel safe here, cocooned by their love.

Joel parked up on the gravel forecourt and she unlocked the door, taking him down the hallway to the large open-plan kitchen that spanned the back of the house. The room was set out with the kitchen at one end, the dining table in the middle and a sofa at the other end, next to a woodburning stove, with views through patio doors up to the moors.

Mack went straight over to the sofa and curled up in his favourite spot, while Joel filled the kettle and put it on. She pulled mugs from a cupboard, and grabbed the milk from the fridge, finding comfort in an old routine.

'I'll go and get my bag from the car,' Joel said, once he was sure she was okay, leaving her to make the tea.

Just when she was wondering what was taking him so long, she heard the front door open and shut. 'Tea's ready,' she called.

'How cosy,' said Ethan, as he walked into the room, a long, bent piece of metal hanging from his hand. It took her a moment to recognise it as a wheel wrench, for tightening up the bolts on a car wheel. Something red was dripping off it onto the limestone tiles of the floor, leaving a trail behind him.

CHAPTER THIRTY-EIGHT

Ethan was so angry and pumped up with adrenaline, he felt like his veins might burst out of his body. He'd seen the wrestlers on WWE thumping their chests with a fist before they went into a fight. He'd seen them yelling, their head stuck forward, mouth wide open, the tendons standing out like wires in their neck. Footballers did it too, rugby players, people heavily invested in winning a game. He felt like he was winning, and he couldn't resist letting out a primal scream. Oh my God, that felt great. He laughed as he moved towards Nicci, who had backed into the corner by the fridge-freezer, shrinking against the wall.

He felt bigger than usual, could feel the power surging through him and he yelled again, letting his rage loose like it was a caged animal hurtling to freedom. At which point, Mack started barking and snarling round his ankles. Damn, he'd forgotten the wretched animal. He picked him up by the scruff of the neck and threw him into the pantry, slamming the door shut before he could escape.

Thankfully Nicci hadn't moved, still cowering against the wall, eyes wide and fearful, her face pale, except where she had a big red scrape on her cheek. It glistened in the kitchen lights, and he knew it would be sore. She also had her arm in plaster, hung in a sling. For a second, he wondered what had happened, but then realised it didn't matter and he didn't care.

He walked over and slapped her face, right on the graze, making her gasp and whimper, tears springing to her eyes. Then he stood back and swiped at her broken wrist with the wheel wrench. Her scream was a piercing, gut-wrenching sound, the sort of sound that would turn heads and bring people running to help. But there was nobody to hear, no neighbours within shouting distance. They could make all the sound they wanted.

He smiled to himself. She deserved what was coming to her. It was all her own fault. All of it.

She was pitiful, bent over and gasping as she cradled her injured wrist in her hand. She looked up at him, then glanced away, eyes darting all over the room, no doubt searching for a weapon. He moved towards her again, the wheel wrench raised in his hand, ready to strike and she screamed before he'd even hit her.

Right, he thought, satisfied he had her full attention for once.

'Tell me, my love,' he said sweetly. 'What was it you didn't fully understand about our wedding vows, hmm? What about the forsaking all others bit?' He cocked his head to one side. 'Are you having trouble with that concept?'

'I don't... I don't know what you mean,' she stammered, tears coursing down her cheeks.

'Oh, I think you do. I think you know exactly what I mean. I saw you and Joel getting cosy in his car.'

Her eyes grew wider. 'You *were* following me.'

'I was.' He shook his head slowly. 'You see, unfortunately, I no longer feel that I can trust you. Not when you decide to believe your corrupt pseudo-friend Stacey over me. Not when you throw baseless accusations at me. Accusations that the police would want to follow up.' He pointed the wheel wrench at her, and she winced as if he'd hit her again. 'We promised not to say or do anything to harm the other. That's what we said. And yet... you've decided, actually, you'd rather not do that.' He tutted. 'Nicci, my love, that's not how vows work. They are serious undertakings and we promised to keep ours till death us do part, remember?'

He could see her shaking now and he relished the power of his words. The power of suggestion. Her mind was making it real, terrifying her without him having to do much at all. That's how fear manifested itself, and he realised he rather liked the effect he was having on her. Making her crumble before his very eyes.

She glowered at him, her face red and blotchy, eyes narrowed.

'You never loved me, did you? Our marriage was never about love.' He could see now that he'd been mistaken. That wasn't fear in her eyes, no, that was fury. She was spitting and hissing like a cornered feline, and he was impressed by her bravado. Not that it was going to make a difference, but he'd let her have her say, in case there was something he should know. 'This was all about the business,' she continued, her jaw set. 'And now Dad's dead you're going to get what you want.'

He beamed, unable to suppress his delight at the way fate had played his cards. 'I know! And it's all happened so much faster than I imagined.'

'Stacey told me about you and Dom,' she snarled. 'I've seen the video.'

He pulled a faux shocked expression. 'Did she now.' He gave a slow shake of the head. 'That woman's a danger to herself, isn't she?'

The thing was, he didn't care. None of it mattered at the moment, he'd deal with Stacey in due course. All he cared about was getting rid of the problem he had married before she went and confessed to the police. Started stirring things about Pete's accident, putting ideas into their heads, and making them look more carefully at the cause of the crash. He couldn't risk that, not when he was so close to achieving his goal.

He gazed at Nicci, thinking how fortunate it was that she'd managed to disable herself. *And* present him with the perfect stage on which to set her untimely demise. He laughed. Stupid woman had made this ridiculously easy.

He watched her inching her way along the wall, spotted the umbrella propped in the corner that she was heading towards. He had to give her full marks for trying. 'Now, my love,' he said, more gently than he felt, his teeth clamped together as he prepared for his finale. 'It's time for you to get ready for a nice long sleep.'

She glared at him, he smiled back, then swung the wheel wrench like a golfer striking a tee shot down the fairway, hitting her under the chin. The force of his shot made her head snap back with a loud smack against the wall, blood spattering the white kitchen tiles. He watched, satisfied, as she slithered to the floor. He loved it when a plan came together, especially when he'd had to think on the hoof. But adrenaline was a wonderful thing, making his brain work at twice the normal speed. He'd even impressed himself.

He frowned as he surveyed the scene. It was messier than he'd anticipated and he could see droplets of blood had splattered him as well as the wall.

'Christ, is nothing ever simple?' he muttered to himself, but it was a reminder that he needed to be more careful and make sure he got it right. He rummaged under the sink, found a couple of carrier bags and put them over his shoes. Then he found Pete's work overalls in the cloakroom and put those on, along with a safety helmet and goggles. Now he was ready and sure that his DNA could be contained.

. . .

An hour later, Ethan was putting the finishing touches to the scene. He was cursing himself for letting his anger take over and make such a mess, but he'd come up with a plan he was pretty happy with.

He'd picked Joel up from the parking area outside, where he'd collapsed when Ethan had felled him like a tree with the wheel wrench. One well-placed strike, with Joel oblivious to what had happened. It had been a bit of a struggle getting him off the ground and into a fireman's lift, but with a lot of huffing and puffing he'd managed. Then carried him through the house, into the kitchen and dumped him on a chair at the table. He was alive but unconscious, a wound at the back of his head still seeping blood, so Ethan had to go back and cover his tracks, scuffing up the gravel to cover any bloodstains, then giving the hallway a mop.

Once that was done, he picked Nicci up and sat her on the chair opposite Joel. Her head lolled back, but he could see the throb of a pulse in her neck. Humming to himself, he got to work setting the table, opening a bottle of wine, and pouring them both a glass. Then he took a couple of ready meals out of the freezer and put them in the gas oven, leaving the door open. Not wide open, just a smidge, like they'd forgotten to close it properly. He found some tins of peas and carrots in the cupboard and emptied them into pans, putting them on the gas hob. Then he moved the scented candle from the fireplace by the sofa and put it in the middle of the table.

He stood and surveyed the scene, giving a satisfied nod. This was looking grand. A cosy meal for two. He thought it would work well. Once the gas had exploded, and this lovely couple had been blown to smithereens, there would be no trace of the injuries he'd caused or any evidence that he'd ever been here.

He found a bin bag in the cupboard under the sink, took off his trainers, which were blood-stained, and put them in the bag.

He stripped, putting his clothes in the bag too. Then he hurried upstairs and had a shower in the family bathroom, washing all the evidence away. In Pete's bedroom, he found some joggers and a T-shirt and put those on, looked at himself in the mirror. Almost the right size, although Ethan was taller and broader than Pete so the clothes were a little tight, but they'd do.

He walked down the stairs, his heart racing faster than he believed possible. All he had to do now was turn the oven on, and the gas rings, light the candles and run. He'd left his phone at the cottage, so that would be his alibi. One last glance round the scene and he was satisfied all was well.

'Goodbye, Nicci,' he said to his unconscious wife. 'Thanks for everything.'

He whistled as he walked out the door, the bin bag swinging from his hand. He shut the front door behind him and climbed into his car, peeling the rubber gloves from his hands and putting them in the bin bag with the rest of the items for disposal.

That night, after a generous nightcap to help him sleep, he lay in bed going through his story, the one he would tell the police when he was inevitably questioned. Of course he didn't know she was cheating on him, they'd been married less than two weeks. But there would be evidence from Louise that Joel had been in love with his wife. He'd seen that message and presumably it was still on Joel's phone even if he'd deleted it from Nicci's. Thank goodness he'd thought to leave Joel's phone outside on the gravel, where it had dropped out of his pocket when he'd picked him up. Any explosion would leave it intact and give the police a lovely piece of evidence to support his version of events.

He'd been following Nicci through the fields, but Joel had got to her first. Thankfully, they hadn't seen him when they were stood on the corner, unaware that he was hiding behind the wall, listening.

He hadn't been able to follow them into the hospital, but knew that's where they were going. Like a concerned husband, whose wife had gone out to walk the dog and not come back, he'd gone straight up to Pete's house, the logic being she would want to be there after her father's death. His phone records would show that to be the case. When he hadn't been able to find her there, he'd driven around looking for her, to no avail. His phone records would show that too. Then he went back home to wait, sending message after message, with no response. And he'd left his phone at home for the final act, so he could say he was nowhere near the place when the tragedy happened.

He would tell them Nicci had become violent and abusive, unhinged by her father's sudden death. He'd say she'd threatened him, become psychotic before dashing out of their cottage. His internal narrative came to an abrupt halt, making him sit up in bed, as a troublesome question popped into his head. A question he couldn't ignore.

CHAPTER THIRTY-NINE

Nicci could smell gas. Why would she be smelling gas? Their cottage was all electric, including the heating. Her head felt fuzzy, thoughts coming and going before she could see them properly, like figures emerging and disappearing in the mist.

She knew there was a problem, but she couldn't quite grasp what it was. Apart from the pain, the awful throbbing pain in her jaw, her wrist.

Move, come on, you need to move!

A voice in her head was shouting at her, but her body seemed to be stuck, her muscles so stiff they refused to work. Her eyes blinked open and she found she was staring at the ceiling, her neck seemingly frozen in place. She recognised the light fitting in the corner of her vision, it was one of the three hanging above the dining table at her dad's house. So that's where she must be but she had no recollection of coming here. None at all.

Her arms were hanging by her sides, and she tried to lift them, but they felt too heavy. Way too heavy. Especially her left arm which seemed to have a weight attached, pulling her in that direction. Gradually, she rocked her neck from side to side, hearing it creak and crack as she increased the range of movement, ignoring the shards of pain that stabbed at her.

It seemed impossible to lift her head from its uncomfortable position and the more she moved her neck, the more aware she was of the burning ache in her jaw. She closed her mouth, which had been hanging open, gasped at the sharpness of the pain. There was blood, she could taste it, her tongue tender and sore.

A flash of a memory lit up in her mind, a split-second image of Ethan holding a wheel wrench. Swinging it at her. What had he done?

Is he still here?

Panic tightened her chest and she started gasping for breath, adrenaline spiking in her veins. She tried again to sit up, but her head was too heavy, so she rolled to the side instead and slid to the floor with a thump, giving a guttural scream as her hand hit the floor. The white heat of pain made her light-headed and nauseous. Acid burned the back of her throat and she closed her eyes, trying to keep herself calm.

Oh God, what's happening?

Now was not the time for a panic attack, not when she knew with every fibre of her being that her life was in danger. She opened her eyes, scanned her immediate surroundings. That's when she noticed the plaster cast and a fuzzy memory fought its way out of the mist. Being chased. Falling.

Joel.

The smell of gas was not as bad down here and the cold of the floor tiles beneath her seemed to wake her up a bit. She was grunting with the effort of moving, but knew, intrinsically, that she must.

Gas. Danger. Get out of here.

She noticed a pair of trainers, someone else in the room and with an enormous effort she pulled herself up on the chair until she was standing, swaying as she tried to focus. Shrieking when she realised what she was seeing. Joel slumped in the chair opposite her, his chin on his chest.

More memories emerging from the mist. Ethan talking, blood dripping from the wheel wrench. He'd hurt Joel, but was he still alive?

The smell of gas was much stronger now. The flickering of the candle on the table caught her eye and her heart skipped. She had to blow it out, but her jaw was swollen and she couldn't puff at all. Instead, she licked the fingers of her right hand, pinched the wick, happy to see the curling column of smoke.

Gas. Turn off the gas.

She moved towards the cooker, the only gas appliance in the house and saw that the oven door had been left open, could hear the hissing from the rings on the hob. She turned everything off and staggered to the back door, flinging it open to let the fresh air in and allow the gas to disperse.

Feeling dizzy and nauseous, she sat on the back steps for a moment, while her lungs dragged in the fresh air, the mother of all headaches pounding in her temples. She tucked her left arm back in the sling and that felt better, the throbbing pain easing in her wrist. Gradually, her thoughts started to clear and she understood what Ethan had done. He'd set everything up for a gas explosion, killing her and Joel in the process. Boom. All evidence of foul play blown to pieces.

She shivered in the cool night air, wondering how she'd been fooled so completely by her husband. *Joel. Is he still alive?* The need to check on him gave her the strength to get to her feet and go back inside, moving towards him at a speed that felt slightly faster than slow motion. Her limbs weren't functioning properly, her mind still hazy.

'Joel, Joel,' she called to him, gently shaking his shoulder. Her tongue was thick and heavy in her mouth, blurring her words, but there was no movement and he seemed exactly how she'd left him. Unconscious. She moved her hand from his shoulder, and her heart clenched when she saw streaks of blood down the back of his neck. When she took a closer look, she realised his black T-shirt was soaked with it. She could see the wound now, at the base of his skull, his light-brown hair matted and dark.

An ambulance. I need to call an ambulance.

Her phone wasn't in its usual place in her pocket, and she desperately scanned the table but it wasn't there either. She hauled herself round to where she'd been sitting, thinking she must have dropped it, but froze in place when she heard the front door slam.

CHAPTER FORTY

Ethan was standing in the hallway and as she gazed in horror, he walked towards her.

A vein pulsed in his forehead, his eyes bloodshot, his fists curled by his sides, fingers tensing and straightening, like he was warming up to use them. His jaw was clenched, eyes narrowed and he looked like his temper was a whisker away from exploding. He hadn't been like this before, when he'd hit her earlier. She remembered him laughing, euphoric, like he was playing a game, not taking people's lives. He'd been in high spirits then and for that she was weirdly grateful, because if he'd been in the filthy temper he was in now, she knew she'd already be dead.

What is he capable of when he's all riled up?

She backed away from him, her breath pumping in and out as if she'd been running, a terrible trembling in the pit of her stomach, spreading through her body. She whimpered. Never in her life had she been this scared and there was nobody who could help her. If she was going to get away from him, it was going to have to be her doing, and hers alone.

He was watching her, watching every move as she shuffled backwards. Her eyes scanned the kitchen, looking for ideas, a means of defence, and out of the corner of her eye, she noticed her phone on the floor under the table. It must have dropped out of her pocket when she'd fallen off the chair earlier. She couldn't let her eyes linger on it, though, couldn't let him see what she was looking at. Instead, she fixed her gaze above his right shoulder, widening her eyes as if she'd seen something.

He turned his head to look, checking there was nobody there and as he did, she sank to the ground next to her phone, switching it on and hiding it behind her back as she scuttled under the table, where she at least had some protection.

The table was made of solid oak, lovingly constructed by her father when he and her mother were just married and had little in the way of furniture. He'd made the chairs too, so heavy they were hard to move if you were having a bad day. She'd hidden under here when she was a child. Throwing a blanket over the top and making a den, sneaking under when she was sad, or one of her parents was cross with her. It felt safe, like being in a cave.

'What do you think you're doing under there?' Ethan asked. She watched his feet walk closer, inched herself back a little further until she hit Joel's legs. Her hand grabbed his ankle, feeling for a pulse. *Is he still alive?* She thought she felt something, the faint throb of a heartbeat and she allowed herself to hope it wasn't too late.

Ethan moved closer, taking his time. Her breath hitched in her throat, her chest getting tighter and tighter.

What's he going to do to me?

There was no doubt in her mind he was here to kill her. He must have come back to check that his plan had worked, and the house had exploded. She was certain he'd make sure he didn't fail a second time.

Adrenaline fizzed round her body, her mind much clearer now the gas had escaped out of the back door, which was still wide open. She could feel the breeze against her skin, raising a rash of goosebumps. There had to be a way to get herself out of this, there had to be.

Think, think, think.

While he wasn't looking, she pressed buttons on her phone, hoping she'd hit the right ones before slipping it behind her back again, so he couldn't see. She was clutching at straws, trying everything she could think of and she couldn't rely on it working. In fact, she had to assume it wouldn't and think of another way to escape.

He crouched down and suddenly they were eye to eye. Her heart missed a beat.

'I think you put yourself in a cage, sweetheart.' He laughed then and the sound brought a chill to her bones. He sounded mad, unhinged. And more than a little relieved.

Was he scared as well? Scared that his plan wouldn't work, that she might escape, and he'd get caught? He'd started a process, an extreme course of action that now had a momentum of its own. He was fully committed, had used up all his choices and in that moment, she knew there was hope. Frightened people make mistakes. The trick was for her to stay calm, not let her own fear cloud her judgement.

'What a night,' he said casually, as if they were talking about a drunken session in the pub. 'I obviously didn't hit you hard enough, did I?'

She noticed that he had no weapon with him. Had to assume that he'd already disposed of the wheel wrench somehow, thinking the job was done. She recognised the T-shirt he was wearing as one of her dad's and her body tensed. It had a picture of Jimi Hendrix on the front, her dad's favourite musician, and it felt so wrong for Ethan to be wearing it.

How dare he take that?

Anger flared in her heart. She couldn't allow him to get away with this, but she'd only get one chance to escape and she had to make sure, when she acted, that it was her best shot. He seemed in no hurry and she wondered if he wasn't sure what to do now Plan A had failed.

He moved a chair to one side so he could see her better.

'I'm glad you're still here because there's something I want you to know. I think I would have regretted it if you'd died before I could confess my sins.' He laughed again, a wild look in his eye.

He paused for effect. 'I want to let you into a little secret. I know I denied it, but I did actually want Joel to be dead. In fact, after I saw his message on your phone, I planned for Joel to die. That's why I suggested we drive home the back way. Right past the place where he'd asked you to meet him. And that's why I yanked the steering wheel to make sure we hit him.'

She had to pretend she was shocked, although she'd known this already, not believing his earlier denials.

'It's been fun letting you take the blame, and after your untimely demise, if anyone should happen to try and pin anything on me, I can point to the fact that a group of people saw you getting behind the wheel of my car.' He laughed again. 'Your name will be mud, but I'm hoping it won't come to that. I have a feeling if I bide my time, the whole thing will go away.'

'You bastard,' she said, lisping because her tongue was swollen and her jaw wasn't working properly. 'You enjoyed letting me think I killed someone, didn't you?'

'I know and I did,' he said, looking smug, like it was the best compliment she could have given him. 'More rewarding still was letting you think you'd killed your lover.' He heaved a sigh. 'Such a shame that it wasn't him we hit. You know, I was confident it was. Until he showed up tonight.' His eyes glanced over the top of the table at Joel. 'Looks like I might have succeeded now, though.'

Now, now, now!

He was momentarily distracted and she had to take her chance. She kicked the nearest chair at him with all the force her legs could muster. He was balanced on the balls of his feet and taken unawares, the chair knocked him backwards, sending him sprawling on the floor. She slid forward, knocking another chair on top of him and before he could free himself, she was out from under the table and running out of the back door, slamming it behind her.

There was no way she had the strength to overpower him when she had a broken wrist, but there was nothing wrong with her legs. She ran for her life.

CHAPTER FORTY-ONE

The problem, she realised, was there was no easy way out of the back garden. It was surrounded on three sides with a stone wall and a fence on top and she wouldn't be climbing over that with a broken wrist. She went round to the side gate, but it was closed and although she yanked at it, she couldn't get it to open.

She stifled a groan, her heart racing so fast she could hardly breathe.

Aware that it would be a matter of seconds before Ethan came after her, she abandoned the side gate and headed towards the end of the garden, keeping close to the wall on the left, in the shadows, until the point at which the lights from the kitchen no longer filtered through the gloom.

It was a long, triangular-shaped garden, at least a hundred yards from one end to the other, and once she hit the darkness, she was thankful that the layout was simple, the ground laid to lawn with nothing to trip her up. There was a shrubbery growing against the side wall on her right that she could hide in as a last resort, but it wouldn't take much imagination on Ethan's part to find her there.

The moon slid out from behind the clouds for a brief

moment, lighting up the summer house and she knew that was the best hiding place. She hurried towards it, tried the door, but it was locked. Thankfully, she could feel the key. Her heart had lost its normal rhythm now and she was convinced she was having palpitations. With fumbling fingers, she grasped the key and tried to make it turn, but it wouldn't budge. All the while she was listening for signs that Ethan was coming after her, constantly glancing over her shoulder.

The summer house was her mum's creative space, some-where she came to work on interior design ideas for their garden buildings, making samples on the sewing machine she had in there. Once her mum had passed away, her dad hadn't used it, leaving it untouched, like a shrine to the woman he loved. Nicci thought the lock mechanism must have seized up with lack of use and two winters of bad weather. Okay, she could break a window, but then she wouldn't be able to get herself in and by that time Ethan would know exactly where she was.

The sound of footsteps made her abandon her efforts, and she slid round the edge of the building, until she was at the back of the summer house. A mistake, she realised, because she couldn't see what he was doing. She clenched her teeth in frus-tration, immediately regretting it as spikes of pain pierced her damaged jaw. It was all she could do to stop herself from crying out, but she had to keep quiet, had to keep him guessing where she was.

Her mind was racing, scrolling through idea after idea and rejecting them all. Perhaps she could outwit him and sneak back to the house while he was still looking for her in the garden. Lock herself in? Then she remembered he had his own set of keys and there were no bolts on the inside of the doors. Her parents had never seen the need to fit high-security locks as in the time they'd lived there, nobody in the surrounding neigh-bourhood had been burgled. Probably because the road up to the house was narrow and winding and didn't make for a quick getaway.

The scrape of a foot moving towards her had her creeping the other way, her back flat against the summer house as she inched down the side, towards the front of the building. Her eyes had got used to the dark now and as she peered round the front of the structure, she was startled to find herself face to face with Ethan.

'Looking for something, are we?' he asked with a grin, his teeth glinting in the moonlight. She'd been expecting him to be going anticlockwise round the building, but he must have doubled-back.

She screamed as he grabbed her arm, fingers digging in, his grasp so tight it was like a tourniquet. There was no way he was going to give her any chance to wriggle free.

I can't let him do this.

She let out another scream, but this time it wasn't a scream of shock or pain, it was an ear-splitting scream of attack. Instead of trying to pull away from him, as he might have expected, she moved towards him, aiming a knee at his groin with all the force she could muster. He yelled and doubled over in pain. She brought her knee up again, into his face, then kicked at his shins but still his fingers grasped her arm. As a final move, she jabbed two fingers into his eyes. It felt awful, but it was a life and death situation and finally he let her go.

Thank God for those self-defence classes she'd attended last winter. It had all come flooding back and every technique she'd practised then had worked now. Saying a silent thank you to the instructor, she dashed back to the house, running in through the back door, through the kitchen, down the hall and out of the front.

Ethan's car was parked on the gravel, the door still open and she could see the keys hanging from the ignition. She jumped in, started the engine, and managed to get it in gear, using her right hand. Breathing hard, she sped off down the lane, jamming her foot on the brake after fifty yards when she realised driving with one arm was not easy and she would end up in a ditch if she wasn't careful. It was impossible to change gear while she was moving as she only had one arm and she needed that for the steering wheel, so she had to stay in first gear and use the clutch, disengaging the gears if she wanted to go faster.

I can't take any more, she thought, wondering how her heart could be hammering so fast, the air rasping down her throat as she dragged in huge breaths. She stopped and pulled her phone out of her pocket. Switched it on. But the screen remained blank. Nothing happened. Even when she tried ringing the emergency number, there was no ringtone. It was dead.

She smacked it down onto the passenger seat in frustration. There was no way to call help for Joel.

The sound of footsteps slapping on the tarmac behind her made her check the mirror and there was Ethan, pounding down the lane, catching up with her.

She drove on down the road a little way, then stopped again to think. She was not fit to be driving and she was scaring herself, sure she'd end up going off the road.

Joel was still in her dad's house. She couldn't leave him to die, couldn't just run away and save her own skin. She'd felt a pulse in his ankle when she'd been cowering under the table and if he was still alive, she had to do whatever she could to get him medical assistance before it was too late. She'd already thought she'd lost him once and there was no way she was going to let that happen again. Her phone may not be working, but her dad had a landline. With a feeling of dread, she knew she had to go back. It was the fastest way to get help and she could try and give first aid while she waited for the ambulance to arrive.

With much difficulty, she managed to turn around. Her

eyes closed for a second while she gathered herself. And when she opened them again, she saw a figure in the headlights. Ethan. The man who'd made her believe she was a killer, who'd browbeaten her into not telling the police about the hit-and-run accident, who'd gone on to kill her father. The man who'd tried to kill her and Joel that evening.

He was evil. He was dangerous and she couldn't seem to get away from him.

She gritted her teeth, revved the engine and drove straight at him.

CHAPTER FORTY-TWO

Ethan lay half on half off the road, trying to work out which bit of him hurt the most. Gingerly, he tried moving different parts of his body. He didn't think anything was broken, but his shoulder wouldn't move properly and he felt a bit sick and dizzy after flying over the car bonnet. He honestly hadn't thought she'd do it and stood his ground until the very last minute when he tried to dive out of the way. Not fast enough to avoid the car, unfortunately.

He'd landed head first in a ditch full of stinging nettles, but he was grateful it had been that and not a stone wall. Thankfully she hadn't been going fast, that old Land Rover not being too speedy from a standing start. He was lucky, he decided, that it wasn't worse.

Slowly, he inched his way backwards out of the ditch, his face on fire with nettle stings. He tried to get on his hands and knees but he couldn't push himself up, pain jabbing and stabbing at his shoulder whichever way he tried to move. He flopped back on the tarmac. There was no way he could get back up that hill. Not before the police arrived, because she'd be calling them any time now.

He closed his eyes, his breathing gradually getting back to normal. Christ, his eyes hurt where she'd poked him. And his groin. He'd never thought she'd have it in her to fight back like that. He'd definitely underestimated the opposition.

What the hell am I going to do now?

He pulled his phone from his pocket and rang Dom. It was time they had a proper conversation, not all this childish behaviour, the not speaking to each other, ignoring messages. Okay, so he knew he was mightily annoyed with him for going through with the wedding. He'd even threatened to tell Nicci about their affair in a last-ditch attempt to call a halt to their plans. Ethan was convinced he wouldn't go through with it and had ignored his pleas to think again. 'You've got to think longer-term,' Ethan had told him when they last met. 'I'm doing this for us and I need you to be patient.' But Dom wasn't the patient kind. He was fiery and passionate, things Ethan loved about him. He could also throw almighty strops like this one, where he'd refuse to speak to him for days on end. Anyway, he needed him now like he'd never needed him before.

No answer.

But while he'd been waiting for Dom to pick up his call, he'd had an idea. There was a way out of this if he kept his wits about him. Damage limitation.

He rang for an ambulance for himself. Then he called the police, saying he was the victim of a hit-and-run. *Fighting fire with fire.* It was the only way he was going to wriggle out of this situation. At the moment, as far as he could work out, it was his word against hers. Circumstantial evidence. And as things stood, he was looking very much like a victim.

If he stayed in the middle of the road, nobody was getting past him until he'd been properly seen to. That should delay things up at the house. Hopefully long enough for Joel to die.

. . .

He wasn't sure how long he'd had to wait because he'd blacked out for a bit, waking to find a paramedic calling to him, gently shaking his shoulder. He blinked, finding it hard to focus, an ungodly pain banging in his head.

'Can you tell me what happened?' the paramedic asked before he started his assessment.

'My wife knocked me down.' His mouth was dry, his voice croaky. 'She took my car and she drove straight into me.' He winced, even the sound of his own voice was too loud. 'I flew over the bonnet and into the ditch.' He had to stop speaking as his stomach heaved and he puked onto the tarmac. He moved his head to avoid the pile of sick, the smell of it making him feel nauseous all over again, the pain as he moved making him grunt. 'My right shoulder isn't working properly. And I couldn't stand up.'

'Okay, let's see what's going on.' The paramedic started a gentle but thorough examination. Another paramedic appeared with a clipboard. 'Can I ask your name?'

'Ethan Watts,' he murmured. 'My father-in-law died today. In a car accident and my wife, she's completely lost the plot. She up at his house now. At the top of this road. God knows what she's doing. She tried to attack me with the wheel wrench out of the car earlier. I called the police so I hope they'll be here soon. I tell you, she's terrifying.'

'I believe the police are on their way,' the second paramedic said as he started asking more questions, filling in his handover chart.

The police arrived as Ethan was being wheeled into the ambulance, off to hospital to be checked over for possible concussion and a suspected broken shoulder blade. The two officers were of a similar age, probably mid-thirties at a guess.

He told them the same story he'd told the paramedics. That Nicci had gone crazy with grief. 'She's blaming it all on me. Saying stupid things like I caused the accident that killed her father. I don't know what she's thinking but, you know, be careful if you're going up to the house because she was swiping at me with a wheel wrench earlier.'

He sighed, almost done with talking. It was far more exhausting than he could cope with, but he had to give them his version first, so they would view the scene at the house from his perspective. With the best will in the world, nobody was completely impartial and if he could skew their interpretation of events, he was in with a chance. 'She blames me for everything. If there was an earthquake tomorrow, that would be my fault too.'

The paramedics were in a hurry to leave, another ambulance waiting behind and they were blocking the road.

'We'll come and talk to you later,' one of the officers said. 'It doesn't look like you'll be out of the hospital in a hurry.'

Ethan lay back on his pillow, finding it impossible to rest in a position that reduced the pain. The paramedic put a cannula in his hand, then gave him an injection. 'Morphine, mate. That should make things easier.'

And, very quickly, it did.

What a shame things wouldn't be getting easier for Nicci, he thought, allowing a satisfied smile to play on his lips. Imagining how she would explain herself to the police.

'There you go, told you that would help,' the paramedic said with a wink. 'Enjoy the trip.'

Ethan thought he just might.

CHAPTER FORTY-THREE

Nicci couldn't believe how long it was taking for the ambulance to get there. She rang again, and they said they were on their way. Joel was still unconscious and his face was so pale, his skin so cold, it was hard to believe he was still alive. She was sure she could feel a pulse in his neck, though. Faint, but there all the same.

It was hard to know what to do for the best, and with little first-aid knowledge apart from the basics, all she could do was try and keep him warm. She filled a hot water bottle. Pulled the throw off the sofa and wrapped it round him. Sat next to him and waited, taking his hand in hers, talking to him, telling him help was on the way. Trying not to think about the wound at the base of his skull. Hopefully it wasn't as bad as it looked, but she was pretty sure she could see the gleam of bone amongst the congealed blood.

It was hard to think about herself when Joel was so badly injured but her jaw throbbed and swallowing was still an issue. At least with her wrist back in its sling, it wasn't feeling too bad now and she'd had another couple of painkillers while she'd been waiting for the ambulance and police to turn up.

Finally, she heard a vehicle draw up on the gravel car park and she dashed through the house, throwing the front door open, relieved to see the ambulance. It was two women on duty and she led them through the house while she told them what had happened.

'My husband attacked us with a wheel wrench off his car,' she lisped, finding speaking an effort. If she kept her teeth together it made it easier. 'He smacked me in the jaw and hit Joel on the back of the head.'

The paramedics exchanged a glance before hurrying through to the kitchen.

The younger woman, with a thick blonde braid hanging down the centre of her back, went over to assess Joel, while the older woman, with short dark hair, had a look at Nicci's jaw.

'You've been in the wars today,' she said, with a nod at her arm in the sling.

'My husband has been trying to kill us,' she said. 'He already managed to kill my dad this morning.'

The paramedic gave her a long look, like she might not believe her, glancing over her head at her colleague.

'The police are following us up here,' she said, all matter-of-fact. 'So, you can tell them all about it. Can you open your mouth?' Nicci shook her head. 'Not much and it hurts like hell.'

'Yes, I think your jaw's broken. We'll have to take you in to get someone to look at it.'

'Skull fracture here,' her colleague said. 'I'll ring it in so they know what's coming.' She walked through to the front door to make her call and Nicci wondered what she was saying that couldn't be said in front of her. Fear wrapped its tentacles around her.

Don't let him die. Please don't let him die.

How would she live with herself if he did? She'd set this whole catastrophic series of events in motion by pursuing her friendship with him. She should have ended it the moment she knew their relationship had veered onto forbidden territory, given that both of them were in long-term relationships.

It's not *all* your fault, a voice in her head corrected her.

Ethan had deleted Joel's message from her phone, knowing that if she'd seen it, she may have stopped the wedding. Then he'd caused the accident, thinking he was killing Joel, while he ended up killing some random stranger who happened to be in the wrong place at the wrong time. That action had frightened her into making a vow that she'd keep the secret.

'It's my fault,' she muttered to herself, still unable to apportion all the blame to Ethan. She had to accept that once she'd threatened to break her vow, everything had spiralled out of control. Her actions had been the catalyst. 'All my fault.'

Her mind drifted as she watched the paramedics getting Joel onto a stretcher, praying that he would survive. The sound of another car pulling up yanked her out of her thoughts. She heard talking outside, but she couldn't summon the energy to get up off the chair. Once the paramedics had arrived, she'd seemed to wilt, her energy evaporating like puddles in the summer sun. Now her body felt heavy and sore and her head was aching, despite the painkillers. She'd had the adrenaline high while she was fighting off Ethan, but now she was getting the inevitable low.

Two police officers walked into the room. Youngish men. They stood and looked around the room before they came to talk to her.

Wearily, she told them everything that had happened and one of the officers took notes, while the other concentrated on the questions.

'Can I ascertain how you left your husband? After you ran him over... What condition was he in?'

She shrugged. 'I don't know. I had to get back here to call an ambulance for Joel.'

The officer pondered her answer for a second. 'So... you are saying you deliberately ran over your husband and didn't stop to check if he needed medical attention?' There was a flicker of something on the officer's face. Disapproval?

'He was trying to *kill* me,' she insisted. 'He broke my jaw.'

'And you were having a meal with your... lover?' He glanced at the table, set out for dinner, the wine glasses still full.

'No, no I wasn't. My husband set it up to look like that's what was going on. Then he tried to cause an explosion by leaving the oven on.' There was no way she could prove this, no evidence of the intention to blow the house up and glancing at the table now, she could see how it might look. The skin seemed to tighten over her scalp, her mouth dry.

The paramedics came back in then, wanting to take Joel and Nicci to hospital.

The police officer who was taking notes flipped his book shut. 'I'm sure we'll have a few more questions,' he said. 'But that's enough for now.'

She could tell by the look on his face and the tone of his voice that he wasn't sure whether to believe her, but there was nothing she could do. At least she'd got her story out and hopefully they would go and talk to Stacey. She'd tell them in no uncertain terms what Ethan had been up to.

When they arrived at the hospital, Joel was taken away for urgent treatment and she was put in a cubicle in the emergency department, awaiting assessment. She was relieved to be able to lie on a bed and close her eyes and feel safe. There was no point worrying about the police interview, they would be back, and she could do a better job of giving them her side of the story. For now, she could rest.

It wasn't long before the doctor arrived, a harried-looking man who was rail thin with hair sticking up all over the place, like a mad professor. His face looked careworn, like he'd had a difficult life.

'Your jaw is definitely broken, but we'll send you for an X-ray so we can see what type of break it is. Then we'll know if you need surgery or if it will heal on its own.'

Two hours later, she'd been to have an X-ray but was still waiting for the doctor to come back and see her. She was lying on the bed, dozing, when a hand grabbed her ankle.

Her eyes blinked open, her heart rate doubling its speed as she looked into the eyes of her husband.

CHAPTER FORTY-FOUR

Nicci stifled a scream. Ethan smiled at her, his fingers digging into her skin. His left arm was in a sling, but his right hand was wrapped round her leg.

'I think we need to have a little chat, don't we?' His voice made it sound like they were planning a picnic.

He let go of her ankle, patted her leg, and pulled up a chair to sit next to her. She'd been put in a side room because the police wanted to speak to her at some point and it would give some privacy for their conversation. It had felt more comfortable being on her own in here, out of the madness of the emergency department, but now she was trapped with the man who'd tried to kill her, it was the last place she wanted to be.

She looked around for the call bell, but it was in its holder, on the wall behind the bed, out of her reach.

'No need to look so scared,' Ethan said, like nothing had happened. 'I just think we should talk, get our story straight.'

'I don't need you to tell me my story,' she lisped, desperately trying to work out how she could grab the call bell. She sat up, thinking she could launch herself off the bed and grab it.

Ethan seemed to work out what she was trying to do and

grabbed the bell himself, letting it drop to the floor where she couldn't reach it, his body blocking the way. There was nothing she could do except keep as far away from him as possible and she shuffled to the far side of the bed until her back was against the wall.

'Let me tell you what the police believe. They think you intentionally ran me over, then drove off to attend to your lover, leaving me to possibly die of my injuries.' He nodded when she didn't answer, as if confirming he was right. 'You can't deny that's what happened.'

She couldn't. That's exactly what had happened, but it had been done out of self-defence. Had she mentioned that to the police? She couldn't be sure, licked her lips, nervous now.

Ethan sat in the chair next to the bed, his voice so calm and even that you'd think he was talking about what filling to put in their sandwiches. 'I think this has all got out of hand. Let me tell you what I'm thinking.' He leant closer, his hand stroking her leg. 'I think we should drop charges against each other, tell them we had a tiff over your friendship with Joel, which is true, but we have sorted out our differences now and we are sorry for wasting their time. No harm done. We're both still standing. We might get charged for wasting police time, but that's about it.'

Her eyes narrowed. 'You're forgetting Joel,' she hissed. 'The terrible injuries you inflicted on him.'

'He had an accident,' Ethan said, deadpan, giving a dismissive shrug.

She shook his hand off her leg, raised her knees to her chin so he couldn't reach her. 'That's not what he'll say when he comes round.'

Ethan raised his eyebrows. 'Perhaps he's not coming round.'

Her body tensed. 'What are you saying?'

Ethan sighed, reaching over and taking her hand in his. 'You're missing the point, sweetheart. I don't know if it's deliberate or if you're over-tired or what. But if we stick by what really happened, we are both going to prison for a long, long time. If we cancel our stories out, then we go back to our lives.' His eyes met hers, the silence unbearable. 'I hope you can remember what we promised each other in our wedding vows. Or shall I remind you? Because the thing you need to bear in mind is that we said we would keep those vows until death us do part.' He laughed then. 'Despite what you think, I don't want you dead.'

Nicci was lost for words. Not a single one would come out of her mouth even though her mind was full of them, clambering over each other to be heard. She couldn't make sense of what he was saying, given he'd tried to kill her several times already.

Ethan carried on talking, trying to persuade her round to his way of thinking. He honestly believed he might be able to sway her thoughts in his direction. But he was wrong, very wrong. He didn't know what he was up against. Had no idea what she was capable of. She wasn't going to spend her life telling lies, keeping secrets, living in fear that the truth might come out. She'd tried that for a short while and understood it was no way to live.

She was going to tell the police the truth and face the consequences, whatever they might be.

Ethan stared at her before playing his trump card. 'Joel will always be in danger. You understand that, don't you? He's a dead man walking unless you agree to my version of events.'

'Joel will tell the police the truth.' She glared at him, her defiance wavering, terrified he might be serious. Then she saw a hardness in his gaze that told her he was and her heart sank. He meant what he'd said.

'Do you honestly believe that a man with a skull fracture is going to remember what happened to him?' Ethan scoffed. 'Even without that, he wouldn't know for definite what hit him. I crept up behind him, you see. He didn't know I was there.

One minute he was standing up, the next he was out for the count.' He laughed. 'He isn't a witness to any crime, if that's what you're counting on.'

He squeezed her hand. 'If you tell the police my version of events, I promise you he will be safe for as long as you keep our secrets. So you see, my love, his fate is tied to your decision. What's it going to be? Are you going to kill Joel to speak your truth, or shall we forgive and forget and get back to how we were?'

Without waiting for her reply, he ran through the version of events he wanted them to separately tell the police. They'd had a domestic. She'd fallen down the steps when she was chasing him round the garden. That's how she'd hurt her jaw. She hadn't intentionally run over him; he'd jumped out in front of the car. They found Joel outside. He'd come to visit when they were about to have their evening meal and they had no idea how he'd come by his injuries.

A nurse popped her head round the door. She looked startled when she saw Ethan. He gave her a sheepish grin. 'This is my wife. We're just... making up, aren't we, darling?'

Nicci nodded. He had her trapped, and for now, until she could think of a way out, she would have to do what he wanted.

'Well, I'm pleased to hear it.' The nurse smiled. 'Looks like you've got matching slings! I wondered where you'd got to, Ethan. The doctor said you can go home now, but take it easy for the rest of the week. You'll get a physio appointment for your shoulder. And the police are here to talk to you. They want to see you separately.'

'Okay,' Ethan said, standing up and leaning in to give Nicci a kiss. 'I'm ready.'

Nicci watched him leave the room, her heart racing, feeling utterly desolate, not sure what she was going to say to the police, or whether they would believe a single word she said.

CHAPTER FORTY-FIVE

Three days later, the police contacted Ethan to confirm they were taking no further action now that he and Nicci had told them the truth and owned up to blaming each other. They accepted that their injuries had been accidental, and they'd used them as a way of getting at each other. He was told that Joel had regained consciousness but the last thing he could remember was driving Nicci back to the house from hospital after her earlier fall. His recollections from the night were muddled and he couldn't say for sure that he hadn't fallen and hurt himself, so they wouldn't be pursuing it further.

Ethan ended the call with a feeling of immense satisfaction. He'd pulled it off. He really had. He went back into Pete's house – now their house – to find Nicci and tell her the news.

She was still a bit hostile, but he thought her icy demeanour was starting to thaw a little. If he carried on with his charm offensive, she'd come round, he was sure she would. Especially when he passed on the news about Joel. He knew she had feelings for the man, but it was hypocritical of him to take exception to that given his relationship with Dom. This was a marriage of convenience and as soon as Nicci began to understand that the better. They could rub along quite nicely for the time being, couldn't they? Then they could discreetly operate an open marriage. If he got to live in this lovely house and be boss of the business, that was all he needed for the time being. After all the accidents, he was going to tread carefully for a while, until the time was right for Nicci's final tragic event.

The next thing to get through was Pete's post-mortem.

He'd asked the police about it on the pretext of wanting to organise the funeral, and they said they'd have the results shortly. Nothing more specific than that, so the burial would have to wait for a little while.

Nicci had suggested the move to Pete's house as she wanted to be close to memories of her father and be around his things and he had been delighted to agree and be out of that dingy cottage. She was sleeping in her dad's bedroom for now – with the door locked – and Ethan was in a guest bedroom. Not that he minded. It was only temporary after all and at least he didn't have to pretend he wanted to make love to her any more. Hopefully those days were over.

You couldn't rush things. He was going to have to leave a decent interval between events now, however much he wanted to move on to the final phase. Anyway, there was plenty to sort out in the meantime. He had to get all the legalities squared away and ownership of the business and the house clear. Joint names for everything, that's what they'd decided. Well, it's what he'd told Nicci they were doing and now he had this lovely big threat hanging over her, there was nothing she could do about it.

Funny how life changes things around. He'd thought Joel was the biggest threat to his plans, but now he found he was the glue that was sticking them together.

He put the kettle on and made himself a cup of tea, put one down beside Nicci, who was sleeping on the sofa. She did a lot of that these days. And crying. She did a lot of that too. He went to sit outside in the late summer sunshine, quietly celebrating the end of the most dangerous period he'd ever had to live through, and looking forward to better times ahead. Fortunately, he hadn't broken his shoulder, just damaged tendons and ligaments, so physio should sort that out. And after a couple of days of headaches, the concussion had faded away. In fact, apart from a bit of muscle soreness, he felt remarkably chipper.

His phone pinged and he woke with a start, realising he'd fallen asleep, no idea how long he'd been there. He whipped it out of his pocket to check the message, hoping it was Dom. But it wasn't. It was Stacey. His heart sank, his mood instantly soured as he glowered at the screen.

What does she want now?

CHAPTER FORTY-SIX

EARLIER

Nicci heard the door bang shut and climbed up off the sofa, peering out of the window. She could see Ethan outside, sitting on the garden bench. Now was her chance.

Ever since they'd come out of hospital, three days ago, Ethan had been glued to her side and she'd had little time on her own. She knew it was because he didn't trust her, wanting to make sure she was keeping to their agreement. He'd even done an online shop so the groceries would get dropped off and he didn't have to go out and leave her.

As soon as they'd got home, she realised she might as well be in prison. In fact, she was in a type of prison and was probably in more danger at home with Ethan than she would be if she'd been convicted of a crime. He'd even taken her phone and disconnected the landline so she couldn't ring anyone. Isolated and afraid. That about summed up her situation, she thought as she lay on the sofa for hours, crying and dozing and crying again.

She was still deep in grief for her father, a loss that had knocked her feet from under her. At least she felt safer up at her dad's house, where she could sleep on her own. And lock the door. Ethan had readily gone along with the move and why wouldn't he? It was what he'd been aiming for all along. He also didn't seem to mind sleeping in one of the guest rooms, but now she knew about his affair with Dom it all made sense. He didn't *want* to sleep with her. It had all been part of his plan to get hold of the business, to move up in the world by taking what was hers via their marriage.

She had no doubt that, at some point soon, she would be surplus to requirements and there would be an unfortunate accident. How could she not think that after the things Ethan had done? Whatever promises he might make, they were never going to be genuine, because he didn't trust or love her. However, as she mulled over her situation, she did think she probably had a bit of time now to decide how to make her move and get herself out of this terrible situation. If she had a fatal accident, so soon after everything else, suspicion would definitely land at Ethan's door and the police would probably look at all the other events in a different light. She felt safe for the time being.

But today, something had happened that changed everything, and she was now ready to make her move.

Earlier that morning, she'd found her mum's old phone down the side of the sofa. She'd been lying there, trying to get comfy and her hand had felt something solid. She'd teased it out and when she realised what it was, she knew she'd struck gold. She'd stuffed it back where she found it, waiting for a chance like this, when Ethan wasn't around. Thankfully, it looked like he'd relaxed his guard duties for the time being, thinking she was asleep again. For the first time, he'd gone outside and left her alone. This was her chance.

She pulled the phone out of its hiding place, dashed upstairs and locked herself in the bedroom. The phone was old, with no password protection, so if she could charge it up, she'd be able to use it. She opened the drawer in her mum's bedside cabinet and started looking for the charger. Her heart was racing, a feeling of excitement stirring in her belly. This could be it. Her chance to escape. There were a couple of chargers in the drawer and Nicci felt her heart flutter with hope.

But neither of them fitted. They were obviously for other devices her mum had owned. Maybe even older phones. She sat on the bed, elbows on her knees, head in her hands, the euphoria sliding into the familiar feeling of defeat. Her eyes noticed something on the floor, and she did a double take. It was the end of a charger, snaking underneath the bedside cabinet, still plugged into the wall socket. Her dad had left it there all this time. But then he'd left a lot of her mum's things about the house, like she still lived there, and she supposed it had given him comfort, giving him the feeling that nothing had changed.

Suddenly, there was a glimmer of hope lighting up the darkness of her world. Would it still work, though? It was two years since her mum had died. A long time since this phone had been used.

She plugged in the phone and waited. It seemed to be taking too long, but then there was a buzz and it started charging. Her heart did a backflip and she waited for a few more minutes before she made her first call. It was going to be awkward, but it was her only choice.

All the time spent dozing had allowed her mind the freedom to wander and it had stumbled upon an idea that she needed to check out.

If she was right, it would be an absolute game changer.

CHAPTER FORTY-SEVEN

The next day, Ethan picked at the loose thread that was coming away from the hem of his T-shirt as he waited. He was meeting Stacey in a coffee shop on Skipton High Street. It wasn't ideal as he didn't want their conversation to be overheard, but he supposed she felt safe in a place where she wouldn't be alone with him. Who could blame her after Pete's 'accident'? She wasn't daft. She knew she'd had a lucky escape and that was fine by him. It gave him the weapon of fear.

He'd suggested meeting down by the canal. By the bench where she'd seen him kissing Dom, but she was adamant she wasn't going to go along with that. Which was a shame. Few people walked down there. He could have sorted out this situation permanently, but instead, here he was, and he had a feeling it was going to go on and on unless he could think of an alternative solution to the Stacey problem.

It was early morning, the coffee shop had just opened and there were only three people in there. He'd taken a table at the back where they would have a bit of privacy. He'd had to secure Nicci in the bathroom while he went out, knowing she would try and escape. But he'd put a bolt on the outside of the door, and the window was far too small for her to get out of, so he was confident she was secure for the time he'd be away. He had to make this trip out as short as possible, though, because she was being a bit weird this morning. She'd actually been smiling, so what was that about? It could be a positive, though... Perhaps she was finally coming round to his vision of the future.

The bell rang every time the door opened, and he kept looking up but eventually there she was, late as usual, striding over to the table with a grin on her face. Well, it would be interesting to see how long that stayed there, he thought, as he smiled back at her.

'I'll get you a coffee,' she said. 'Black, no sugar, right?'

'You remembered.'

'They reckon people who drink black coffee are a bit psycho, did you know that?'

He laughed as she went to the counter. The one thing he did enjoy about Stacey was her sense of humour, he thought as he watched her. She brought the drinks over and sat down on the chair opposite him, taking a look round the rest of the coffee shop, no doubt making sure they could talk in confidence.

He sipped his coffee, put his cup back down on the saucer. 'I'm interested to know what this is about,' he said, his eyes meeting hers. He'd always found her gaze unnerving. Something intense about it and her eyes were an unusual colour. A pale grey with dark rings round the edges. Now, her pupils were little black dots, and he could feel the distaste coming off her. So strong it was almost visible. Oh yes, despite all the smiles, he knew exactly what she thought of him.

'How's Dom?' she asked.

'Fine,' he said, tight-lipped now. *Not this again.*

'He hasn't been around for a while,' she said, giving him that sly smile.

What's she playing at?

He could feel that she was toying with him, enjoying some secret game. God did that annoy him. His shoulders tensed but he tried to look nonchalant, not letting her see that she'd hit a nerve.

'He's gone to visit his parents,' he said, playing with his teaspoon, his eyes no longer able to keep contact with hers.

'I don't think so,' she said, leaning forward. She tapped a finger on the table. 'I saw him yesterday.'

His eyes flicked up, his heart giving a jolt that felt like an electric shock. He was sure hope must have been written all over his face before he managed to rearrange his features. 'Where? Where did you see him?' He heard the neediness in his voice and gave a nonchalant shrug. 'Perhaps he's just got back.'

'I don't think so.' Again, that sly smile.

His teeth clamped together, and he had to stifle the urge to slap her. She paused, stirred sugar into her latte and took a sip, taking her time and all the while, he was sitting there, waiting for her to tell him, like a dog waiting for a treat.

How pathetic I am.

He hated this about himself, this need to hear about Dom, but he couldn't help it. That's what love had done to him. He missed Dom and was desperate to speak to him because the last time he'd seen him, they'd ended with an argument. After a heap of empty threats, including telling Nicci about their affair, Dom had stormed off saying if he went through with the marriage, their relationship was over. His heart clenched now when he thought about it, hoping he could make amends.

'Stop playing games,' he snapped, annoyed now. 'Spit it out, will you?' Then he frowned as he realised what her game was. *This is about money again.* 'How much do you want this time? Just tell me and let's get this over with. But it's going to be the last payment I ever give you. Any more demands and I'm going to the police.'

'I don't want anything.' She gazed at him over the rim of her coffee cup. 'In fact, I have something for you.'

He looked puzzled. 'You do?'

She gave a slow nod. 'A gift.'

He gave a derisive snort. 'Don't be stupid. Now you're talking in riddles.'

'Okay, you're right.' She put her cup down, sat up, her face serious now. 'I'll tell you straight.' She leant over the table. 'I saw Dom... at the hospital.'

Ethan felt himself crumple. 'That's where he's been. I wondered why he hadn't—' He stopped himself, hating the vulnerability in his voice. He couldn't sound so desperate. Not in front of this witch of a woman.

'He was in the morgue,' she added. 'Dom is dead, and you killed him. He was the hit-and-run victim. I went and identified him yesterday afternoon.'

His jaw dropped. He didn't believe a word she said. How did she even know about the hit-and-run? Unless... the truth dawned on him. *Nicci.* One more example of what a liability that woman was. Perhaps he was going to have to speed up his plan and arrange for her to disappear sooner than he'd anticipated. He hadn't really taken in what Stacey had said, too bothered about how she'd known about the accident.

When his brain finally caught up, her words hit him like a sledgehammer to the side of the head. Time stood still, a coldness running through his veins.

Dead? Is that what she said? Dom is dead? His hands flew to his mouth as his stomach lurched, the horror too much to bear.

She took another sip of coffee. 'It's the God's honest truth. You killed your boyfriend while you thought you were killing Joel.'

Ethan swayed in his seat, feeling light-headed, like he might faint. 'I can't have done,' he murmured, talking to himself as much as Stacey. 'The person I hit was wearing the same coat that Joel wears.' He was hyperventilating, felt far too hot. 'It wasn't meant to be Dom.'

Stacey smiled, finished her coffee and stood. 'Karma is a bitch,' she said as she turned and left.

CHAPTER FORTY-EIGHT

Nicci was holding her breath as she listened to the conversation between Ethan and Stacey, hardly daring to believe her plan might work. My God, Stacey was playing it cool. She'd called her before she went in and Nicci was recording everything on her phone, ready to give to the police. She would have loved to have seen Ethan's face. But she thought it might be a long time before she saw him again.

As soon as Stacey delivered her parting words, Nicci stopped recording and took a deep breath. Now she had her evidence, she was ready to ring the police, telling them her husband had locked her in the bathroom and she was frightened what he might do to her.

After a barrage of questions, she was informed a police car was being dispatched and she sat on the loo seat, waiting, hoping they would get to her before Ethan returned. But if he did get back first, she was ready with the bleach spray which her dad used to clean the tiles round the bath. A quick squirt of that in his face and he'd be out of action, she thought, her leg jigging up and down as she waited.

· · ·

Fifteen minutes later, she heard the sound of a car engine, tyres crunching on the gravel outside. The bathroom Ethan had locked her in was upstairs, at the front of the house, and she stood on the toilet seat and opened the tiny window, checking it was the police.

'I'm up here,' she called and the officers looked up at her. Relief washed through her as she recognised them as the same officers who had attended a few days ago. 'You'll have to break in, he's locked the house as well as locking me in the bathroom.'

They gave her the thumbs up and got a big red hammer device out of the boot.

Satisfied she was going to be rescued, she climbed off the toilet seat. Happy that she wouldn't have to go through her story again because they already knew her version, even if she'd been forced to retract it later by Ethan's threats.

Will they believe me now?

Ethan and Nicci had both been told they'd been lucky not to get a caution after the last call out. Would they think this was some domestic weirdness, some sort of game she and her husband played, rather than take her seriously? She chewed at her lip, nervous, not knowing what sort of reception she was going to get. At least now she had the evidence to make them listen, though. She had the conversation between Ethan and Stacey recorded on her mum's old phone. She'd also recorded him on her own phone, three days ago, when she'd been hiding under the table, admitting to attacking Joel. She knew he carried her phone with him, so once he was arrested, she was hoping they'd be able to access his confession.

Is it enough, though?

All she could do was hope.

She listened to the loud bangs at the front door, then footsteps thumping up the stairs. She went to the door. 'In here,' she shouted, thankful to hear the two bolts being drawn back and finally, the door opened.

This was it. Her hands were slick. Time to confess, to get the whole truth out in the open.

Later, in the police station, she was sitting in an interview room, with the duty solicitor by her side. She'd told him the full story before the interview and said she wanted to confess to her part in the hit-and-run. She'd told him she wanted to be able to tell the whole truth and had been advised about the possible consequences, but still insisted. She was not going to be saying 'no comment'.

'That's quite a story,' the detective said once she'd finished, and she'd played them the conversation on her mum's phone. She'd guess he was about forty, with a square face, brown eyes and a buzz cut, his hair thinning at the front. He had a weary look about him, like he wasn't getting enough sleep. The other officer was a dark-haired young woman with a pudgy face. She looked like she'd had too much coffee, never still, pen tapping, fingers twitching.

Looking at the expressions on their faces, Nicci wasn't sure they believed her after the last occasion, aware that her actions then didn't make her look like a credible witness.

'I have more evidence,' she said. 'I recorded a more detailed confession from Ethan on the night he tried to kill me. It's on my phone. This is my mum's old one, but he has mine. He carries it with him so I can't contact anyone.' She looked from one officer to the other, silently pleading with them to take her seriously. 'And what sane man locks his wife in the bathroom when he goes out?'

Another glance between the officers. 'Okay,' said the man. 'We're going to follow up some of this information and then we'll be back.' He stood and stretched. 'Might take a little while. Just ring the bell if you need anything.' He indicated a buzzer on the wall by the door.

She was left alone for a long time, the duty solicitor taking the opportunity to go out and make some phone calls. Someone came in and offered her a drink. Another person came and brought her a sandwich, apologised for the delay. Eventually the young officer bounced back in.

'Your husband has been arrested. You're free to go. But we'll need to check the house over as a crime scene. Is there anywhere else you can stay?'

Nicci felt so weak, it was hard to stand. 'I can stay at the cottage. That's where we lived before. But I need to get the dog. He's still at the house.'

'Don't worry about the dog, we'll bring him to you, okay? I'll give you a lift to the cottage.'

Nicci nodded. 'What about me? Am I... going to be charged with anything?'

The officer gave her a sympathetic smile. 'We'll have to wait and see.'

'I swear, everything I told you is true.'

The officer nodded. 'I believe you. But we can't rely on circumstantial evidence. It can't be your word against his. The CPS won't go for a prosecution. What we need is hard evidence. So, I need you to think about that and help us find it, okay?'

Her words hit Nicci like a punch. If Ethan wasn't in prison, he would kill her. But what evidence could she possibly give them?

EPILOGUE

Eight months later

Nicci was hanging up the washing in the back garden, Mack snuffling in the flowerbeds, when she stopped to admire the view. It still felt fresh, this change of scenery. Instead of looking at the gritstone edges of the moors above Skipton, she now saw an oak wood, which stood about a hundred yards from the back of her cottage, stretching up the narrow valley. Trees as far as you could see.

She loved it. Loved the sound of the breeze whispering through the leaves, the cool canopy they made and the architecture of the twisted limbs laid bare in the winter. In the other direction, she could see the sea, sparkling in the cove down below.

It was spring now and the sun had a bit of warmth to it. Enough to make her think about tidying up the garden and tackling the overgrown borders. Creating a nice space to sit outside and enjoy the beautiful views.

It was peaceful, quiet, secluded. Exactly what you needed when you were running away from something.

Mid Wales had a lot to offer, and it had turned out to be a great place to hide, the property reasonably priced, with lots of detached cottages like hers, where you didn't have to mingle if you didn't want to. She was still at the stage where she preferred to keep herself to herself, but maybe in time, she'd feel confident enough to make new friends.

She heard a car engine and then saw a flash of red. The postman. He was always friendly, and although he probed for information, she was careful to be vague. That's what the police had advised her to do when she decided she couldn't risk staying in Skipton.

It had been a busy few months and she'd been running on adrenaline for a lot of it. Now that the court case was over, she was starting to relax, but it was going to take time. Thankfully, she had the support of a therapist who was helping her to cope with the constant fear, the worry that Ethan would pop up and take her life.

She was still processing everything that had happened, including the death of her father. The accident investigators had taken a closer look at things once the post-mortem had shown no medical reasons for loss of control of the car and she'd told the police of her suspicions. They did lots of tests, looked at the marks on the road and goodness knows what else. Their conclusion, after several weeks, was foul play. The brakes had been tampered with and there was an issue with the steering.

At least she'd got justice for him, and for Dom, now that Ethan had been convicted of two counts of murder. Forensic evidence had been found linking Ethan to both deaths and along with the recorded telephone conversations that Stacey and Nicci had managed to capture, he knew he was cornered. He pleaded guilty to reduce his jail term. He'd also been convicted of GBH against Nicci and the attempted murder of Joel, the police finding the wheel wrench hidden at the back of the wardrobe in the cottage. He'd done a poor job of wiping it clean and they'd found his fingerprints, along with DNA from both Joel and Nicci. There was also a wheel wrench missing from his car's standard toolkit and the one they found matched the ones Land Rover used to supply to that make and model of car. It was pretty much a slam dunk in terms of damning evidence.

He was given concurrent life sentences with a minimum of twenty years to be served. It sounded like a long time, but Nicci was determined he would have no chance of finding her. The police had helped her to change her identity and checked in on her at regular intervals and she felt as secure as she ever would. Anyway, for now, she didn't need to worry because he was behind bars, but she did sometimes wonder if he might send someone to look for her. She wouldn't put it past him, so it made sense to take precautions.

Thankfully, he hadn't made a fuss about the divorce and that had all gone through smoothly. Any claims he might have had to her assets were nullified by his crimes. She supposed she had nothing that he wanted anymore, so her value to him as a wife was zero. What a relief it was to be rid of him.

She'd sold her dad's business to a new company set up by the employees and she was sure he would have approved of that. She'd also sold her parents' house, which meant she was financially secure, with enough savings to be able to spend the next three years training to be a teacher. Her course would start in the autumn, at Aberystwyth, and in the meantime, she was learning Welsh, so she'd be able to teach at a local school.

She'd also given a chunk of money to Louise to help with the baby. It wasn't to assuage her guilt, but more to help a friend. She knew life wasn't easy for a single mum, and she wanted to offer support. At first, Louise had refused, but when Nicci had pointed out the money wasn't for her, it was for baby Lily, she'd reconsidered.

Stacey had been convicted of blackmail and sentenced to

six years, so she'd be out in three probably. She'd confessed to Nicci that she'd needed the money for the renovations of their house, having underestimated the amount of work that needed doing. Nicci had been appalled and although Stacey had helped her at the end, she could never forgive her for thinking blackmail was in any way acceptable. It was ironic that Stacey's approach to get a confession out of Ethan had meant she'd incriminated herself. She really hadn't thought it through.

Dom's death remained a puzzle. Why would he have been standing on the corner on such a filthy night? She had no definitive proof but she did have a theory. He'd asked her to meet up with him three times before the night of the accident, saying he needed to speak to her, but each time something had come up and she'd put him off. She couldn't imagine that whatever he had to say to her was that important and with all the wedding stuff to organise, it hadn't been a priority.

His last message to her, though, when she'd read it again, made her wonder.

There's something you need to know and I want to tell you to your face.

She'd thought it was about him having to go back to Spain and not being there to support her when she was booked in to do her Spanish exam. But what if he'd wanted to tell her about his affair with Ethan? What if he wanted to make her stop the wedding?

Whatever he was doing, standing on the corner in the pouring rain, it was the act of a desperate man. She could only hope he hadn't known what was happening. That he hadn't suffered.

A shout made her turn and Joel walked into the garden holding up a letter.

'I got the job,' he called. 'I only went and got the flippin' job!' He ran towards her and picked her up, twirled her round. 'Now I can afford to keep you in the manner to which I want you to become accustomed, Mrs Finnegan.'

She caught sight of her ring finger, the single gold band, studded with tiny diamonds, sparkling in the sun. She'd only been wearing it for a month. But this time the wedding ceremony had been simple and joyous, no nerves, or second thoughts. It felt so right that he was the groom, and she was his bride.

Meanwhile, in HMP Wakefield, a high-security prison nicknamed 'Monster Mansion' because of its six hundred high-profile sex offenders and murderers, Ethan was making friends. The place had certainly opened his eyes to new opportunities, and he now had plans to take his career in a different direction. Much more lucrative and way less effort.

In fact, he'd already started. Seems you didn't have to be on the outside to get involved. There was a whole plethora of activities co-ordinated from inside, which was kinda fun. And crypto currency was such a help in keeping money out of the hands of the authorities. He was a fast learner, knew how to charm people, his sales skills making life a lot easier for him than for others.

He had to face up to the fact that his need to show his father that he was better than him had taken a knock. A setback was how he phrased it in his mind. But he was confident this new scheme he was involved in would outshine anything he could have achieved with Pete's business. He was going to make millions. Literally *millions*. By the time he got out, he would be able to kick back and enjoy himself and make up for the lost years.

He missed Dom, of course he did, and the tears came at

night, sometimes, when his mind took him back over everything that had happened. It wasn't his fault, though. It wasn't. It was Nicci messing about with Joel. If he hadn't thought she might cancel the wedding and choose Joel instead, he wouldn't have staged the accident. It had seemed like the perfect opportunity to get rid of the threat.

Okay, so Dom had messaged him earlier that night and said they needed to talk, but he'd put him off because it was difficult to keep his eyes on the prize with Dom going on at him. He didn't for one moment imagine that Dom would be waiting for him to come home so he wouldn't be able to ignore him. He had no idea what he'd been planning. Maybe he was going to bang on the door and then blurt it all out to Nicci, throw a bomb into their wedding plans. That was the most likely scenario, because he'd threatened to tell her several times. The fact that he hadn't gone through with it had given Ethan a sense of security, thinking it was an idle threat. Wanting to persuade Ethan to forget his big plans and leave. Go to Spain with him and start again. That's what Dom had wanted.

What was done was done, though, and he had to move on and make the best of his situation. It wasn't all bad inside. He even had a new lover, which had made incarceration a lot more bearable. Would it be weird to say the place suited him?

As for Nicci, well he'd put her out of his mind for now. She was a long-term project. With his new-found contacts, he would find her eventually. And then he would play with her for a while before he finished her off. Let her know what real fear felt like. Make her understand that vows had to be kept.

Seems karma wasn't such a bitch after all…

———

Two months later

Nicci was upstairs, hoovering, when she heard Joel shouting her name. She switched off the hoover so she could hear what he wanted.

'Can you come down here, love?' Joel's voice sounded strained and she immediately went to the top of the stairs, looked down to see him peering up at her, his eyebrows pinched together. 'The police are here.'

Her heart leapt up her throat, a sudden fear making her muscles tense. *Why would the police be here?* Her mind flew back over everything that had happened in the last year, wondering if they'd decided to review her one year ban for drink driving, deciding it should be increased or a prison term considered. That worry was never far from her mind and neither were her vows to Ethan. Had he escaped, was he coming for her? Or had he arranged for someone on the outside to track her down?

Her hands, slick with sweat, slid down the banister as she hurried downstairs and into the living room, where two male police officers were standing, making the room feel crowded.

'Have a seat,' she said, indicating the sofa, while she perched on the arm of a chair, her pulse racing. Their faces looked grim and it could only be bad news.

'We just had a call from HMP Wakefield where your ex-husband is being held. Unfortunately, there's been an incident. A fight apparently. Last night.' She sat stock-still, hardly able to breathe, glancing over at Joel who was leaning against the mantelpiece.

'It seems your ex-husband had started up a new line of business inside and trampled on a few toes. Anyway, he's been badly injured. Life-changing injuries, we're told, although I don't have the exact details. He's in the ICU. They're not sure if he's going to make it.'

Nicci was unable to speak, struggling to take in the news.

A radio crackled and one of the officers stood, made his way outside while he took the call. Joel came and sat beside her, putting a protective arm round her waist and she leant into him as she let the news percolate through her mind.

The officer came back in, took off his hat. 'That was an update on your ex-husband's condition. I'm sorry to tell you he's passed away.'

Joel pulled her closer and she found herself nodding, still unable to find any words to express how she felt. Silence filled the room, pressing on her, keeping her locked in place.

'Thank you, officers,' Joel said as the men stood. The sound of his voice was muffled, like she was underwater and she watched him show them out, heard the murmur of conversation.

She moved off her perch and sank into the chair, hands clasped to her face as she began to understand what the news meant. He wasn't trying to find her, or sending people to look for her. There would be no coded warnings landing on her doorstep, no need to wonder if he'd get parole, when he might be out and come for his revenge.

No more hiding. It was over. Ethan was dead. Her vows to him had been nullified. At last, she was free.

A LETTER FROM RONA HALSALL

Dear reader,

I want to say a huge thank you for choosing to read *Bride and Groom*. If you did enjoy it, and want to keep up to date with all my latest releases, just sign up at the following link. Your email address will never be shared and you can unsubscribe at any time.

www.bookouture.com/rona-halsall

The idea for this book came about from a fun chat with my editor, Maisie Lawrence, when we were throwing ideas around for titles and stories. We started with the title and decided the couple must have made a binding vow about something at their wedding, a terrible secret that bound them together. My editor came up with the idea of a hit-and-run just before the wedding – how awful would that be?! – and the storyline expanded from there.

I particularly enjoyed the setting for this one and used a cottage I once lived in as my couple's rental. My grandparents lived nearby and I have very fond memories of Skipton.

I hope you loved *Bride and Groom* and if you did I would be very grateful if you could write a review. I'd love to hear what you think, and it makes such a difference helping new readers to discover one of my books for the first time.

I love hearing from my readers – you can get in touch on my Facebook page, through X, Instagram or my website.

Thanks,

Rona x

ronahalsall.com

 facebook.com/RonaHalsallAuthor

 x.com/RonaHalsallAuth

instagram.com/ronahalsall

ACKNOWLEDGEMENTS

This is the first book I've written since my husband passed away and I'll admit it was a struggle to get started. But once I'd dived into the story and immersed myself in the characters, I wrote it really quickly. Writing was a balm for my soul and having this book to lose myself in helped me through a very sad time.

My publisher, Bookouture, has been absolutely lovely throughout the last two years when my husband became poorly and then after he passed away so I would like to thank each and every one of you for your love, support and patience. Similarly, I would like to thank all my fellow authors who are members of Motivation Station, a Facebook Group run by the lovely Carla Kovach, who have definitely had my back and helped me to press on through troubled times.

My editor, Maisie Lawrence, deserves special thanks, as I was struggling to come up with a workable idea for this book. Thankfully, after a couple of ideas sessions with her, a storyline started to come together and, with her great editing, I'm pretty happy with the way it's shaped up.

Thanks also to my children, John, Amy and Oscar, who have been a tremendous support and have been there when I needed them.

I must also thank the ladies of the St John's Chapel prayer shawl knitting group, including Rev Jo, for their enthusiasm for my writing and for giving me several shoulders to cry on.

Finally, thanks, as always, to my little group of beta readers

– Mark, Dee, Wendy, Chloe, Sandra and Kerry-Ann – for their insight and feedback, which has made this book better in so many ways.

PUBLISHING TEAM

Turning a manuscript into a book requires the efforts of many people. The publishing team at Bookouture would like to acknowledge everyone who contributed to this publication.

Audio
Alba Proko
Sinead O'Connor
Melissa Tran

Commercial
Lauren Morrissette
Jil Thielen
Imogen Allport

Data and analysis
Mark Alder
Mohamed Bussuri

Editorial
Maisie Lawrence
Ria Clare

Copyeditor
Jane Eastgate

Printed in Great Britain
by Amazon

40793965R00162